RORY POWER

BURN OUR BODIES DOWN

MACMILLAN CHILDREN'S BOOKS

First published 2020 in the US by Delacorte Press, an imprint of Random House
Children's Books, a division of Penguin Random House LLC, New York

This edition published 2021 in the UK by
Macmillan Children's Books an imprint of Pan Macmillan
The Smithson, 6 Briset Street, London EC1M 5NR
Associated companies throughout the world
www.panmacmillan.com

ISBN 978-1-5290-2283-4
Text copyright © Nike Power 2020
Cover art copyright © Allison Reimold 2020

Pan Macmillan does not have any control over, or any responsibility for,
any author or third-party websites referred to in or on this book.

1 3 5 7 9 8 6 4 2

A CIP catalogue record for this book is available from the British Library.

Interior design by Trish Parcell
Printed and bound by CPI Group (UK) Ltd, Croydon CR0 4YY

I was so proud not to feel my heart.
Waking means being angry.

—ELIZA GRISWOLD, "RUINS"

ONE

Flick and catch of the lighter, fire blooming between my fingers. It's too hot for this. Late June, sun close and watchful. Here I am anyway. Flame guttering in and out, in and out.

The candle I lit this morning is on the coffee table. Scented, cloves and pine—Mom stole it from work last year and we've been putting off using it, burning every other thing we can find. A bowl of tea lights, clean and bright, or a prayer candle she took from church. But we're running low, and this Christmas shit was the only one left in the box Mom keeps under her bed. Too sweet, too strong. But the rules are more important. They're always more important.

Keep a fire burning; a fire is what saves you. The first, the last, the heart of them all. She taught me that as soon as I was old enough to hold a lighter in my palm. Whispered it to me in the dark. Pressed it against my forehead in place of a kiss. And I used to ask why, because it makes less than any sense at all. But you learn quick when you're Jo Nielsen's daughter. It's answers or her, and you'll only ever get one of them, so you'd better be careful deciding which it is.

I picked her. And even so, I don't get much of her most days.

With one hand, I test the breeze coming through the window I'm sitting at. It's barely anything, but I want to be sure it won't put the candle flame out. She pretends not to care about that anymore, says the lighting is the important thing—and it is, it is. She watches me do it every morning with this look on her face I'll never understand. But still. I remember the fight we had the first time she came home to a blackened, bare wick. I won't let that happen again if I can help it. Especially not these days, with Mom always in a mood, holding herself open like a trap.

I get up from the windowsill and slide to the floor, tilt my head into the shade. Floorboards sticking to my thighs, salt on my tongue every second. Above me I can see the smoke gathering, blue against the crackling ceiling. Nothing to worry about. Detectors disabled ages back. Mom ripped them down herself, paid the fire department to stop coming around. They turned off the electricity that month, but it was worth it. To her, anyway. And me, I went to school, and I came home, and I did my homework with a flashlight between my teeth. Made a life for myself inside the mess of my mother's head, just like always.

I think I'd give anything to know what happened to leave her like this. As long as it's not waiting to happen to me.

The sun's dropped and left the room dim by the time I hear the station wagon rattle up outside. Mom back from her shift at the funeral home. She works at the front desk and takes all the calls, tells people if the coffin they picked is too short, helps them order enough whiskey for the wakes.

Footsteps on the stairs, but I don't stand up. My whole body languid and heavy, the humid air pinning me down. Mom can carry the groceries by herself.

She's a mess when she gets inside. Hair loose, sticking to her mouth, and a coffee stain on the lapel of her shirt. We look so alike that people are always calling us sisters, and not in a way that's flattery. The same somber mouth, the same streaks of gray at our temples. Mine came early, so early I don't remember what I looked like without them, and sometimes I catch Mom staring. Sometimes I catch her about to cry. I used to think maybe it was that I reminded her of my father—the man she never talks about, the man who must have given me something. But then I stopped thinking about him at all. Started wondering about where Mom came from instead. About who gave her the face that looks so much like mine.

"Hey," she says, squinting over the top of the grocery bag at me, and there's a smudge of something at the corner of her left eye, just above the scar there, spreading and raised and older than me. That's one thing we don't share, at least.

I peel my legs off the hardwood and hug my knees to my chest. We're having a good day so far. Both of us out of sight, both of us quiet—it's the talking that's gonna ruin it. "Hey," I say.

"You want to help me with this?"

She sets the groceries down on the rickety table by the door. I can see her checking the apartment. Everything the way she likes it, the candle burning strong in the center of the room, but her expression curdles anyway.

"You couldn't have closed the window?" she says. I don't answer as she crosses to it, her knee brushing my temple where I'm sitting on the floor. I can hear her rock the window in its frame, working it shut. It was only an inch. An inch, and if she were someone else's mother she wouldn't mind, wouldn't notice, wouldn't have these rules in the first place. But she's right. I should've closed it.

And still, it could be worse. She hooks her fingers through mine and pulls me to my feet. My stomach twists at her touch. We go for weeks without it, sometimes, her body flinching if I get within a yard or two.

"Help me," she says again, something nearly painful in

the strain of her smile. "You can stand in front of the fridge."

It's even hotter in the kitchen, and fruit flies we can't get rid of cover the fluorescent bulbs under the upper cabinets. Mom scrapes her hair off her face and starts unbuttoning her work shirt while I bring in the grocery bag. I can't see everything inside it, but what I can see isn't promising. She never learned how to grocery shop, and when it's just her she comes home with melba toast and cherry tomatoes, or seltzer and string cheese. Enough for both of us, if I'm lucky.

It's not that she forgets about me. I really don't think that's it. More like Mom usually has only enough energy to look after one person, and that person's always her.

It's easier when I'm in school. Lunch in the cafeteria, people who call themselves my friend as long as I'm right in front of them, and the lingering looks of the teachers who notice that I'm still wearing summer clothes deep into fall. I can pretend Mom's just like the other parents, pretend there's more for me than this apartment, than waiting for her to want me again.

Because she does, sometimes. Tucks me into her body and whispers, "Nobody but you and me." Good, because she's decided she loves me, and bad, because the hooks we've got in each other are too deep to ever come out, no matter how much we pull at them. But I don't care. Me, and Mom, and the whole world right here.

Today she's brought home a six-pack of seltzer and a bag

of baby bell peppers. I know what she'd say if I shopped like that—we have tap water at home, and produce is too expensive—but I've watched her in the grocery store, watched how she freezes, how the sight seems to drain from her eyes. I stay quiet, put everything in the fridge alongside the hot dogs and American cheese from her last trip.

"What should we make?" I ask. I'm picturing it, the two of us at the counter together, our dinner disgusting and oddly assembled, but ours.

That's my mistake. Maybe it wouldn't be one on a different day, but I see it happen in her. See her jaw tighten, her eyes narrow.

"Make?" she says.

I can save it. I can pull it back. "Yeah," I say, grabbing the hot dogs from the fridge, ignoring the horrible slide of the liquid in the package. I have to show her I meant I'd do it for the both of us. That I don't expect anything more from her than what she's already given. "I could sauté the peppers, or—"

"If what I brought home isn't good enough," Mom snaps, "you can go back out yourself."

She pulls the car keys out of her pocket, tosses them down on the counter. I will myself into stillness. If I take the keys, the argument has started, and I won't be able to end it without getting into the driver's seat and weaving to the nearest gas station for a bag of pretzels. Mom's like that. So

6

am I—I learned it from her. Ride it until the end, no matter what.

"No," I say carefully, "it's fine."

But she's picking up steam. "Take some of my money, too, and just go get whatever you want." She leans into me, pressing the keys against my chest, the metal cold and scratching. "Go on. If you don't want to drive, you can walk."

I knot my fingers together, squeezing tight to keep from snatching the keys and taking the bait. She's feeling guilty. That's why she's picking a fight. But understanding that doesn't make it feel any better.

"Really," I say. "I didn't mean it like that."

That's not what she wants from me. I know it's not. But if I can get out of this without giving that to her, I will.

"Do you want me to make you a plate?" I try instead. I can end this fight. I can. I've done it before. "I'm not hungry."

"Since when does it matter what I want?" Mom says, turning away from me and going to the sink, twisting the tap until water is pouring over her wrists, cooling her blood.

"It always does." And fine, fine, if it gets us out of this stalemate, I will give up some ground. I will take another piece of blame—those pieces are the only things I can really call my own. "I'm sorry," I say. "It was my fault."

For a moment she doesn't acknowledge that I've spoken.

And then she looks up, an emptiness in her eyes like I'm one of the bodies she sees at work. The water running over her paper skin, until I reach across her to turn it off.

She blinks. Reaches up to touch my cheek, brushing the spot on my skin where the scar sits on hers. Her palm is cold and wet, but all the same I can feel my face flushing, feel my eyes flutter shut.

She moves then, and there's a tug at my hairline. When she draws back, it's with a long gray hair pinched between her fingers. She went gray right at my age, later than I did, but I can't remember who told me that, and suddenly it's seeming like it couldn't have been her.

"Oh," I say, blinking back a moment of dizziness to watch as she winds the hair around her finger so tightly the skin turns red.

"What a shame," she says, almost to herself.

She leaves me to handle my own dinner and disappears into her room. Runs the bath all night, and at first I think she must be cooling down, but when I go in later to brush my teeth, the mirror is fogged and the taps are hot.

How to keep a fire burning. How to stitch a fight up until it's only a scar. That's the kind of thing you learn with a mother like mine. Mostly, though, you learn how to be loved without any proof. Seventeen years and I'm still getting that part wrong.

TWO

Mom wakes me up before she goes to work. My room is right next to hers, not even really separate. A speckled beige partition we bought at an office supply store, a foot too short, cutting the room in half, and on the other side, her bed. Now, in the early gray light, she perches on the foot of mine, yesterday's candle cupped in her hands.

I sit up, rub the sleep from my eyes, and fumble for the lighter on my nightstand. The day's already too hot, my sheets sticking to my legs.

"Let's go," Mom says. "I'm running late."

Her hair damp from a shower, dripping onto her lilac work shirt. She'll leave the windows down in the car and it'll be dry by the time she gets to the funeral home.

"Sorry," I say. "Okay."

The flame jumps up, stands steady and stark. My hand used to shake when I did this, but it doesn't anymore. No nerves as I hold the fire to the wick until it catches. No fear as I let the lighter go out, lean in to feel the heat on my skin.

This is the part that matters to Mom. Watching me. On good days it comes with a kiss to my temple, with her favorite rule whispered in my ear. On most days it comes with nothing at all. Just the feeling that this is a test, somehow, and I've only barely passed.

"All right." She gets up, firelight gathering under her chin. "Go back to sleep."

She leaves the candle on my nightstand. I lie down, turn my back to it. One of these days it'll burn us both down. I don't even know if I'll care.

It's late, full morning when I wake up again. Don't bother checking my phone—my data's run out, and besides, nobody's looking for me. Now that school's out I have nothing to do, and nobody to do it with. Too many days laid out in a line. Nothing to put inside them. It used to be Mom would take me to work with her. She'd stick me under her desk and I'd watch her stomach move, watch her suck it in whenever the phone rang. The gaps between the buttons of her shirt, the paleness of her skin and the wrinkles pressed red into it. For a while that was what I thought of when I pictured her. That shadow and curve, and the smell of the funeral home, like powder, like roses, like dust.

I get to my feet. I can hear the kettle whistling. Just faintly, but there, and when I lean out my door I can see through the living room to the kitchen. Burner still on. She must have forgotten to turn it off. I can picture her rushing, gulping down a cup of weak tea, no breakfast because she bought all the wrong groceries. Shut my eyes, ignore the pang in my chest.

I love her so much more when she's not here.

Our fight yesterday wasn't new. We've had a hundred just like it, and we'll have a hundred more. But I still feel sick after every one, still find myself trying to wring something out of this town that will qualify as amends, since I know I'll never get them from her. Not that there's much to get out of Calhoun, either. Why Mom chose to settle us here is beyond me, but I think I'd say that about anywhere. There's never been one minute Mom's looked like she was somewhere she wanted to be.

I shut off the burner. Get dressed quickly, pull on some shorts and a T-shirt, braid back my hair. For a moment I pause halfway through it, think of the gray wings at my temples, think of how easy they'll be to see. Mom doesn't like it like this. But I'm doing enough for her already.

I slide on my sneakers and head downstairs, a breeze slipping up from the open door off the street. Still, the heat, with a pulse and a cling, and my hair's collecting sweat by the time I'm out on the street.

We live above an empty storefront tiled in a too-bright teal, the word *Entrance* on the door all that's left of the signs that used to hang there. Most of Calhoun is like that, with gaps where life used to exist, where time has just stopped. Next to our building is a barbershop, open for business like always, with absolutely nobody inside, also like always. Across the street a warehouse stands empty, the windows broken, the brick striped with graffiti. I find my favorite one as I pass by—*you're already dedd,* it tells me in a neon-pink scrawl—and keep going, my eyes nearly shut against the sun.

I'm heading for what passes for the center of Calhoun, one block back from where the highway cuts through. Town's empty this time of the morning. Even Redman's diner is quiet between meals, with just one customer propped up at the counter staring into a cup of coffee. I kill time there some evenings, if Mom looks close to the end of her rope. Watch my classmates come in and out, smoke ringing their shoulders, their eyes bored and wanting.

Most of them live north of town, where the houses are spread out, lawns sprouting between them. When we were younger, some of those kids were my friends, and I'd spend afternoons on their couches in front of their televisions, eating their food. But then they'd ask where I lived, and I'd think of my house, with its cloying smell and its empty fridge, and it would be over. Now I see those same faces in class, see their preowned cars parked outside the movie theater that's barely holding on, showing movies from half a year ago.

The woman who owns the theater is our landlord, but we haven't seen her in a few months and Mom's stopped paying rent, which is just as well. The more money she keeps, the less likely it is that she'll notice I've been stealing some.

Not for fun. I never spend it, never even look at it. Just tuck the cash inside the envelope I keep under my mattress and try to ignore the twist in my gut as I think of ways to leave Mom behind, as I imagine what she'd do, how she'd wake up to an empty apartment. Would she look for me? Or would she finally be able to relax, because maybe that's what she was after all along?

It's not like I haven't tried to leave before. I get close. Sometimes I even get out the door, never mind that I'm only seventeen, never mind another year of school on the horizon. But then I hear it—*Nobody but you and me.* Like a curse we can't shake. So I stay with Mom, because she's all I have, because she says this is where I belong, and maybe it's spite or maybe it's love but I can't really tell them apart anymore.

That doesn't keep me from looking for another way out. If I can't find the will to leave on my own, I'll need someone else who wants me. Another Nielsen. Another shot at family.

I asked Mom about it once. Just once. I was ten, and a

girl at school came in with a batch of cupcakes for her birthday, said her grandmother had baked them. And I'd known about grandparents, and I'd known about fathers, but she set a cupcake down in front of me and I had to throw up in the trash can by our teacher's desk. The nurse asked me later if I was sick. I said yes because that seemed easier than explaining. Easier than telling her I'd just realized there was a part of my life left empty.

When I got home I asked Mom where our name came from. I started with my father because that seemed easier, seemed like it would matter less to her, and I was right, because that she brushed off. But my grandparents. It was the first time I couldn't recognize her.

She didn't say anything at first. But she got up and she locked the apartment door, and she sat down on the couch, leaned back with her arms crossed over her chest.

"We're not moving," she said then, her voice flat, eyes fixed on me, "until you promise to never ask that again."

I remember I laughed, because of course she didn't mean it. We would get up to eat dinner, to go to the bathroom, to sleep. But that laugh died in my throat as I kept watching her.

"Not an inch," she said. "We'll die right here, Margot. I don't care. Unless you promise me."

If we had that conversation now, I wouldn't be able to let her win. We'd sit there deep into winter, until one of us gave up. But I was small and I was hungry and I said, "Yes." I said, "I'm sorry." I said, "I promise."

So naturally I went looking the second I got the chance. Bought a notebook from the Safeway, wrote my last name on the first page and started pecking away at the library computers, flipping through the archived newspapers. But all I ever turned up were phone-book listings and disconnected numbers, or other confused Nielsen families who'd never heard of a Josephine or a Margot.

I gave up. There were more important things to keep track of. Me and Mom, for one. That's what's in the notebook now, tucked under my mattress next to the money. Fights we've had, word for word. Moments she looked at me like she wanted me with her. All of it evidence that things happened the way I remember. You need that with someone like Mom, someone who fights more about whether things happened than whether they hurt.

Yesterday's not worth writing down, though. There'll be dozens more days like it before the summer's over. Break, and break, and bleed back together. That's how it goes with us.

And when I can help it along, I do, which is why I've got a fold of that stolen money tucked in my pocket, why I've got my eyes fixed on the storefront across the street. Heartland Cash for Gold, where Frank's got half of Mom's belongings in his display cases. She goes through cycles— spends too much on groceries she won't eat and then sells

Frank a jewelry box full of fake gold earrings; saves money on rent and buys half the earrings back. It's ridiculous. The buyback price goes up every time, and it's not as if she has to keep them out of someone else's hands. She could leave them in that pawnshop for half a century and nobody would touch them. But try telling her that.

I don't know what I can afford with the bills in my pocket, but whatever it is, I'll bring it back to her and hope it buys me a few days of quiet. A few days when it doesn't seem like the wrong decision to stay.

I cross the road, asphalt burning through my sneakers, and hurry into the pawnshop. The bells on the door jingle softly as I ease it shut behind me. It's dark in here, cool from the fan working overtime in the corner, and for a second I think about just sitting down on this grimy gray carpet and never moving again. But then there's a noise from the back of the shop, and I hear Frank's low, tuneless humming.

He's in one of his short-sleeved button-downs. Sweat stains the armpits, darkening the plaid, which looks better suited to the holiday season. He's nice, Frank. Never turns Mom away when she brings stuff to sell, even though it's all shit. Never cuts her a deal when she wants to buy it back either, but I wouldn't if I were him.

"Margot," he says, waving me over to the counter, where he's thumbing through a stack of receipts. "Your mom coming?"

It's not one of her rules, the way the candle is, but I'm not supposed to be in here without her. After all, this is her life in boxes, her life before I came into it. I hesitate, wonder if I should just go home. No, this is a nice thing I'm doing for her. She'll appreciate it. I'll buy her back a pair of earrings, or some old clothes she can take to the tailor and make new again.

"Not today," I say, crossing the shop toward Frank. There's a display case running along each wall, and two shelving units split the space left in the middle, objects cluttered and close. Their tags flutter lightly as the fan turns, the breeze catching each handwritten price, a slash drawn through it and a lower one written just underneath.

I step up to the case against the back wall, the register on one end, Frank's stool waiting behind it. "How's your wife?"

"Still dead," Frank says, just like he always does, and he waits for me to laugh, even though I never do. "You all right?"

I roll my eyes. "Better than ever." I wonder if I'll ever mean it.

Frank sets the receipts down and leans forward, his arms braced on the display case. "Well?" he says. "What'll it be?"

I should've counted my money outside. But I forgot, and now that I'm in front of Frank I'm not about to empty my pockets. It's a pair of twenties, probably—Mom doesn't pay

17

our rent in singles anymore—but I know better than to let Frank see. "Not sure yet," I say, backing away and meandering toward one of the cases where Mom's stuff usually is. "Just browsing."

"Her shit's not out here," Frank says, coming around to stand next to me.

"What do you mean?" Frowning, I turn to see an array of ratty baseball cards and a pair of fake diamond studs where some of Mom's stuff used to be.

"I mean," Frank says, impatiently, "that you two were the only people buying it. Not exactly running a wide margin here, am I?"

"So where'd you put it?" I can't hide the panic tight in my voice, the fight already stirring in my body. If it's gone, if he's ditched it, it'll be my fault somehow.

He gives me the same look most people in town do once they've met my mother. Disbelief, and a little bit of worry—which I hate more than anything else, because what right do they have to worry about me? She's my mother, and when I hurt, I know she does too. "Just put it in the back, that's all," he says, and nods toward the door behind the register. "Take it easy."

"Sorry." I swallow hard, force myself to relax. "Can I see?"

He gestures for me to follow and heads to the back room. It's stacked so high with junk it's probably supporting the whole building. Clothing, books and enough watches to cover both my arms all the way up to the elbow. At the far side of the room, a table that looks antique but is probably particleboard is covered with five or six battered boxes, the sides peeling away from each other. *Nielsen* written on each one in fading black ink.

"There," Frank says. "Told you."

"Thanks." I shift from foot to foot, suddenly cold. "You don't have to stay in here with me."

"So you can smuggle half your mom's stuff out under your shirt?" He sounds like he's joking, but he leans against the doorframe, arms crossed over his chest. Something about the sight of his kneecaps poking out below his cargo shorts makes me feel sick. "Figure out what you want. Prices should still be marked."

I ease toward the table, trying not to let Frank see that I'm nervous. They're Mom's belongings, things she decided she didn't need. I've never really looked through them before—she does it herself, has me wait where Frank is standing now. And whenever I've come here without her, it's been for myself, usually to see if Frank's willing to sell me a better phone for half the marked price. He never is.

"Any day now," he says, grabbing one of the tagged watches to tap it impatiently.

"It's not like you have a bunch of customers waiting for you," I say. Meaner than he deserves, but I'm on edge, and it's true. "Just give me a minute."

I open the first box and peer inside. It's mostly empty except for an odd assortment of silverware and a frying pan coated with something unspeakably pungent. I cough, my eyes watering, as Frank lets out a delighted laugh behind me.

"That one'll get you," he says as I turn to get a breath of fresh air.

"Why the hell would you buy that from her?" I ask. "I didn't take you for a charity."

"Shows what you know," Frank tells me, his chest puffing up proudly. "I'm the nicest guy in the world."

I look back at the boxes of Mom's stuff. If the others are like the first one, Frank might be right. It's junk. All of it junk. And it's sad, really. My mother's life. Thirty-five years. This is all she has to show for it? She had me young, I know that, but it's hard to remember that when she's as far from me as she is. Hard to realize that in the eighteen years before I came around, she barely had a chance to live at all.

I ignore the tightness in my throat and tug the smallest box toward me. I've never seen this one. Inside is mostly fabric, and at first I think it's clothing and maybe we could take it to the tailor, like I planned. But then I tug one piece all the way out and it's not clothes. It's a blanket. Small, and soft, and a pale new pink.

"That's what you want?" Frank says. "Cheap enough, I guess."

I don't answer. Can't answer. This was mine. It has to

have been mine. There's no monogram in the corner, no name written on the small white label, but this box: these are all my baby things. A catch in my throat, a prick in my eyes. The very beginning of me, packed up and sold, and she couldn't keep it and couldn't get rid of it either. Just the way she is with me.

"Not this," I say, my voice rough and low.

"Fine. Hurry up, then."

I set the blanket down on the table and root through the rest of the box. Here a board book, bright colors and no text, the edges warped with humidity. Here a T-shirt, cut up and stitched haphazardly into a onesie for someone unimaginably small. You, I remind myself. This was for you. But it stings too much to linger. This was a bad idea. I should go.

I take one last look before giving up. At the very bottom, the dim light is bouncing off something bright. I reach in and take it out carefully. A Bible, the words stamped in gold across the white cover. It doesn't look like the ones I've seen whenever I can be bothered to sidle into the back of a church service. This one's bigger, nicer, a pattern bordering the cover, the edges of the pages all gilded and thick. I open it to the first page, the spine creaking. There, written in blue looping cursive, is a message.

> *If it be possible, let this cup pass from me;*
> *nevertheless, not as I will, but as thou wilt.*

—For my daughter on her twelfth birthday.
With all my love, your mother. 11/8/95

I've spent a long time looking for proof that there was somebody before Mom. That our family existed, somehow, in some form. This is the first of it I've seen. Somebody wrote this. My mother was a child once. And I knew that, of course I knew that, but not the way I do now.

"This," I say. "How much for this?"

"You could check the tag," Frank grumbles, but he comes over and reaches for the Bible. I don't give it to him. Just turn the spine toward him so he can see. "That?" He raises his eyebrows, and I do my best to keep my own expression blank. "Weird choice."

"You want to sell it or not?"

"I'm just saying, that's all." He props up the cover and frowns at the price scrawled on the top corner of the title page. "It's forty."

I should haggle, but I can't stand to be here a minute longer. I fish the bills from my pocket—turns out two twenties is all I have—and slap them into his palm before heading back through the shop toward the door. The leather cover of the Bible is sticking to my chest and the sun is too bright. Mistake, I tell myself over and over. A mistake.

THREE

I can't go home. What am I supposed to do—just wait until Mom gets there? It's too much, and not enough, and I end up at Redman's, in the back booth, a glass of water in front of me and no money to pay for anything. If it were any busier, they'd kick me out. But as it is, it's just me and the waitress, and a guy slumped over at the counter who I'm mostly sure is still alive.

I watch a bead of condensation run down the side of the water glass to pool on the table. Now that I'm not faced with the spread of Mom's stuff, the panic has started to wear off, but there's still an uneasiness in my stomach, a sourness on my tongue that I can't swallow, because I figured out why I'm doing this.

It takes a while, sometimes. To understand. It would

mean something to me to have a gift from Mom, and so it'll mean something to her to have a gift from hers. That's what I told myself when I went to Frank's. But Mom's spent my whole life hiding us from her past, and this isn't a gift. I'm punishing her. I'm trying to hurt her.

According to her, I try that a lot. Usually I don't mean to, but this time I do, even if it took me a second to realize it. I'm going to show her that Bible and say, "Look what I found. I've been breaking your rules this whole time. You can't keep me from my family forever."

I open it again, trace the handwriting with my fingertip. Twelfth birthday. I can't imagine Mom that young. Can't imagine her reading a Bible, for that matter. Did her mother take her to church? Read her Scripture as she dressed for bed?

Her mother. I press the heels of my palms to my eyes and breathe deeply. My grandmother. This is my grandmother. My name and my blood—they came from her. She was real. And she still might be.

I just have to find her.

I turn a few more pages. Here and there in the margins I spot bits of handwriting. Underlined passages, and a game of tic-tac-toe scrawled across one of the headings.

"Can I get you anything else?" the waitress asks me. I jump, shut the Bible too hard on my fingers.

"No thanks," I say. She stares pointedly at the empty spot in front of me where a plate of food should be. I put on a smile. "Maybe some more water."

She picks up my full glass and then sets it back down. "There you go."

As soon as she's gone I flip the Bible back open. Something inside's been nudged just out of place, poking out like a bookmark. Carefully, I turn to the spot where it was placed deep in the press of the pages, near the back of the book.

A photograph. Its edges are crisp, but the glossy surface is dotted with fingerprints, as though someone has spent a long time tracing the features captured in the picture. I bend closer. It's of a house, or part of one, white paint fresh and proud against the sky, and the sun is bright enough that it's nearly washing out everything else. The wide roll of the fields covered in snow, the blur of trees on the horizon. Everything except the girl in the foreground. She's young, her face still round and full, unscarred and smooth, her arm outstretched toward the person behind the camera, and she's smiling so wide I can see a gap where one of her front teeth has fallen out.

Mom, I think. It looks like her. Like me, when I was that age. This must be where she grew up.

Gently, I tug the photo free of the pages. I'm not telling her about it. The Bible she can have. This I'm keeping for myself. She was like me once, but I won't be like her.

I flip the picture over, ready to fold it up and tuck it into my pocket. There's handwriting here too. The script matches the dedication on the front page of the Bible. It must have been written by the same person. By my grandmother.

Fairhaven, 1989, Nielsen Farm. Followed by: *Remember how it was? I'll be waiting. Come when you can.*

After it, luckier than I ever have been before—a phone number.

I'm smiling, a laugh nearly tipping out of me, before I can help it. All those days looking and looking, and it was right here. Someone calling me home.

Calhoun only has one pay phone, smack in the middle of town. I'd rather use my own phone, an old one with no touch screen and no caller ID, but we use pay as you go and my card ran out early this month after I spent a whole afternoon playing a game at the library and forgot to join the Wi-Fi network. So it's the phone booth outside the center of commerce, and it's right now, while Mom's still at work and the streets are empty. With any luck, nobody will see me, and I'll be able to keep this hidden from Mom a little while longer.

The booth is empty when I get there, like it always is, so I sidle in, drop the Bible onto the plastic shelf under the phone, and slide the photograph from my pocket, unfolding it carefully. The phone number is still on the back. I didn't imagine it.

Can it really be as simple as this? A photo in a book, a

quarter I stole from the tip jar in the diner and my family on the other end of the line?

Maybe the number will be out of service. Maybe it'll be another Nielsen who doesn't recognize my name. Or maybe it'll be my mother's parents, who've been waiting and waiting and wishing for me.

I shut my eyes for a moment, square my shoulders. Stop stalling, I tell myself. Do what you're here to do. Life with Mom will always be this way, and you have a shot at something else.

But I can still hear her as I reach for the phone, as I lift it off the hook. *Nobody but you and me. Nobody, nobody, nobody.*

The phone feels too heavy in my hands, and I clutch it tightly, feel the slip of sweat against the plastic. The quarter I swiped from Redman in my pocket. My family waiting for me to find them. Now, Margot. It has to be now, before Mom comes back, before the door you managed to push open slams shut.

I drop the quarter into the slot and dial the number. Take a deep breath and wait for the line to connect.

For a moment it doesn't. Worry rippling through me— the number's too old, it's out of date, and I'll never find my family, not ever—but it fades as the line clicks on and starts to ring. Once. Again. Again, and again, until finally.

Quiet. What sounds like the slow draw of breath. Then,

a woman's voice. Real, and in my ear. "Nielsen residence, Vera speaking."

I open my mouth. Wait for the words to come out of me, but they don't. I should've practiced, I should've planned what to say, but how could I have prepared for this? For another Nielsen on the phone, for the answer I've been looking for since I was ten years old?

"Hello?" But I can't answer, and in the silence that follows, the woman on the other end of the line—Vera, her name is Vera—says, "Josephine? Is that you?"

My heart drops. Will I ever be somewhere my mother hasn't been first?

"No," I say. I stand up straight, try to wrestle back some composure. "This is—"

"Who is this? If you're one of those telemarketers, I'm sorry, but I won't be buying anything you have to sell." Impatience and urgency in a low voice, roughened with age. Like my mother's, but with a core of iron running through it that Mom's never had. It has to be her. The woman who wrote that dedication, who left Mom her phone number— my grandmother.

And I should just tell her, just say my own name. But I want my grandmother to know me already, to recognize my voice. I want to have mattered enough to my mother that she told people about me. Even people she's spent my whole life keeping me from.

"It's me" is all I can give her. Please, please, let her know. Please.

"Oh." I hear a staggering sigh. Don't know if it's mine or hers. "Margot. You're Margot."

Something hooks itself behind my chest. Tugs hard enough that I feel it in my whole body. This is what it feels like to get what you want. "Yeah," and I'm embarrassed by how close to crying I sound, after barely any words between us. I squeeze my eyes shut, try to picture the woman on the other end of the phone. All I can conjure up is my mother's face. "That's me."

"That's you," she says, and I'd bet all the money still under my mattress that she's as close to tears as I am. "That's my little girl. That's my granddaughter. God, it's good to hear your voice, honey."

A strangled laugh lurches into my throat, and I swipe at the fresh sting of tears. She sounds like she means it. "You too."

"I've been hoping I would," she says. A pause, one I recognize in my bones, one you take when you're weighing the risk of what to say next. Is that where Mom learned it? Is it part of our line, like our gray hair? "Your mother keeps you to herself," she goes on finally. "But I've been thinking all about you."

"So have I," I say, and it's eager, embarrassing, but none of that matters. My grandmother. My family. Somebody who isn't Mom.

"Where are you these days? Are you well?"

How much does she know? About how we live, Mom and me? "We're fine," I say, a touch of annoyance sneaking into my voice. We're fine, and even when we aren't, that's our problem.

"All right," my grandmother says gently. "I'm glad."

None of my searching ever turned up even the outline of this woman, the empty space she left behind. It certainly never taught me how familiar I should be. "Do I . . ." I clear my throat. "Do I call you Vera, or . . . ?"

She laughs, sharp and clear. Immediately I think I've ruined it, made a fool of myself.

"I get to pick," she says, "don't I?"

Oh. "Yeah." It's just something funny. She's laughing and it's not at me, and it's not because I said something I shouldn't have. It's just something funny.

This might be the nicest conversation I've ever had.

"I never liked Granny," she says. I hear something in the background, like the creak of floorboards. "And I'm much too sensible for something long like Grandmother."

It's real. It's real because she said it. Proof, I think, and I want to write it down in my notebook.

"What about Gram?" she says.

Maybe it would be more polite to just call her by her first name for a while. But if she's opening a door, I'm going through it full speed. "I like that."

"So do I," Gram says. It's easy to start thinking of her that way. I've been wanting this my whole life, after all. "Listen, Margot, I'm glad you called."

I can feel my cheeks fill with heat, a silly smile tugging at my mouth. "Really?"

"Of course. I've been hoping to meet you for a long time, but, well. You know your mother."

"How about now, then?" I'm being too eager, I know it, but I will never get this chance again. "I'll come see you. I'll stay the summer."

"As much as I would love that," Gram says, "it wouldn't feel right to steal you away from Josephine. The two of you should visit together."

I barely hold back a laugh. Me and Mom, dropping by Gram's house like a regular family. "I don't know," I start, but Gram's determined.

"It's been too long," she says. "Bring her home to Phalene; there's a good girl."

Phalene. That must be where Fairhaven is. That's where I need to go.

"I'll try," I say, and it's half true. I'm about to ask for something more, for a promise that Gram will be there waiting, when I hear the squeal of brakes behind me and the slam of a car door. Engine still running, the smell of leaking oil trailing toward me.

"What the hell are you doing?"

FOUR

I freeze. Mom's voice, knifing through the heat, finding me right between my shoulder blades. She's supposed to be at work, north of the high school and nowhere near here.

"Margot?" Gram says in my ear, but I don't respond. A shiver in my skin, breath coming shallow. I keep the phone pressed to my ear, the cord clutched in my fist, and turn around.

Mom's standing on the sidewalk, our station wagon idling at the curb behind her. Hands in the pockets of her work trousers, head tilted, and my body rattles with panic. She's too relaxed. That's how she is before the worst of it, always.

Lie, I tell myself. Lie, and apologize now, before she can ask for it. If I pull the pin myself, the grenade will hurt me less when it goes off.

"I was just calling your office," I say. She's been out— she won't know it's not true. "I was gonna see if you wanted me to bring you lunch, but—"

"Give it to me."

She holds out her hand. Gram's gone quiet in my ear. Just the hush of her breath. She's waiting too.

"It went to voice mail," I start.

But Mom just says, "Now." It jolts through me, sends me stumbling to one side, making room for her in the phone booth before I realize I'm even moving at all. I drop the phone into her hand.

She doesn't say a thing. She's looking right at what I left on the counter. The Bible I bought back from Frank. The photo of Fairhaven, and the message written on the back.

She knows. She has to know who's on the phone, what I've done. Still, she lifts the phone to her ear and she says, "Who is this?" Like she's hoping more than anything she's wrong.

She isn't. And Gram must say something, because I watch it happen. I watch Mom turn into me. The look on her face, suddenly nervous, frightened, and the hold of her body, the hunch of her shoulders, one arm curled around herself. That's mine. That's what she gave me, shelter and cower.

Vera is the woman who taught her to be this kind of mother. A flash of pity in Mom's eyes, of recognition, because she knows. She knows what it feels like and she still did it to me.

"No," she says into the phone at last. Her voice is a quivering little thing. "I can't."

This feels wrong. I shouldn't be watching. But I can't stop, because I've seen Mom angry and I've seen her afraid, and I've seen her with a fire between her fingers and a smile on her face, but I've never seen her like this. I've never seen her belong to anyone. Not even to me.

A pause while Gram talks. Mom turns her back to me. I watch her clench her fist tight, nails digging deep into her own skin.

"No," Mom says again. "I told you then I was never coming back, and that's all I have to say."

Gram's turn, but it's quick, and Mom shakes her head. "I'm not," she says. "I'm not doing this." Stronger now. She means it. If Mom has her way I will never see Gram, and whatever bridge we just built between us will never be crossed. And I can hear Gram now, loud and wordless from the speaker. If I listen hard, if I wish harder, I can make it my name she's saying. *Come home, Margot. Come home.*

Mom takes the phone from her ear. For a moment she doesn't move. Neither do I. Both of us holding our breath, until she hangs up so hard the receiver clatters back off the hook and dangles there on the cord, swaying back and forth.

"Hey," I say, as gently as I can, but Mom whips around, so close the ends of her hair snap across my cheek, and I stagger back, into the sprawl of the sun.

"Why would you do that?" she says, frantic. Her skin flushed with anger, scar standing out white. The Bible on the ledge behind her, catching the sun. "You went to Frank's? You went through my stuff? I told you never to go to Frank's alone, Margot. I told you."

"What?" Another fight for the notebook. "No, you didn't."

"Yes, I did."

"Just like you told me about her?" I say, gesturing to the phone. "Just like you told me about Phalene?"

She flinches, and of course she knows the name of that town. It's the place we've been hiding from all my life.

"You don't know what you're talking about," Mom says. Something animal about the curl of her lips, something I'd be afraid of if I were smarter. "You have no idea, Margot. You talked to her for thirty seconds and you think you can give me shit?"

"For lying to me? Yeah, I do." It's climbing up my throat, the real thing I've been wanting to ask her ever since that first day I wrote *Nielsen* at the top of that notebook page. "Why didn't you tell me about her, Mom?"

"I'm not doing this here," she says, straightening her shirt and tucking her hair behind her ears. "I'm not fighting with you in the middle of the street."

She's locking herself back up, but I won't let her. There's nobody around, the sidewalks empty and glazed with heat-shimmer. And I've kept this down for so long, so long. Until today, when I heard Gram say my name. "Didn't you want me to know I have family?" A tremor in my voice, a break. I hate when I get like this, when I let her see how much I care. "Didn't you want me to know there are people out there who love me?"

"That woman," Mom hisses, "does not love you."

I let out a bark of laughter. "What the hell would you know about it?" And I shouldn't, I shouldn't, I shouldn't take it so wide when there's plenty to be mad at right in front of me. I am supposed to be quiet, I am supposed to be good, but I was born at war and I can only keep from fighting for so long. "You barely even know I'm here half the time. I take care of myself—I do that for you. You could thank me, you know."

"*Me* thank *you*?" Mom smiles. I can't stop my mouth from curling in answer. Fighting is when I feel closest to her. She drops her guard and lets me near enough to see her then, because that way she can hurt me.

"Yeah," I say. A flare in my gut, a warning. This is bait, and I shouldn't be taking it. But it broke something inside me—Gram on the phone, and Mom nowhere near remorse for keeping me from her. She doesn't care, so why should

I? Why should I pull any punches for her sake? "Yeah, you thank me. Thank me for making a life out of your mess."

For a second she looks like I've hit home. It can't be real, though. When has anything I've ever said mattered to her that much? And it's gone in a moment, papered over by a grim determination. It must have been nothing. Just the sun in my eyes.

"Listen to me very carefully," she says through gritted teeth. "I am your mother. Do you know what that means? It means your life is mine. I gave it to you. And I am the only thing keeping you alive. Keeping you safe. So thank me for that."

She's handing me a way out of our fight, and every other time I have taken it. Every other time I've given ground, tried to rebuild a peace between us because it was worth it. Because she was all I had. But I don't think that's true anymore.

"What about everything after?" I say. "Huh? You gave me my life, but there's more to being a mother than that."

She shakes her head. "Stop it."

I can't. Not now, not when I'm finally saying everything that's been beating in me like blood. "Don't you know? The shit you do touches me, Mom. It fucking hurts."

"You think it doesn't hurt me?" Her eyes are overbright, her hands trembling as she pushes her hair out of her face. "What about that? What about me, Margot?"

As if we haven't been answering that question my whole life. And that's all it takes. That's the whole of my decision, in one heartbeat. Mom, with me in front of her, with me in pain and alone, and she asks, "What about me?"

"I don't know. It's not my job to know," I say. Maybe it should be harder to talk to her like this. But it feels like relief, drifting and cool. "Honestly, Mom, I don't care."

I expect some sort of reaction. Some sort of pain, or even my relief mirrored in her. But she only laughs. That same dismissive look on her face as at the end of every fight. I don't understand how she can swing back and forth so fast, how things can stop mattering to her from one second to the next. "I told you, Margot," she says. "I'm not doing this. It's my goddamn lunch break and I'm just not doing this." She nods to the phone booth, to the Bible and the photograph. "Sell that back to Frank. It's not worth whatever you paid for it. And we'll talk about where you got the money later."

She doesn't understand what's just happened. I have to tell myself that as she steps away from me, as she gets into our station wagon and pulls away from the curb. She doesn't understand that this, this conversation, this rejection— that's what I needed. I'm ready to leave her.

Even if she did get it, I'm not sure she'd ask me to stay.

I spend the afternoon in Redman's, don't go back to the apartment until dark. She's already asleep when I get there. Doesn't wake as I sneak into the bedroom to get the rest of my money from under the mattress. Doesn't wake as I pace through the night in the living room, waiting for dawn.

Nobody but you and me. She doesn't think that'll ever change. I didn't used to either.

When the sun breaks the sky, I know it's time. I leave three twenties stuck between the pages of the Bible and hide it in one of the cupboards above the stove, the photograph and the rest of the cash safe in my pocket. She'll find it if she needs it. I can do that, at least.

Outside, the air is just touched with chill. I take my hair down from my braid, let it hang around my shoulders. No phone and no ID, but ahead there's the lure of the streetlights along the highway. There's the rush of a passing car, and east or west, wherever it is, that's where I'm going. Phalene.

FIVE

Morning finds me in the back of some guy's pickup. He passed me on the sidewalk outside the Safeway in Calhoun, and if he'd looked at my bare legs for a half second longer I wouldn't be here. As it is, he told me I could ride in the cab or climb into the truck bed. I picked the bed.

Johnny—that's what he said his name is—didn't know what the hell I was talking about when I told him I was looking for Phalene, but he typed it into his phone and said sure, he could drop me in the town center. It startled me, how close it looked on the map. Barely three hours away on the back roads. I expected it to be over in the east, near Omaha, or even out of state, but instead it's practically next door by Nebraska standards. As if Mom ran as far as she could, and it turned out to be not very far at all.

It's taken us longer than it should, though. Johnny insisted on a too-long nap at a rest stop just before Crawford, and I spent the whole thing ready to bolt if another truck pulled into the lot. But we're close now. And here I am, sky fresh and wide overhead as I sink farther into the pile of burlap and tarps and hold tight to a bungee cord Johnny's got hooked to the side.

Just get to Phalene. Just find Gram. She'll take care of the rest.

This far northwest, Nebraska's not as patched-up with farmland. The ground we crossed on the drive seemed layered with long grasses and low, broken hills. Here, it's starting to level out. Now and then I can spot a house dropped into the middle of nothing a mile or two back from the highway.

Lives going on like nothing happened. I wonder what Mom's doing at home. Whether she's noticed that I'm gone. Whether she's already on her way after me.

I grip the bungee cord so tightly that it cuts into my palm. That's not happening. Mom's probably as happy to have lost me as I am to have left. She doesn't matter anymore. I left her behind. I picked something else.

Gram, and maybe more. Maybe a grandfather, aunts, uncles, cousins. The kind of family you see in pictures. As long as Phalene's still on the horizon, I can wonder, and I can hope.

If I'm remembering the map right, we're coming in from the east, through what should be fields thick with green. But they're stripped bare, flattened, with barely the slightest hint of any furrows for planting. Someone used to farm here a long time ago, but there's nothing more to get out of this land. It's dead.

The town starts all at once, sprouts from the black earth on either side of what passes for a highway. It's only been one lane in either direction since Calhoun, but now the pavement starts to fracture and gape, and houses press in, their shapes familiar, like they were all built from the same plans. I let them glaze past me. None of these is Fairhaven, the house I saw in the photograph. This might be Phalene, but it's not Nielsen land.

After a few blocks the houses drop away and the town opens onto a square. That's where Johnny leaves me, on the sidewalk in front of a laundromat, his truck's exhaust sticking to the back of my throat as he disappears.

Late morning. Barely anyone around, and it's quiet, the air stale as I squint through the sun to get a look at the town. There, laid out like a handkerchief in the center: a park, lush and well kept, with a circle of brick in the middle, where two spigots are spraying out a high arch of water, rainbows ricocheting onto bronze statues of children playing.

It's empty in the way Calhoun is, ramshackle and

weathered, but there's a quaintness to it that's unfamiliar. Buildings border the park, low storefronts and flapping awnings in colors that used to be candy-bright, the sort of thing you'd see in a snow globe or a picture book. Most of the stores seem empty from here. A grocery, the name on the crooked sign different from the name in painted letters on the big front window. A pharmacy—Hellman's, by the neon flicker over the door—where there at least seem to be some people inside. And behind me the laundromat, its door open, all yellow tile and peeling linoleum. An older woman sits behind the counter, her eyes shut as she listens to a commercial on the radio.

This is it. Phalene.

This is *it*?

I told myself I wasn't expecting anything. But of course I was. Something inside me thought I'd set foot on Phalene land and feel it burrowing into me like roots—a belonging. Something inside me thought Gram would be waiting when I pulled into town.

She's here somewhere. I'll find her.

As I'm watching, a group comes spilling out of Hellman's, their laughter carrying across the park. They seem about my age, maybe a little older. I shove my hands in my pockets and start to walk slowly around the park toward them. At the very least they can tell me where I can find some breakfast.

The closer I get, the more I can pick them apart. Three

people gathered around a fourth, a girl with a long dark ponytail pulled so tight on her skull that it hurts just to look at her. She's holding something in her hands, glancing over her shoulder into the pharmacy with a bright laugh.

"Hey," a voice says, "I see we're shoplifting for fun now," and she twists around.

"It's just a pack of gum, Eli," she says to a guy standing a few steps back. Her voice is low, hoarse, like she's been yelling all night, or like she was asleep until just a few seconds ago. "Besides, you really think Hellman's gonna ask the police to arrest his landlord's daughter?"

"His name's not Hellman," the boy says as she doles out pieces of gum to her friends. "What, you think the workers at Wendy's are all named Wendy?"

The girl rolls her eyes. I'm near enough now that I can see how pretty she is, in a strange, almost secret way. Wide-set eyes, brown like her hair, and a pale, thin mouth. She's wearing a version of what I am, shorts and a loose T-shirt, only hers looks fresh from the store, the rips in her shorts done just so.

"Calm down," she says, popping a square of gum into her mouth and chewing with her obscenely white teeth. "It's a buck fifty, max. I'll pay him next time."

The boy—he feels too old for that word, but not by much—kicks at a crack in the sidewalk and sighs. That kind of resignation you feel when this is just how someone is. I know it from Mom.

"Hey."

I look up. She's watching me from the hold of her friends, between the swing of their summer-blond hair. They haven't turned to face me yet, and I don't think they will. That's all right. I'm not interesting to them, and vice versa.

"Hey," I say back. It doesn't sound right. I'm good with parents who ask where my father is, with the librarians who ask if I'm sure I don't want anything from the vending machine, their treat, but girls like me—I don't know what everything means. Just like with Mom, every word has some different meaning hiding inside, but I always guess the wrong one.

My heart trips in my chest as the girl slips free of her friends and steps toward me. A minute ago I would've said she was perfect, but now I can see the sweat at her hairline, the damp gleam of her throat and the chips in her pale pink nail polish. The color matches the pack of gum she's holding in the palm of her hand.

"You want a piece?" she says, holding it out. Head tilted, voice too innocent, too friendly. But there's a smile on her face like encouragement. And I unravel her in my head, because that's what you do when you don't have anybody there to fill the hole of your life, and here is this girl, waiting for somebody to join her, to take up her dares, to be the person on the bike next to her as she whips through midnight on her way out of this town.

Sure, I think. I could do that with you.

I don't get the words out, though, before she's shrugging and turning back to the others. I watch her knit herself back into her friends, arms around waists and ankles knocking, and they cross the road, onto the grass. Passing laughter between them like a joint, and the boy follows, reluctant, slow. For a moment I let myself imagine me with them. A fourth girl in that line. My hand in someone else's pocket.

Doesn't matter. I shake my head, clear it. A girl with needle-narrow legs and skin she lets the sun touch—that unnerves me more than anything. Terrifies me, that I want to be one. That I want to be *with* one. That I want to slice one open to see just how it works when you live like that.

I head for the door of the pharmacy, ignore the drift of voices from the park as I step through. The AC is on full, buffeting down so hard that my hair flickers into my eyes, and for a second I just stand there and let it push the summer out of me.

At the far end is a long pharmacy counter, a man propped up on his elbow behind it, flipping through a catalog. I duck into one of the aisles. I'm not hiding. I just hate that first moment when an adult sees me, when the good girl inside slips herself over my body like a goddamn couch cover.

Of course I picked the aisle stacked high with tampons. My face goes hot, blood rushing under my skin, and I hurry past pads and things that shouldn't embarrass me, that maybe wouldn't if I had a mother who didn't make it seem like the very existence of my body was a personal affront.

"Can I help you?" the man at the counter calls just as I'm about to turn up the next aisle. I freeze, feel the tug of my public smile pulling at my cheeks. It's already on tight by the time I turn around.

"Yes," I say, starting toward him, careful to sound like I know what I'm doing. "I'm looking for Fairhaven. Or Vera Nielsen?"

I'm expecting a shrug. An idle gesture in one direction or another. Instead the man's ruddy face goes pale as I get close.

"Nielsen?" He straightens. "Who's asking?"

"Nobody," I say immediately, my mother's caution an instinct I can't shed. But the damage is done. His eyes are wide, his mouth slack.

"Jesus," he says, "you look just like them," and I think of Mom, of the face I share with her. Gram must be the same. Here in Phalene, that doesn't seem to be a good thing, if the look on the clerk's face is anything to go by.

"Never mind," I say, eager to leave. "I just got turned around."

"No, hang on." And he almost sounds kind, but he's reaching for the landline next to the register. "I'll call the station. They can help you if you just wait a minute."

I don't. I give him that same public smile and exit the way I came, through the gust of the AC. And out in the heat, someone is waiting for me.

SIX

It's the girl from before, her phone in her hand, the glow from the screen washed out by the sun. She looks up as I let the glass pharmacy door slam shut behind me.

"You're new," she says. Behind her, at the center of the park, the others are laid out on the grass, one girl pulling off her shirt. She's got a bathing suit on underneath, and she shrieks as the boy shoves her into the spray of the fountain.

The girl in front of me clears her throat. I haven't answered her fast enough.

"Yeah," I say. I check over my shoulder. Through the door I can see the clerk on the phone, looking right at me as he speaks. "Margot," I say, facing her again. "I'm Margot."

"Margot what?" She smiles when I don't answer, smug

and amused. If she knows what I am, she doesn't seem surprised, the way the clerk was. Instead she just tilts her head so her glossy ponytail falls over her shoulder. "I'm Tess."

Laughter from the others. I look over at them, but Tess doesn't move an inch. Watches me, and watches, and pops her shoplifted bubble gum.

"Where are you from?" she says.

I have to not be standing here anymore, right where that man can see me. I don't know who he called. The police, maybe, and if I stay here I could be letting them find me. Could be letting them send me back to Mom.

"Calhoun County," I say. I step around Tess and into the road. I've learned my lesson about being direct. I can still get what I need; I just have to be more careful. "You know a good place to get something to eat? Or you got anything more than gum?"

"Yeah," Tess says. "The Omni's open." She points across the square, to the grocery store with its mismatched signs.

"Can you show me?" This is the kind of girl who knows everything about her town, the kind of girl who can put the whole thing into her pocket without missing a beat. Calhoun has one of them, but she's never gotten within three feet of me. Still, Tess can't be that hard to work. I'm betting that if I can keep her talking, she'll tell me where to find Fairhaven.

Tess raises her eyebrows—the Omni is right there, after

all—but gives me an indulgent little smile that makes me feel about five years old. "Sure."

I follow her down the middle of the road, checking behind me to make sure nobody's shown up to answer the clerk's call. But there's nothing. Nothing at all. Just the hum of crickets and the press of the sun, and Tess and her friends and the pharmacy clerk could be the only people alive, the only hearts beating in the whole town.

The boy watches as we turn the corner of the park and pass by. He's too far away for me to be sure, but I think he's frowning. Tess is supposed to be over there, stretched out, keeping up with her tan. Instead she's here, with me.

The Omni looks pretty much exactly like the pharmacy. Same brick face. Same poorly fitted door that squeaks egregiously as we push it open and sidle through. The lighting inside is even the same, fluorescent and yellow and fizzing. The air-conditioning isn't working, and the cashier is fanning herself with a tabloid magazine.

"Hey, Leah," Tess says. The cashier ignores her, but Tess doesn't seem bothered. She just keeps going, leads me down the first aisle—half of it empty, like the whole place has been raided or, more likely, understocked—toward the back, where a row of clear freezers covers the far wall.

She props herself against them, the chill raising goose bumps on her crossed arms. I look away, busy myself reading the prices on a rack of bruised produce.

"Margot," she says, like she's trying it on. "So, what are you in for?"

"That's what they ask in prison, right?" I say, frowning.

Tess only laughs. "Where do you think you are?"

Something curdles deep in my stomach. I don't know this girl, don't know a thing about her, really, but I know what money looks like, and I know how it sounds when a person doesn't understand what they have.

Fuck you, I think. I'd give a lot to be in your kind of cell.

"What's so bad about it?" I ask, turning a particularly damaged banana over in my hands. It's too soft, like just the slightest pressure would split the peel. Quickly, I put it back.

"Oh, you know." Tess straightens up, strands from her ponytail sticking to the door of the freezer. She smiles when she notices me watching. "Middle of nowhere. Boring. But I guess it's not boring if you're here for Fairhaven."

I go still. "For what?"

"Oh, come on," she says. "Really?"

Is it that obvious who I belong to? If not for our ages, Mom and I could be sisters, could be twins, and maybe it's the same with Gram, but I didn't expect anyone to recognize me.

I could tell her. I was ready to when I got here, with no reason to hide. But the panic that wrapped around me as the pharmacy clerk reached for the phone—I can still feel it. *Not safe, not safe,* over and over in my head.

"Have it your way," Tess says, when it's clear I won't respond, and I can see the interest leak out of her, see her summer smile sliding back on.

So she doesn't care. If I'm not going to entertain her, I'm worth less of her time. But I still need to find Gram. And I know Tess can tell me how, if I can only find a way to ask that doesn't mean giving her something in exchange.

I should talk about her. She'll open up that way.

"Your family own this place too?" I say, grabbing a bag of chips from the rack. She frowns, and I wave it off. "I heard you before. Landlord's daughter."

"That's me," she says, giving a wide, sparkling smile for a moment before it drops and she's rolling her eyes. "Yeah, they bought up half the town."

The storefronts, maybe. Or the land I passed on the way in, flat and dry, furrowed from long-ago planting. "Are the fields yours too? They looked pretty wrecked."

Tess takes the chips from me and opens the bag, fishes for a handful. "Out east? If it's wrecked it's not ours. Everything else is, though. It's all a mess. Phalene used to be a big farming town when the Nielsens owned it, but after the drought, the land went bad and nobody could afford to grow anything."

I swallow my questions. Not yet. Not yet.

Tess bites a chip, bits of it falling to the floor. "Didn't

53

you see? On the way in?"

I nod. That could ruin a town. Acres and acres, wasted and barren all at once. Too many people. Not enough work. I wonder if that happened to Gram.

"I mean, we still plant," Tess continues, "and I guess so does Vera, if you can really call it that. Her whole farm seems like an exercise in futility, but tell that to her." She shakes her head. "God, why anyone stays in this town is truly beyond me."

"So leave," I say. Mom left Phalene. And I left Mom. You can always make it out of somewhere, if you want it badly enough.

"Yeah," Tess says, a moment too late. Something's there, moving under the tight mask of her smile, but she's not about to let a stranger see it. "Anyway."

She heads for the register, waving to the cashier as she fishes out another handful of chips. I hurry after her.

"One fifty," the girl says, not looking up from the tabloid, which she now has open on the conveyor belt.

"Thanks, Leah," Tess says, and then she's outside, the chips still with her. I sigh, hand Leah my money and wait for change before following.

"Can I have some?" I ask, not waiting for an answer before I take the bag from her. "Listen, about Vera—"

"Tess!"

We both startle, and I follow Tess's gaze to the park,

where her friends were a few minutes ago. Now it's just the boy, standing by the bike rack with one hand raised to keep the sun out of his eyes.

"Hang on," she calls back. When she turns to me, she's got almost an apology on her face. "That's Eli," she says.

I don't bother looking at him again. I've seen enough boys to know he has the sort of face I think I'm supposed to like, but how can any of that matter when there are girls like Tess in the world? I clear my throat. "Are you guys . . ."

She laughs, shrugs one shoulder. "Depends who you ask."

I'm asking you, I want to say. She's gone before I can, crossing the road and stepping onto the grass, beckoning for me to follow.

Eli nods in my direction as we approach—that, apparently, is how boys say hello in Phalene—and then wordlessly holds his phone out to Tess. She takes it, biting her lip as she scans the screen, and then lets out a laugh.

"Holy shit," she says. "Really?"

"Yeah. Will says he passed it on his way to work."

I feel ridiculous standing here, watching them have their own conversation, so I reach into the bag of chips and come up with a handful. It crinkles so loudly that Eli looks my way just as I'm in the middle of shoving it into my mouth. So what. I'm hungry.

"We should go see," Tess says. She's practically bouncing, her smile real and shining. "If it's happening again."

If *what's* happening again?

Eli takes his phone back, shoves it in his pocket and moves toward one of the two bikes propped up in the rack. "You know I hate when you get started with that." I want to ask what he means, but he's already waving Tess away. "Come on. Let's do something else."

"What's going on?" I say.

"Oh, you'll want to see this," Tess says even as Eli makes a noise of protest. "Somebody lit the Nielsen farm on fire again."

It sweeps over me, a panic so wild and sudden I don't understand it. Gram. That's Gram's land, and it's burning. "On fire?" And then, as the rest of Tess's words sneak inside: "Again?"

"Yeah," she says. "Just like before. A new fire for a new Nielsen."

She says it like it's a story she's telling, excited and eager. But this is real, and it matters. It matters that she knows my name. It matters that somewhere out there, my grandmother's fields are on fire. What if Fairhaven is burning? What if Gram's injured?

"Is everyone okay?" I manage to ask.

She shrugs. "Will didn't say."

I'm too close for it to all disappear. I won't let it.

"We should go," I say. "Now. We should go now."

SEVEN

The sun is high as we follow the main road out of town, Tess riding in front, standing up on her pedals. Eli stays steady; I'm perched on his handlebars, his arms bracketing me. It's uncomfortable, and I can tell he'd rather I weren't here, but after the first block I stop holding my body so stiff, stop focusing so hard on keeping my skin away from his, and manage a look around.

Outside the town center it's more of those houses I passed on the way in, identical and rotting. Paint flaking like shedding skin, beams at an angle, the whole place swooning in the summer heat. Some houses are shut up and dark, mail piled on the porch. Others I can see into the kitchen, can watch a woman pick at crusted food on her apron as her microwave runs, can watch a toddler scream and scream from their high chair, red-faced and alone.

Mom was here. I can picture it, can put her on any one of these porches, in any one of these houses. I wonder if she was born wanting to be anywhere else, or if this place put it into her. If there were already stories about her last name or if the stories are about her.

It's three more blocks before the town ends. Just like that. One moment it's houses and streets that might have been tree-lined once, cars scattered like litter, and then it's gone. Land smothered with crops, and the almost painfully empty stretch of the sky.

"Oh," I say, before I can help myself, and I feel Eli's chest jump behind me, like he's laughing.

Tess said her family still plants, and said my grandmother does too. Or tries. This must be the land, hers or mine. The earth, dark and gritty and dry as we pass, and everywhere the yellow rise of the corn. This time of year it should be chest high and a bright, new sort of green. I've seen enough of it around Calhoun to know. But it's not. And I know what Tess meant when she described Gram's farm. Because this is all wrong.

The corn is too tall, maybe eight feet, and a strange, flat yellow, like it's dying even as it grows. I wait for it, for the moment when we hit just the right angle to see all the way down the paths reaching empty and clean between the planting rows. But it never comes. The ranks are long gone, and what's left is a tangle, stalks knotted together, the smell strangely bitter and almost chemical. I want to shut my eyes, to pretend Phalene has something else to give me, but I can't. Because there, pluming black and heavy. Smoke on the horizon.

"Come on," Eli calls over my head. "This is close enough."

"No way," Tess says. "Let's keep going."

"It's getting dangerous, Tess."

"I think you mean it's getting good."

"Jesus Christ," Eli mutters. "It's a fucking fire." I don't think he means me to hear, but I'm glad I do, and when he sends us riding after her, I feel a little better, always more comfortable in the breath of a fight.

He's right, anyway. Tess is acting like this is all happening a hundred miles from her, like it's a movie, a dream. It would unsettle me if I didn't feel almost the same way. Out of my body, all in my head, just wanting and worry.

We keep going. The sky closer and closer, dropping to wrap us in bitter gray, until I can actually feel the fire against my skin, a heartbeat of heat; can hear the rush of the burn in my ears and the wind carrying it toward us as Eli pedals after Tess, her ponytail streaming behind her.

Up ahead, the road widens to a gravel shoulder that juts into the corn. Tess swerves onto it, and Eli follows her, braking so hard I tip off the handlebars.

"Sorry," he mutters, but I'm not paying attention, because from here I can see the fire. Maybe half a mile out, maybe less. Ripping through the farmland like a bullet, pushed by the wind.

For all the time I've spent with a lighter against my palm, this isn't any fire I know. Wild and bright and red, red, red, and it drifts up off the crops in waves before breaking, crashing in a spray of spark and ash.

"Shit," Eli says. "Guys, we should go."

Tess leaves us behind, steps right up to the edge of the gravel. The fields drop off on either side of the highway, dipping to a ditch before stretching out flat. From here we can see over the top of the corn, can watch the fire take more of the earth with every minute.

"Where's the fire department?" I ask. "Shouldn't they be here?"

Tess has her thumbnail between her teeth, scraping at the underside of it until she swallows, and I forget to look away.

"It'll take them a while," she says, "if they show up at all." Shoots me a grin, no hint of sympathy or anything close to it. "Nielsen land isn't high priority."

"Is this all Vera's?"

Tess nods. "The house is that way." She points toward the fire, and the air's too clouded for me to see anything, but she keeps going. "Out near mine."

"Will your house be okay?"

I expected her to care about her own, at least, but she just shrugs and says, "Probably," like she hasn't really thought about it until right now. "The wind's taking it toward town anyway."

Eli steps up next to her. My stomach sinks as he drapes his arm over her shoulders, tugging at her until she leans against him. *Are* they together? Or is this just how people can be?

I look away, stare out over the fire. This is where my mother came from. And somewhere behind all this is a woman who wants me.

That's when I see it. A twitch in the corn, rippling, and the flash of something pale in the sweep of yellow and gold. I squint hard, try to make out any shape through the smoke. For a long moment, there's nothing, just my own breathing and the trip of my heart, but then there it is again.

"Do you see that?" I say. "I think someone's out there."

"What?" Eli says.

I barely hear him. It is; it's someone, out in the crops, fire tumbling toward them. Too slow. They're moving too slow, if they're moving at all. They won't make it to safety.

I'm breaking for them before I realize it. Scrambling down the bank, gravel pouring down the slope with me. The corn sways and crackles, beckoning me, and I can hear Eli calling out, but somebody needs help.

I crash in, leaves snapping against my raised arms,

stalks bending, arching over my head to close out the sky. The air thick and thicker with ash, and I can't remember where I saw it, that slip of skin, of someone. It already hurts to breathe too deeply, the smoke sliding like water down my throat.

"Hello?" I yell, before my voice dries up. No answer, or nothing I can hear, so I keep on. Heat coming in, screaming up my skin, the fire rolling like fog. Already my arms are red, already my mouth is dry and thirsty. It would be smart to go back. It would be smart to never have come here at all.

Instead I crouch, peer through the gathering smoke. I'm farther out than I realized, closer to the burn, and the ground is warm where I press my palms into it, leaning on them to get a better look, because there it is, just like I thought. A person, sprawled on their side, and it's a girl, a girl with long dark hair, and she's not moving.

"Hey!" I yell, crawling forward. Thirty yards away, maybe. I can't stand back up, not if I mean to keep breathing. The sky blotted out overhead, my lungs catching closed. Closer now. The girl's skin is too pale, and her body too still. "Can you hear me?"

She's wearing a dress, faded and too small for her, seams stretching and pulling across her ribs. Finally I'm near enough to touch her. I reach out, palms stained ash-black, and shake her arm. She doesn't move.

"Are you okay? Hello?"

The fire cracks, hisses and spits, and I throw my arm up to keep a spray of sparks from my eyes. The wind is carrying it too quickly—if I don't move soon, my way back to the road will be cut off, and I'll be trapped. But I can't leave her here. I don't know who she is or how she got out here; I just know I can't leave her.

I get to my feet, my body bent in half to keep out of the smoke, but it's no use. My tongue fuzzy with the taste of it, my eyes watering. I grab her hand, hold my shirt over my mouth with my other hand, and pull as hard as I can. Her body jerks toward me. Hair falling across her face, gauzy air clinging to the shape of her. I try again, only manage to get her a few inches farther before I have to let go and catch my breath.

She's too heavy, and the smoke is too thick, and I need help. I can't do this on my own. Most everything I can, but this is too much. The fire is too close. I cannot do this by myself.

"Hey!" I yell over my shoulder. "Eli! Someone!"

There's a shout, and I turn to see Eli's tall figure coming through the gray, his elbow raised to shield his face.

"You've been out here too long," he calls, and I could cry. Somebody came after me.

"There's a girl," I say. He closes the last distance, his eyes red, a streak of soot across his cheek. "I think she's hurt."

Or worse, but that doesn't matter. "You have to help me carry her."

"I'll do it," he says, stepping around me. "You go ahead."

But I can't leave her, not just like that, so I watch as he bends and hoists her up like she's nothing. Drops her over his shoulder, her head hanging down, fingers curled delicately.

A gust of wind. We both flinch as a lick of fire whips past us, and Eli shouts, his voice breaking with panic, but he's yelling, "Go, Margot, go!" so I run. I run so hard I can feel every step shuddering up through my bones, so hard I forget to breathe, and when I do the air burns me from the inside out. Fire is not like this, not the way I know it. It's swallowing the field, the dry scorch stealing the life from my skin. I don't last long before I'm gasping, the air turning to dust in my lungs. Eli behind me somewhere, but if I turn around I'll see it, the reach of the flame, and I have to keep going.

Ahead, a break in the smoke, and there's the road, the shoulder a bank of broken glass and gravel. Tess is waiting, her phone pressed to her ear, lit red and blue in the flash of police lights. A cruiser parked across the highway, and sirens muffling the scream of the fire.

One more step. Another. It's gonna be okay.

"Hey!" Tess yells when she sees me. "There they are!"

A man in uniform kneels at the top of the bank, reaching down. "Come on, honey," he says, his eyes fixed on Eli behind me. I let him haul me out of the corn, to the safety of the road.

He lets go as soon as I'm up, and I pitch onto my hands and knees, the air so fresh it's almost cold. I forgot what breathing was like.

Somebody crouches next to me. "You're okay," they say. Tess, her face knit tight with concern.

"Help!" I hear Eli yell, and I try to get up, but Tess keeps me still.

"They're right behind you," she says, smoothing her hand across my forehead. I shut my eyes, gulp down another breath.

"Shit," one of the officers says. I open my eyes in time to see him using his uniform hat to smother the girl's dress where a spark has caught, burned it black and left her skin scorched red. Eli's jaw is set, his eyes wide as he hurriedly passes her into the other officer's arms.

Tess helps me to my feet. Something's different about her, about the look on her face, like in the rush of everything she forgot to put on that perfectly bored expression she was wearing before.

There's a fire truck barreling past us, but it's probably no use. The fire is spreading too quickly. It'll take this land, and more besides, and when it dies, it will be because it's finished, not because somebody decided it was.

"I'm going to set her down," the officer carrying the girl

says. "Just until the ambulance gets here."

Eli collapses onto the gravel. "I don't think you'll need one."

I step closer as they lay her out. Her dress is flowered, with a high neckline and sheer, puffed sleeves that cut into her arms. She looks like she's from twenty years ago. A hundred. I kneel next to her, ignore the warning from the officer.

Her head is tilted away from me, hair across her face—all I can see is her mouth, only just open. I adjust her head. She's still warm, the heat of her leaking into my hands. One of the officers grabs my arm, tells me to stop, but he's too late, and her hair's falling away, streaks of gray at the temples, and "Shit."

I scramble backward into the officer's legs, breathing hard.

Pale freckled face. Strong nose and stronger chin. Eyes open, dark and staring and empty, empty, empty. I know that face. It's mine. It's my mother's.

Nielsen land, I think, for one wild moment. A Nielsen body on Nielsen land. I can hear the officers talking, can hear Tess say my name, feel her hand on my arm, but none of it matters.

Because there is a stranger wearing my face. And she's dead.

EIGHT

I only have a second to tip over onto my hands and knees before my stomach is seizing and the chips I ate are spattering onto the pavement in a mouthful of bile.

"Jesus," one of the officers says, and the sound of it, of somebody else, brings the world slamming back into me. First the officer's hands on my arms, tight and binding as he lifts me up. Then Tess next to me, her jaw slack, her eyes wide.

"Who is that?" she says. "I don't understand."

And I don't either, because I am here, I am breathing, and I am laid out on the highway in a too-small dress, and for a second, for an age, I can't tell which of us is which. Whether I'm living or not. *Sister, sister,* the word running through my blood, but that can't be right. There can't have been another of me. I would know. Wouldn't I?

No, a voice at the back of my head whispers. *Never. Your mother has spent your whole life building walls around the both of you.* Maybe this was why.

"I need you to step back, Miss Miller," the officer holding me says to Tess. Officer Connors, according to the name tag on his chest. I focus on the letters, on the fade and scratch of them, because that, at least, is real. He's got his other hand on his gun, casually, like he doesn't mean to. I don't buy that for a second. "Right now."

"What for?" Tess asks even as Eli pulls her away. "Margot. Margot, are you—"

"I said," Officer Connors repeats more firmly, "step back."

He still hasn't let go of me. I don't think he will anytime soon. I don't know, really, what this looks like. Just that it doesn't look good. And I wish, I wish I could explain it to them, but how does any of this fit together in a way that makes sense? She's still there. Staring up at the sky. A sister of mine that Mom left behind? Or something else—my mind giving me what I wanted and making it a nightmare.

The first police officer, Officer Anderson, steps in front of me, blocking my view of the body. I let myself be relieved until I catch the look on his face. Suspicious and accusing, and I don't like it, but at least it's familiar. Just like Mom.

He's tall, his face beaten with sun, his dark uniform drenched in sweat. "I'd ask you your name," he says, "but I think I can guess."

"It's Margot," I say, before I realize that's not what he meant. Nielsen. What else could I be, with a face like mine?

"We should get everybody back to the station," Officer Connors says next to me. "Leave this to the techs."

Anderson doesn't move. "Not yet," he says, eyes fixed on me. "Margot? Okay, Margot. Can you tell me what happened? What were the two of you doing out there?"

A fire engine blares past, its sirens at a shriek, the sound so loud it seems to shake the whole world. I can feel my body trying to get back to normal, trying to settle in spite of the adrenaline racing through my veins.

"The two of us?" He must mean me and Eli. Unless—

"You and your sister here," Anderson says.

It jolts something loose in me, hearing it from him. "No," I say, and I manage one step toward him before Officer Connors hauls me back, fingers tight around my arm. "No, that's not. She's not. I've never seen her before. Not ever." I want to keep talking. I have to make him understand. I have to understand it myself—that this girl is not mine. She is not my mother's. She can't be.

"Never?" Anderson raises his eyebrows. "Not once? I'm sure you can understand why I have a little trouble believing that."

"Margot was with me all morning," Tess says from over his shoulder.

He barely blinks. "And I'm sure you can understand why I have a little trouble believing Miss Miller."

"She's not lying," Eli calls. His face flat and pale with shock, his fingers flexing like he's trying to shake the feeling of that body in his arms. "We brought Margot out here. She didn't do this." His eyes meet mine for a fraction too long. I can almost hear him ask it: *Right*?

"I swear," I say, my voice unsteady. "I just came to Phalene this morning." It feels ridiculous to be standing here talking about this when there's a body like mine laid out on the pavement. But she isn't impossible to them like she is to me. She's just another girl they've never seen before. A simple story. Two girls go in, and one comes out.

"All right," Anderson says. Indulgent. Fake. "You just got here and you've never seen this girl before. Let's say that's true. So what happened?"

"Tess and Eli heard there was a fire," I say. I want to look to Tess, want her to confirm it, but I know if I look away even once, Anderson will call it guilt. "They wanted . . . we wanted to see. So we rode out here."

"And you're sure it had already started?" Anderson says.

"Yes." I try to remember what happened in town, whether it was Tess or Eli who got the message. "Someone saw it and told us."

"Because this is Nielsen land." Anderson nods to the fields, to the fire sweeping closer. "And you can tell me any kind of lie you like, Margot, but you two are Nielsen girls. That means something in this town."

"And what's that?" I ask. A challenge, sure, but more than that, something I need to know.

Anderson smiles grimly. "Trouble."

The blur of adrenaline is leaving my body, and pain is taking its place, prickling over my skin, throbbing and fuzzy. "I'm telling the truth. We were watching and I saw someone out there." I sway suddenly, the heat gripping me hard and letting go. I need some water. I need to sit down.

Take a deep breath. Eyes back on him. "So I went to look."

"You just ran out into a fire?" Anderson leans in. "You weren't scared?"

I have to be careful. I'm alone here, and there's a reason they're not talking to Eli, even though he's the one who carried the body out of the field. Treat it like Mom, I tell myself. Only what you'd say to her on her very worst day. "Of course I was scared," I say. "But I thought someone needed help."

"Sure." Anderson nods like he believes me, but nothing about him relaxes. "So you went out there to help. Then what?"

"Leland and Polk are on their way," Connors says. He nods to the third police officer, the one setting up traffic cones across the highway behind Tess and Eli. "Mather can hold the scene until then. Let's go, yeah? They need some water and a medic."

A medic. I glance down at my flushed hands, feel the sting of a burn along my hairline like it only just now occurred to my body to feel any pain.

"Then what did you do?" Anderson presses, ducking to meet my eyes. "I want to get you looked after just like Officer Connors does, but we have to do this first. We have to do it now, Margot."

Ignore it, I tell myself; ignore the flush of your skin and the roar of the fire, still there, still in your veins. Get this over with. "I tried to lift her. But I couldn't. So Eli came. He carried her out. And that's when you got here."

For a moment nobody moves. I think maybe I've done it. Maybe this is just a mess we're all in together, and there's no blame hiding in any of it.

Then Anderson sighs. "I really wish you wouldn't lie," he says. "It'd be so much easier."

"I'm not," I say. It's all I have the energy for. I am so tired and I don't understand any of this. These men, asking about the fire when the real question is there on the ground, her eyes open, her heart still. Half of me wants to kneel over her again, to touch my forehead to hers and make sure I saw what I think I did; the other half is sick at the thought of it.

"All right," Anderson says. "Then we need to go to the station."

Connors adjusts his grip on me, holding my elbow

loosely. "And we need to call Vera."

"Well, sure," Anderson says, rocking back on his heels. "But not just yet. Margot still has some things to tell us."

"Hey," I hear, and I watch Tess push off from Eli and come toward us. She gives the body a wide berth, but apart from that you'd never know she'd noticed it at all. There's nothing in her of that fear I find under everything I do. "You can't just take her, okay? Everybody here is a minor." Her shoulder just brushing mine as she edges in front of me. "And like I said, Margot's been with me all morning. So whatever you think happened, you can drop it."

Anderson shuts his eyes briefly. "Save it for the station, would you?"

"She has to come too?" I ask.

"Of course. All three of you do." Anderson nods to Connors, who turns away and speaks into the walkie-talkie strapped to his shoulder. "You can call your families once we're there."

Our families. Mom. I haven't even thought about that. But I should've. I should've been worrying about that from the start, because they'll tell her where I am, the trouble I'm in, and she'll be so angry.

"It's all right," Tess says to me. And when I look at her I'm surprised by the earnestness I can see shining out of her. I can't really fit it together with the girl from town, the one with stolen bubble gum and a sly smile. "My dad will take care of it. I'll talk to him."

"You do that," Anderson says, and the bare amusement in his voice makes me nervous. He's enjoying this. A mess, a nightmare, a girl out of nowhere. And he's enjoying it.

They walk me to the nearest cruiser. I guess I'm lucky they don't handcuff me, but I haven't done anything, I haven't.

Still I can't ignore it. Her face, staring, and I can see it even as they load me into the backseat, the vinyl sticking to my thighs, the seat belt too hot as it grazes my arm. I can see her looking at nothing, and I can see her looking at me.

The Phalene police station is back in town, on a corner opposite the pharmacy. It shares a parking lot with a church and with the town hall, a two-story brick building with dirty windows and a sign out front missing half its letters.

The station doesn't seem like it's in much better shape, but I barely have time to get a good look at it before Anderson is hauling me out of the cruiser and marching me through the lobby into an open room full of desks, the kind they call a bullpen on cop shows.

He leaves me there, in an uncomfortable plastic chair pulled up next to his desk, and disappears into an adjacent conference room, but not before telling me I won't go anywhere if I know what's good for me.

It's cold in here, the air-conditioning running so hard that the window unit leaves a puddle underneath it, dark on the carpet. I wrap my arms around myself, think longingly of the clothes I left behind in Calhoun. It used to get cold like this in the winter, money too short to turn the heat up, and we'd stay up late, sitting on the couch, Mom's body pressed close to mine, keeping me warm whether she wanted to or not. That's the best care I got from her. The kind she didn't mean to give.

What did she do when she noticed I was gone? Did she try to call me, realize I left my phone behind? Is she looking for me at all? Or is this what she's waited for my whole life? For me to decide to leave on my own so she doesn't have to make me?

I don't know which would hurt me more. I left to get away from her, and I left to get closer, and I try to imagine explaining it, sometimes, to other people. That yes, it's exactly what they think, and nothing like it, and a hundred other things at once. I will always wish I were hers, and will always want to be only my own. I haven't found a way yet to make the two fit.

Today only complicates it. The police will call her, they'll call her to tell her what happened, and for her it'll be like a gift. Here it is, a reason to stay as far away from me as possible. I know something I shouldn't. I've seen something she didn't want me to. My sister.

Because that's the only way to put this together. Maybe I imagined it, the way our faces matched, but everyone else saw it, too. Anderson said it himself. Me and my sister, a girl I never knew. Will never know.

But I can't swallow it. It won't work. Mom, in the hospital, two babies in her arms. Mom, choosing me. Keeping me. That's the impossible thing of it.

Why didn't she leave us both?

And if she had a choice, why was I the one she wanted?

Maybe that's where all of it comes from. The wrong choice, the wrong girl, and Mom with resentment souring in her blood. I slump forward, rest my head in my hands. I came here looking for my grandmother, looking for family, and this is what I get. Of course it is.

The bullpen door swings open. I sit up as Tess and Eli come in, Officer Connors behind them with a look on his face like there's nothing he'd rather do than die right on the spot.

"—can't wait to give him a call," Tess is saying, victory in her smile as she turns to face Officer Connors, walking backward, nearly colliding with one of the desks. "Because you really do have to call our parents right away. I'm only seventeen."

"I know," Connors says wearily.

"My dad will want to speak to your captain, and I'm sure they'll sort it out. After all, we'd probably have to cancel that fundraiser we're hosting for you if this goes on too long." She bats her eyelashes, shoots me a grin, and there's the girl I met this morning, sharp and bored and better than you. It's who I might've been, I think, if I'd grown up here. But that's not true, is it? It means something else to be a Nielsen. I'd have been that girl in the field. The body in the burn.

"For the love of God," Connors says, pointing to his desk next to Anderson's, "sit down, and please, just for a minute, stop talking."

He edges around Eli, whose hands are shoved in his pockets, his eyes empty. I wonder if the memory of the body is picking him apart the way it's doing to me.

"Where are you going?" Tess calls as Connors heads for the conference room. "Don't you want to separate us? Make sure we can't get our stories straight?"

The door slams behind him. Through the broad window I watch him toss his hat down on the table and say something to Anderson, who rolls his eyes.

"One day, you're going to annoy someone into murdering you," Eli says, sitting heavily in the chair like mine that's pulled up to Connors's desk.

Tess smiles brightly. "What a way to go." The glitter of it fades as she turns to me, taking in what I'm sure must be a sight. My hair coated in ash. My skin pink, blisters waiting underneath. I got too close for too long.

"Shit," she says. "Are you okay?"

"Yeah." I clear my throat, nervous. "Thank you both. For sticking up for me."

"We were just telling the truth," Eli says. He's watching me the way the police did. Wary. Suspicious. "We were, right?"

"Yes," I say in a hurry. "I know how it looks, but—"

"Lay off, Eli," Tess cuts in. "She was just in a fire."

His hand cracks down on Connors's desk. "Yeah, so was I. I know you think this is a great story, but you have to be serious, okay, Tess? We could get in a lot of trouble."

"For what?"

I stay quiet as Tess steps between me and Eli. She's defending me. I don't know why, but she is. I'm not about to stop her.

"I believe Margot," she keeps on. "She said she came here alone, so she came here alone."

Eli shakes his head, pushes to his feet. "You're being naive."

"I'm being a nice fucking person, actually."

This feels like a fight they've had before. I watch as the two of them eye each other, tense and defensive, and I wait for it to spark into something worse like it would with me and Mom. Instead, Eli goes soft.

"Yeah," he says. "That too."

Tess glitters with triumph, her face shining as she grins

over her shoulder at me. "He's all right sometimes," she stage-whispers. "I mean, it's rare, but it does happen." Eli sighs, long-suffering, as she faces him again. "Can you ask about a first-aid kit? Now?"

"Anything else I can get you?" he says flatly.

"Iced coffee. New car. World peace."

"We're friends why, exactly?"

"Phalene's got limited inventory."

"Oh, very nice." He flips Tess off with a smile, and she does the same before he's off across the bullpen, heading for the conference room door.

"Sorry about that," she says, sitting in Anderson's chair behind the desk. "We just get like that sometimes."

She doesn't seem worried, doesn't seem to care that she's in the station, being held for questioning. It's probably easy to brush off when the world belongs to you. When you know that no matter what, you can't be touched by something like this. Tess is in no danger. She never has been, but she certainly isn't now, not when it was me the police kept pinned between them. Me, with a matching body out on the road.

"You really do believe me, then?" I ask.

"You saw that girl and you threw up. I feel like that's hard to fake." Tess turns serious for a moment, keeping her voice low even though the officers are behind a closed door. "But you get how it looks, right? She must be related to you or something. Whether you know her or not."

I understand, I do. I'd be asking the same thing if I were Tess. And I wish I had a better answer for her, something harder to snap in half.

Somebody must know her. Somebody must have that answer. She was there, in that field. She had to have come from somewhere. "You said you live near Vera, right?" I ask. "If you've never seen her before, do you think she could've been hiding that girl at her house?"

Tess leans back, her glance flicking to the conference room, where Eli is waiting for one of the cops to answer the door. "That's a big secret to keep. And she looked our age. Could you really hide a whole person for, like, eighteen years?"

I'd like to ask my mom the same thing, but I don't say so.

She shrugs. "Then again, Vera doesn't exactly invite people over. I've never even been there."

"Seriously? Not even once?" I find that hard to believe. This is a small town. Isn't it supposed to be friendly?

"She's come to our house before, but we never go to hers." Tess fakes a full-body shiver. "Vera's like Medusa if Medusa knew what a casserole was. You'll see when you meet her."

She didn't sound like that on the phone, Gram. She sounded like something better than what I left in Calhoun. I ignore the cold fear that wakes in my stomach. She'll be good to me. I know she will.

I watch as Tess fiddles with a stack of Post-its on Anderson's desk. A few are already stuck to the drawers of his file cabinet, one with a last name on it that looks almost like mine. I lean in, anxious to get a better look, but before I can, Tess takes one of the Post-its and sticks it to my forehead with a smack.

"Beautiful," she says. "Are they calling her for you? Vera? Or are your parents here? And God, how strong are Nielsen genes? You guys look like those 'spot the difference' pictures." She purses her lips, considering me. "But a really hard one. Not the kind they have in those dentist office magazines."

"Okay." I snatch the Post-it from my forehead. "You can stop."

She winces, and I immediately feel terrible. Eli can do that, can knock her back a little, because he knows her. Who the hell am I?

"What?" Connors says across the bullpen, finally opening the conference room door. Eli asks for a first-aid kit, ignores the looks the two of them give me. Whatever damage the fire did to my skin is the least of my concerns.

"So?" Tess says. "Your parents?"

For a second I have no idea what she's talking about, and then I remember. Who will they call for me?

"My mom, I guess," I say. "But she doesn't really count." Which makes sense to me but, judging by the look on Tess's face, doesn't to her.

"Why not?"

If there's a good way to explain how we are, Mom and me, I've never found it. "It's just not how we work," I say. They'll call her, sure, but it won't matter. Mom couldn't even tell me Phalene existed—no way would she actually come here, not even with the police reeling her in. "And I came here for my grandmother, anyway."

Tess lights up. That's what she wanted. An actual admission from me. Yes, that's what I am. Yes, that's who I belong to.

"My mom never told me about any of this," I say. I mean to draw the story out of Tess, to unspool it inch by inch. But I don't have to.

"Not much to tell, really. After the drought Vera ran Phalene into the ground. Pretty much everyone used to work for her. So you can guess how that turned out." Tess starts using the Post-its to cover the screen of Anderson's outdated computer. "And then the whole mess with the fire." She pauses, cocks her head. "I guess we have to call it the old fire now."

"What happened—"

"This," she says, gesturing to me with one of the sticky notes, "being the new one."

"Yeah," I say. "I got that. What happened with the old fire?" If that's what has everybody looking at me like I know more than I do, I need everything she can tell me.

But she just shrugs. "It's like"—she puts on a voice that's probably supposed to be an imitation of her parents—"*something we don't talk about.* But the gist, as far as I know, is that there was a fire at Fairhaven and Vera lost her daughter."

Lost Mom. So that's why she left Phalene? A fire? That can't be everything. She's hidden this town from me my whole life—there has to be a bigger reason. For the secrecy, and for the way the police treat my last name like it's a warning. "And that's why Anderson thinks Nielsens are trouble?"

"That, and the fact that he's an incurable asshole." She grimaces. "And probably the dead body has something to do with it."

Right. I wonder what the police think the truth is. Some of it is clear enough. Me and that girl out there together, setting that fire. But there's my grandmother, too, hovering around every word like an echo. She has to know something. This secret has to belong to her. To Fairhaven. I just don't quite know what it is yet.

"Anyway," Tess says, "I'm sure Vera will be here in a bit to handle everything, and in the meantime you have me on your side. Anderson and Connors can say what they want, but I was with you this morning. I told them, and I'll tell them again. They can't do anything to you, okay?"

She sounds so certain. It's never been anything but all right for her. But I keep thinking of the look on Anderson's face as he loaded me into the cruiser, and I don't think it'll be all right at all.

"Okay," I say anyway, and she leans across the desk toward me.

"Great. Okay, hold out your hand."

"What?"

She nods to the computer screen, now fully covered in Post-its. "I need something else to do, don't I?"

Bewildered, I stick out my left hand, palm up. Tess's little smile breaks wide and she's laughing as she grabs my wrist to turn it over. I watch her methodically tear a sticky note into little strips and start to fit one on each of my fingernails.

"I'm a genius," she says grandly when she's done. "I have such a future in nail art."

"I'll be your model," I say, and Tess snorts. "Take me on tour."

A noise—someone clearing their throat. I look up, startled, and instinctively hide my hands under my legs, the paper strips falling to the floor. I'd forgotten we were here for a moment. Forgotten what was waiting for me.

Officer Connors is waving me over to the conference room, a bright red first-aid kit in his hands, as Eli meanders back toward me.

"Come on in here," Connors says. "You can fix yourself up while we talk."

NINE

At first we just watch each other, Anderson and Connors on one side of the long conference table, me on the other. The first-aid kit is lying open on the table in front of me. I haven't touched it, even with the pain ripening my skin. I had nothing to do with this—with the fire, with the girl. Not even enough to be hurt by it.

"How old are you, Margot?" Connors says finally. He's leaning forward, his hands folded together on the tabletop.

That seems safe enough. And it'll be a reminder to them that there are rules to follow. "Seventeen," I say.

"You have ID?" Anderson says.

I shake my head. "I left it at home."

"And where's that?" Connors says it idly, like maybe we're just talking.

"Calhoun," I say. "Southeast of here."

Connors nods. "I know it. I've been a couple times."

A lie. Nobody goes to Calhoun.

"You're new to town, then?" he continues, like he's the head of Phalene's tourism board.

I try to keep my face relaxed. He can't see that I'm nervous. He'll think it's guilt.

I saw someone out there. I went in. That's all. It's obviously not all to them, though. The fire, and a body they've never seen. A girl with my face. They think I did it. Or we did.

But she can't be a stranger in this town. There's no way. She has to belong to Gram, to Fairhaven. I just don't understand how, yet.

"Sorry," I say. "I just . . . Who do you think she is? You must have seen her before, or—"

Anderson frowns, holds up his hand to forestall me. "We're the ones asking the questions right now, not you. And I'm asking you when you got here."

There's no way I can convince him I had nothing to do with the fire. Not until I've answered every question, proved I have nothing to hide.

"This morning," I say. "I told you that before."

"What time?"

I glance between the two officers, catch Connors watching me with a wariness. Like I'm the ghost of the girl who died out there in that fire. Maybe I am.

"I . . ." I don't know. But I can't say that, can I? And I don't know when the fire started, and I don't who that girl is, or how she got out there, and there are too many traps I could be walking into. I take a deep breath. I can try to answer this. At least we're talking about the slice I understand, so small in the face of everything I don't. "Mid-morning, I guess. Maybe eleven?"

"And you were alone?"

Not technically. Mom taught me that even the smallest thing can be called a lie. "I got a ride in from—"

"Yes or no will do," Anderson interrupts.

"Then yes. I arrived alone."

"Anybody see you?"

I look out the conference room window to where Eli's sitting at Anderson's desk, Tess behind him, kneeling on a rolling chair and pushing herself down the aisle. They don't care at all. This is nothing to them, no matter what Tess told me out there about being on my side.

"They did," I say, nodding toward the window. "They were in the square when I got here."

Anderson scoffs. "It's not a good sign when you're call-ing on Theresa Miller for an alibi."

"I wouldn't know," I snap. I can hold on and hold on, but when the rope breaks, it goes all at once. "Why don't you just ask me what you're really asking?"

"And what's that?"

"Whether I set that fire. Hell, whether I killed that girl."
I settle back, cross my arms. "By the time I got to the fire,
it had already started, and by the time I got out into it, she
was dead. Whoever she is and whatever happened, it has
nothing to do with me."

Anderson's palm hits the table with a crack, and I jump.
"Don't bullshit me."

I grit my teeth, meet Anderson's gaze steadily. If this
is Nielsen business, then it's mine, not his. He can pry all
he likes, but I'm not letting him in. Not before I've had a
chance to find the family I'm after.

Connors pinches the bridge of his nose. "Jesus," he says.
"The apple doesn't fall far, does it?"

I don't know what he means, but I smile anyway, and I
say, "No, it really doesn't."

Anderson gets up, his body blocking the light, blocking
the window, and I reel back, before a voice comes from the
lobby, muffled but still sharp enough to cut through the air
between us.

"Excuse me," I hear. "Where?"

I watch as the two officers make the same face—disgust,
exhaustion and something else I don't recognize. Something
that comes with knowing a person.

"Speak of the devil," Connors says under his breath.

"Damn it." Anderson steps away from the table and

scrubs one hand over his buzz cut. "I didn't want her yet."

I twist around in my chair. Through the conference room window I can see Tess and Eli jump to their feet as a woman comes bursting through. She's tall, as tall as Mom, dressed in pale blue jeans and a flowered button-down with the sleeves rolled up. Silver hair, long and swinging, and skin striped with wrinkles, with sunburn and tan.

"Theresa," I think she says, and Tess nods back, pointing to the conference room, otherwise lost for words, which doesn't seem like a thing that happens very often.

That's when the woman turns. Looks at me through the window and smiles, smiles, smiles so wide it lifts me off my feet.

I know you, I think. And you know me.

When she comes in the door, she smells like smoke, and there's dirt tracking behind her, clumped on her boots, staining the hem of her jeans. I can't take my eyes off her, can't help the slight reach of my hand as she steps into the conference room.

"Gentlemen," she says. The voice from the phone. It's her. "Just what the hell are you doing with my grand-daughter?"

Seeing the body out on the highway was one thing. My face, still and empty and gone. Seeing my grandmother is another.

89

We look alike. Exactly alike. It shouldn't be a surprise—Mom and I match each other just the same way—but after this morning, it is. To see life there, to see her muscles shift under her skin. Nielsen women, just like the clerk at the pharmacy said. *You look just like them.* He's right. I do. This is how everybody knows what I am.

"Gram," I say, barely more than a whisper. Her eyes flick to mine, with just a hint of the smile she gave me through the window.

It's not enough. I don't know what could be—a hug? A sigh of relief? Tears? I don't get any of those. But there's a certainty in her I've never seen in Mom. She'll handle this. I don't know her, but I trust that much.

Across the table, the officers are side by side, Connors pale and strained while Anderson puffs up with indignation.

"You can't just barge in here, Vera," he says, his fingers hooked in his belt loops, elbows sticking out.

"And you can't just keep my granddaughter for no reason," she replies easily, looking away from me at last. I hope she never calls me anything but that. Her granddaughter. Hers. "She's a minor without an adult. You're lucky I got here before either of you took this too far."

"This is serious," Anderson says. "There's another fire on your land—"

"Yes, thank you," Gram says. "Of that I'm aware."

"And we've got two girls nobody can account for."

"I only see one," Gram says. "And I can account for her just fine."

I start to smile before I remember where we are. Why I'm meeting her like this.

"That's because the other's dead," Anderson says. "She's one of yours. No getting around that. You really think we wouldn't recognize her?"

I watch her for it, for a sign that he got it right. That the girl in the field belongs to her. It's the simplest way to explain this—me with Mom, and my sister with Gram. There's nothing, though. No guilt she has to bury, no surprise she has to cover. She just frowns and says, "It's a shame someone died, certainly. But I don't see why she has to be mine."

"We found her on your land, Vera. You been keeping her to yourself?"

It's bait, but Gram doesn't take it. "You hear all sorts of stories about young girls these days," she says smoothly. "Drifters. Runaways."

Anderson scoffs, and for once, I agree with him. She has to be lying. There's no way that girl came from anywhere but her house, on her land. "You'd know a thing or two about runaways, wouldn't you?" he says. "About all of this. Good thing I've got all my dad's old case notes in storage."

He has to mean Mom, Mom and the first fire. Anderson's dad must have worked that case, and now here we are again.

Everything fits together—Anderson is right about that. I just wish I could see the picture it's supposed to form.

"You're more than welcome to get involved with all that again," Gram says. "But it did your father very little good, as I'm sure it'll do you."

"Really?" Anderson says. "That's the angle you'd like to take?"

"I don't have an angle," Gram says, as though she's disappointed in him for even suggesting it. "I wish I could help you, but if you're going to insist on speaking to me this way, I really don't see how that's possible."

It brings me up short, how flat she sounds. How utterly untouched. I wish I could be like that. I wish I could take what I've seen, take my questions and lock them all away. But Gram has to know what's going on. Sure, she's lying to the police, but she'll tell me the truth when we're alone. Right?

"Look, there doesn't have to be any fuss," Connors says, making a half-hearted attempt at warmth. It seems a bit late for that. "If one of you would just tell us what happened, we could close this all up. But your granddaughter doesn't seem to want to help us."

Help? That's not what any of this has felt like. But I don't have to worry. Gram isn't fooled.

"What you need," she says, "is a scapegoat, and you will be finding one elsewhere."

A swell in my chest, bright and sweet. Someone's finally fighting for me. Someone's taking the weight from my shoulders and bearing it themselves. Is this how it's supposed to be?

"There's no need for a scapegoat," Anderson says, heated. "Your name is written all over it. What are you hiding, Vera? What were you doing this time?"

I look at Gram, wait for an answer. Anderson's asking her the questions I want to.

"Honestly, Thomas, this is all a bit much, don't you think?" Gram says, and his face goes bright red. She smiles at me. "Margot is visiting me for the summer, and she just arrived. That's all."

For now, anyway. At least until it's just us.

"So she spent her first day at the scene of a crime?" Anderson says. "Some summer visit."

"What crime do you mean, exactly?" Gram raises her eyebrows, and doesn't wait before continuing. "My farm caught fire, and unless you would like to call that arson—"

"We might."

"Then go ahead. Charge Margot. Charge my granddaughter for setting fire to her grandmother's land."

"She's not who we're after here," Anderson says, glowering.

"I'm glad to hear it," Gram says lightly. "Well then. That's that settled. And as for this other girl, it's a tragedy, surely, but that is, in fact, the only thing you can say with any certainty."

It's impressive. How polite she sounds, how little ground she gives. If I hadn't seen my own face on that body, I wouldn't hesitate to believe her.

"We can say something else, too. She's a Nielsen, through and through." Anderson lifts his chin, and for a second he and Gram just look at each other. "Maybe we don't have enough yet. But we will soon."

It's a threat. But Gram doesn't seem to care. "Looking forward to it," she says with a cheery smile, before holding out her hand to me. "Come on, Margot."

"You can't just take her," Anderson says. "She's got no ID. You have no proof of guardianship. Until we contact her family—"

"You said it yourself. She's a Nielsen. I'm her family."

It's the best thing I've ever heard, and it burns up my questions, pulls me out of my chair, draws me to her side. I would go anywhere for that. Do anything.

She looks down at me then, reaches out and sweeps my hair back from my temple, showing the gray streak there. She smiles faintly. "Just like," she says.

Like her? Like Mom? Like the girl in the fire?

It should matter more to me, I think. It should scare me. That if anybody knows anything, it's her. But nothing's going to keep me away.

"Margot's coming home with me," Gram says to the officers, her hand still brushing my temple.

Anderson and Connors let me leave. I don't think there's anything else to do in the face of a force like Gram.

Tess and Eli are still waiting in the bullpen. Eli's just behind Tess, and he's watching me with a sort of bland curiosity. Tess, on the other hand, looks absolutely delighted. I remember how she sounded, talking about Phalene, talking about how boring it was. Some entertainment at last. It makes me a little ill.

Gram stops in front of them, barely acknowledging Eli before focusing on Tess. "I would say it's nice to see you, Theresa, but it decidedly isn't under these circumstances."

Tess shrugs, playing it easy, but I can tell she's on edge under Gram's scrutiny. "Hopefully you'll see me in better ones soon."

"Oh dear," Gram says mildly. "That sounds ominous. Let's go, Margot. Some alacrity, please."

For a moment I try to imagine Mom saying the same thing, and I nearly laugh. We might look the same, but if Mom got anything else from Gram, I can't see it yet.

"I guess I have to go," I say to Tess. "But——"

She waves me away. "You'll see me. We're neighbors now."

"Yes," Gram says as she leads me away. "And aren't we lucky?"

Gram doesn't speak again until we're out of the station, me rushing after her through the parking lot toward a weathered pickup truck. I chance a look behind me to see Officer Anderson lingering in the doorway, watching us.

"Ignore him," Gram says, and I jump at the sound of her voice. Almost like Mom's. Almost familiar, but not quite. "They're all the same. If they see a chance to knock me down, they'll do it however they can. It's been like that for years."

I wish it were as simple as that. A grudge held and unearned. It's not, though. That girl was real, and she must have come from Gram. There's no other explanation.

I get into the truck. I can feel every inch of my skin, every press of the seat belt. It hurts. All of it hurts. The blisters from the fire, the stares of the police officers. And Gram, meeting me finally and being nothing like what I thought I wanted, simple and sweet and easy.

"Your mother's not with you?" Gram says brusquely as she throws the truck in reverse and rolls the windows down. Like I really am just visiting for the summer. I don't know how she can pretend everything's normal.

"No," I say. I don't want to talk about Mom right now. "She didn't want me coming here in the first place."

We peel out of the lot so fast I careen into the door, let out a hiss as some of my burn blisters pop. She turns onto the road bordering the town square, and I glimpse a few of Tess's friends from this morning, back at the fountain, stretched out to tan. But then Gram's leaning on the gas and we're out of Phalene proper almost before I can blink. Like everything at the station never happened.

"Why not?" Gram asks.

I can barely hear her over the wind coming in through the open windows, and it takes me a minute to remember what she's talking about. Do I want to be honest and tell her how far Mom went to keep her—her and that girl in the field—a secret? I doubt it'll be a surprise. Not with what I've seen today.

I decide on something neutral. A shrug, and I say, "Just how she is."

Gram laughs, a cracking, unruly sound. "That's an understatement, Mini."

"Mini?" My first thought is that she's insulting me somehow, in a way she knows I won't understand. But that's not fair. She's done nothing yet to tell me that's who she is.

The fields stream by as we head in the direction of the fire. My mouth goes dry, my head swimming. Gram doesn't seem upset that her land's gone up. Why doesn't she care?

She glances over at me, one hand on the wheel, the other dangling out the window. "Sorry," she says. "I used to call your mother that."

So, not an insult. But it sits uncomfortably in my chest anyway. I don't want to be like Mom to her. I want to be myself. Her granddaughter.

"She never told me," I say.

"Of course she didn't." Gram sounds bitter, and I know the feeling. "She doesn't know you're here, does she?"

I look at Gram, searching. For disappointment. Disapproval. For the thing that's gonna send me back to Calhoun. But she's just asking, her expression open and curious.

"No," I say firmly. "I didn't tell her. I just left."

"Well, we'll give her a call when we get home."

Home. It's enough to keep the rest of what she said from hitting me, but when it does I lurch across the console, leaning toward Gram, my palms itching to grab her arm.

"Please, let's not," I say. I hate how anxious I sound. "She'll figure it out on her own. And in the meantime, what she doesn't know won't hurt her."

Gram shakes her head, her eyes still on the road. "There is a time and a place for that line of thinking, Mini, but I don't think we're there."

The time and place were at the police station. She had no trouble keeping things from them. But I guess I should be happy, should take this as a sign that once we get to Fairhaven, she'll tell me everything.

And all of this—it should make me more uncomfortable. Even without the fire and the body, Gram should feel like a stranger. But she isn't, really, is she? She's Mom, and she's me, and she's family, and it wasn't that she never wanted me. It was that Mom never wanted her. There was only ever Mom between us, and now that's gone.

The fire's coming up on our right. This is the same path I took with Tess and Eli, twenty minutes on the bike turned into five in the truck. Out across the tops of what corn has survived I can see a fire engine parked on an access road, fighting the blaze back toward where it came from.

But I'm looking up ahead, to where two cruisers are parked across one lane of the highway. When we left the scene for the station, there was only one, and only one officer keeping watch. It felt like half a dream. Like it couldn't be real.

It's different now. Neon crime scene tape, and a stretcher waiting for the body. I can see two figures there, on the shoulder of the road, the body between them covered with a white sheet.

"Don't give it another thought," Gram says, slowing down as we ease into the other lane. "It will all sort itself out."

"How can it?" I say. How can she be so calm? "That girl. She's—"

"She's what?" There's a challenge in her voice that stops me short.

"Nothing," I say. This is still too fragile. It isn't safe.

"No, let's hear it," Gram says, just like Mom when she

99

won't let go, when she makes me make her angry. "Say what you mean, Margot."

Fine. She asked for it. "My sister. She has to be. She looked exactly like me, and she was on your land. And I know you said you didn't know what the police were talking about, I know that, but we're not with them anymore, and you can be honest with me. You can just tell me you were keeping her."

The truck squeals as Gram hits the brakes. I swallow a cry of surprise.

"Excuse me?" she says, turning to me. Dust drifting in through the open window. The heat catching up with us.

"Why did you stop?" My heart racing, my mouth dry. I knew I shouldn't risk it. I knew it, and I did it anyway.

"I must have misheard you," she says. I don't know how to read her yet. Just her expectant face and her dark eyes, and it's Mom and nothing like her all at once. "Are you suggesting that I'm lying?"

"No," I say hurriedly. "No, I didn't—"

"Good." Her face softens. "I would never lie to you, Margot. That's not how family should behave. And we're family. I understand; I know you were there with the police for a long time, all by yourself. I'm sure they told you all kinds of things."

"Not really," I start. "I mean, some things, but—"

"Things like how Nielsens are all kinds of trouble, I'm

sure." She rolls her eyes, and it startles me for some reason. She's sharp in ways I'm not ready for, in ways that will cut if I'm not careful, but warm, too. It coaxes me closer.

"Yeah," I say. "Like that."

Gram seems to relax, and she throws the truck back into gear and eases onto the highway again. The fire is burning in the distance. I wonder if it'll be out by the morning. If this will have happened at all.

"Don't listen to Thomas Anderson," she says. Easy, like this is just an unfair parking ticket. "I've known that boy since he was seven years old. He's no more than a nuisance. His father was the same way."

This isn't safe, I can feel that thrumming through my blood. Familiar, so familiar that for a moment I could be back in Calhoun, Mom in her room and me with a lighter in my hand.

But I'm not. I'm here. And Gram's hiding the truth, and calling me family, and I have to decide which is more important. If I push now, I lose this forever. If I wait, I get Gram. I get Fairhaven. I get another chance to find out what happened.

"Okay," I say. "I'm sorry."

And then she reaches over. Her hand tight around mine. And she says, "Me too. I didn't mean to upset you."

An apology handed back to me. I've never had one from family before. *I'm here,* it means. *I will still be here.*

Not the answers I wanted, but something better.

We keep driving. The crops outside my window are blackened, broken, oozing smoke. Across the ash field I can see the lingering glow of the fire, the plume and spray of the fire hoses, and beyond, the red gleam of the engines. They're parked on another of the access roads that seem to run like spider's legs off the main highway, cutting through the fields.

"Is that where it started?" I ask.

Gram nods. "From what I can tell. But with weather like this, it's hard to say. We'll know more once it's out."

She doesn't seem upset. Isn't this her livelihood? I want to ask, but I don't think she'd take kindly to that.

Gram doesn't say anything more as we pass the last of the fire. I twist in my seat, keep watching it for as long as I can. She sounded like she thought it was an accident. But I know what the police are sure of. Me, and that girl, and a fire all our own.

TEN

Fairhaven isn't much farther. I still have the photo folded in my pocket, the name imprinted on my mind in Gram's handwriting. It looks just the same as we pull up to the long, straight driveway, the house in the distance, set a ways back from the road.

"There she is," Gram says, turning us onto the dirt road, the rattle of the tires nearly drowning her out.

The house is big, three stories and tilting like somebody bumped into it and forgot to set it right. White siding, or it used to be. Now the color's closer to spoiled milk, and the paint is peeling. A rusted weathervane tops the roof, and a rickety porch is striped across the front of the house. I trace the line of it, try to find where it corners, but it feels like the whole place twists around itself.

The corn crawls right up to the edge of the drive-way, golden and crackling, tilting in the wind. It's dead, I think—by that color it has to be dead—and yet it still seems to be growing.

I stare out the truck window as Gram parks. Tess said Gram plants. I'm not sure she's right, though. The corn is growing, but from the emptiness, from the complete absence of any kind of machinery, I doubt Gram has much to do with it.

"Well," Gram says, "let's not dawdle, shall we?"

She's already out of the truck, peering at me through the open window on the driver's side. I get out, stumbling on my weak legs. It's midafternoon, the sun still bright, and I can't believe it. It feels like a year since I left Calhoun.

I round the truck, my shoes kicking up dust, my hair sticking to my forehead. I could drop to the ground right now and never move again, the rush of the day leaving me in a heartbeat. But the shade of the porch beckons, and so does Gram, waiting for me on the steps now, her hand outstretched.

When was the last time someone reached for me? Someone with my mother's face, my mother's last name? I follow her like it's a dream. Up the stairs, boards creaking underneath me, the whole house seeming to sway. I can't feel the pain of my blisters anymore. Can only feel Gram's hand as it closes around mine.

She props open the screen door and pushes back the solid one behind it. Neither locked. Nothing in this whole place kept away from me. "Come on in," she says, so I do.

The entry is close and shadowed, all paneled walls and heavy curtains. Immediately ahead of me, a staircase climbs to the second floor. Next to it an arched doorway leads into a big kitchen, the opposite wall cut through with windows that look out onto the back porch and the fields beyond. Off to one side, a huge set of double doors stands slightly open, showing me a sliver of a dark room dominated by a dining table and chairs.

Fairhaven. The house where my mother grew up.

It looked real from outside. But here I can't keep all of it in my head at once. Just a room, just a wall, just the edge of my mother's body disappearing around every corner. She's not here, I remind myself. Nobody but me.

And Gram. She's ahead of me, waiting in the doorway to the kitchen. "Come on, Mini," she says.

The kitchen is large, skimmed with yellow light. Through the screen door to the back porch, I can see acres of gold. Beyond them, a strange stand of trees on the horizon. Some seem jagged, their trunks bent at odd angles, while others blur into green growth.

Everything here is old, older even than what we have back in Calhoun, but where our apartment is falling down, Fairhaven is neat. Well kept, even as it gets further away from being new. A small table is tucked against the wall, an empty vase perched in the middle of it, one chair pushed in. One chair, for Gram. Nothing to tell me another girl ever lived here.

Doubt drops through me. But I saw her. We all did. She had to come from here—where the hell else?

Across from the table is the fridge, humming, gleaming brightly, like it's just been polished. Gram goes to it, carefully adjusting the fall of a hand towel looped over the oven handle before pulling the fridge open and removing two bottles of water. My mouth goes dry at the sight.

"Finish this," she says, handing one bottle to me and pointing me toward the chair. "The whole thing. You look about ready to faint, and a mess besides."

I nearly drop it, my hands trembling. The first sip feels like neon sliding through my veins, lighting up every bit of blood, shocking me into somewhere else. It's so cold. I've never felt anything so good.

I drink half the bottle before I sit down, the chair rickety underneath me. At the sink, Gram is busy wetting a washcloth, wringing it out, and I watch her, measure her against this house. It's big enough for so many more than just her, but she's all there is. One chair at the table. One cup and one plate in the glass-fronted cabinet next to the fridge.

"Is it just you?" I ask. I mean so many things. The girl. My grandfather, or aunts, or uncles, or anyone. Anyone.

"Just me," Gram says, nodding. "Been that way for a long time."

How long? Since this morning?

"And now me," I say instead. I shouldn't be so eager. I shouldn't show Gram how much I need her to want me here. I can't help it, though, can't help my instinct to throw myself forward at the slightest opening.

"Now you," Gram repeats.

She comes toward me then, draws her fingertips along my jaw before I can flinch and starts dabbing at my forehead with the washcloth. It comes away black, stripping ash from my skin. She's a little too rough, and it hurts, but I go stiff, sit as still as I can. Watch her watching me with stern, dark eyes.

"There," Gram says, stepping back. "That'll do for now. Although you're still a sight, I'm afraid." She tosses the washcloth into the sink, wipes her palms on the front of her jeans. "Right. Let's get you fed."

I nearly faint with relief. Besides the chips from the Omni, it's been almost a day since I last ate, and my body feels like it's flickering in and out. "Please."

"And then I'll call your mother."

Oh. I was really hoping we could avoid that. I look down at my shoes, at the peeling soles. "I, well——"

"With feeling, Margaret."

I jerk at the sound of my full first name. Even Mom never calls me that. "She won't answer," I say. "She won't come."

Gram almost looks proud as she pulls her hair over one shoulder. "It's true that Nielsens are a stubborn sort," she says. "But your mother has nothing on me."

With that she turns and makes for the entryway. "You wait here," she says. "I'll go get your room sorted and find some clothes you can wear."

She disappears around the corner, her footsteps muffled as she climbs the stairs. And here I am. Alone in Fairhaven.

I turn around slowly, scanning the room for any sign of Mom. No framed school pictures, no old holiday cards. Now that I've met Gram, I wouldn't expect anything different. If there was ever any sentimentality in our family—and it still sends a shiver through me to think about it, my family—it was bred out a long time ago.

She would have been here, that girl. Would have sat at this table and lived in this house, and where did all the proof of it go? Did it burn up with her?

But why hide it? Why keep it from me? All I've ever wanted was somebody to be there with me. I would have never let her go.

I finish my water bottle and go to fill it back up. The tap is dripping, hitting the metal sink with a wet smack, and as I get closer, something twists in my stomach. A sugary smell with a bitter tang spiking through it is coming from the drain. I think of the glimpse I caught of the inside of the fridge, the cases of water waiting there. Maybe this isn't safe to drink.

Still, I reach out and hold one finger under the drip. The next droplet splashes onto my finger, and I draw back, hold the water into the light from the windows. At first it seems normal. But the more I look at it, the more I realize: it's pink. So soft and so blushing you wouldn't notice if you didn't look close enough. But the color is there, along with a touch of grit that I can feel as I rub my thumb and index finger together.

I wipe my skin clean on the towel hanging from the oven handle. No sign of Gram coming back yet. Through the back windows, the trees on the horizon look blackened, their branches broken, bodies standing like columns of ash against the sky. That must be where the old fire was. The one Tess mentioned, the one that sent Mom running.

When Gram comes back, I'll ask.

I cross the kitchen, heading out to the entryway. The hallway leading to the rest of the house looks too complicated, full of too many corners and too many closed doors. I choose the other direction, the double doors and the dining room.

Here the rug is plush and thick, and clean. I wince at the ash and dirt covering my clothes, but that doesn't keep me from going in. The table is lined with four chairs on either side, and one each at the foot and the head. Each has elegant scrollwork along the back, gleaming and smooth. There was money here, once.

The table matches. It's covered in a film of dust that's broken here and there by smudges and tracks I think must belong to mice. I step closer, drag my hand along the surface, leaving trails behind. There's a strange texture. I bend down, squint to get a good look.

Scratches on the table, long and thin. Near the edge and close to me. Scars in the wood, biting deep and sliding shallow at the ends.

"Margot."

I jump. When I turn, Gram is watching me from the doorway. She doesn't look mad. But maybe that only means the worst is coming.

"Sorry," I say quickly, and I step back. I mean to head for the kitchen, but something catches my attention. Photographs, hung the whole length of the wall behind me, dusty glass glinting dully. The faces in each of them are almost familiar. None of them look as similar as Mom and Gram and I do, but I can spot our eyes looking out at me from a dozen photographs.

"Is that—" I start, and Gram nods.

"That's us," she says. A catch in my throat, and an ache in my chest. Us. All these people. All this history. And Mom just cut it out of our lives. Closed the door on it and left us out there, alone. What happened to her here? What could be so bad that she'd leave this behind?

I look more closely at the photographs. I'm not sure, but I think they run from past to present, older and more faded closer to the door. More and more people in each one, arranged on what must be the front porch, staring into the camera with only a handful of smiles between them.

"Is there one of you and my grandfather?" I ask. The Nielsen name probably came from him, and I'd like to see him, to see what our line looked like before Gram was part of it. But she shakes her head and points to the far end of the photographs.

I frown, staring at the last picture—a man and a woman, in black-and-white, with a little girl standing between them, her hair in two braids, a stuffed animal of some sort hanging from one hand. The girl's face is immediately recognizable. That's Gram, and her parents.

"You were the Nielsen?" But as soon as I say it, it's not a surprise. Of course she was. I can't imagine her arriving in her husband's car, getting out and looking at a Fairhaven that wasn't already hers.

Gram sniffs disdainfully. "As if I'd give up my own name for anybody."

I look back at the photographs. It seems like they take one of every generation, so there has to be one of Mom's. But there isn't. The whole row's off center, like it's missing something, and there's a slightly paler rectangle on the wall next to the last photo, and a hole where a nail was.

There was one, once. And now it's gone.

"She took it with her when she left," Gram says. "I don't

suppose she ever showed you, did she?"

I can't help laughing. "Of course not." I don't know how to explain to Gram that this, everything—it's more than I would ever get from her, even if I tried my whole life.

"Then what did she tell you, exactly? About us."

There's something careful about the way Gram is asking. But there's nothing careful about my answer.

"She never told me anything," I say. Gram raises her eyebrows, like I'm exaggerating. "I mean it," I say. "I only found your number by accident. Whatever I know, I know from here. From you. From—"

I break off. Gram's already dismissed everything the police said. She'd hate the kind of rumors I heard from Tess. But my face must give it away, because she says, "You spoke to Theresa, didn't you?"

"Maybe."

"That girl loves a good story." She holds out her hand, ushers me through the double doors and back toward the kitchen. "It comes down to your mother leaving home and this town being full of busybodies. Do people say that anymore? Busybodies?"

"No," I say, smiling, and Gram gives it right back.

"One day you'll find yourself left behind just like me," she says, knocking her knuckles gently against my cheekbone in a way I think is meant to be fond. "She got pregnant with you when she was just eighteen. No father in the picture. You must know all that."

The thing is, I don't. I mean, I know how old she was when she had me, but only because I figured it out myself. As for my father, I never wondered. Could never imagine it being an answer big enough to fill the space Mom left between the two of us. No, those years of Mom's before I showed up, they're hers. And she keeps them that way, packed in boxes in the back of a pawnshop.

"Why did she leave, though?" I say as we head into the kitchen. "I mean, I'm sure people talked, but—"

"It doesn't take much in Phalene. But that, and the accident." She points through the screen door, toward the stand of trees. "There was a fire out back that fall. In the apricot grove. She got wrapped up in all of it."

"Wrapped up how?"

Gram doesn't answer. She just sighs, and for the first time since I met her, I hear a mother in her. "It was a lot to put on her," she says. "A girl can only take so much."

I know, I think. Believe me. I know.

Gram sits me down at the table again and heats up a half-empty dish of casserole. The smell makes my stomach growl, but it's too heavy, too rich, and I nearly feel sick when Gram slides a plate of it in front of me, the cheese bubbling, steam soft against my raw skin.

I should've taken the first-aid kit with me from the police station. Although I don't know what I'd do, really. The flush is draining from my arms and legs, but I still feel tight all over, like if I move too fast my skin will split and I'll pour out. Gram sets another water bottle down by my elbow, and when she's not looking, too busy cleaning the already clean countertop, I press it to my forehead to ease the fever I can feel simmering in my veins.

It's still so early, but I barely have the strength to stay upright at the table. I haven't slept in more than a day, not since the last full night I spent in Calhoun, and every time I shut my eyes I see her, the girl, sprawled on her side in the corn, waiting for me to save her.

I wish we'd pulled over on the way here and I'd thrown back the sheet covering the body and said, "Look. Tell me who that is." That way Gram wouldn't be able to stay so calm. So normal. I'd have the proof I need, the proof I thought I'd find here, but there's no sign of anyone else in this whole house, and I can't fit it all together. Sister, twin, and empty space.

I nudge the plate away, take a slow, deep breath. If I have to throw up again I'll do it where Gram can't see me.

"All done?" Gram says. I nod. "I'd prefer a clean plate," she tells me, but she takes it to the counter and starts scraping the leftovers back into the casserole dish. "I'll make an exception for today."

I get up, legs unsteady. All I want is to disappear into the ghost halls of this house. Find somewhere my mother never

114

touched and stay there for a hundred years, until everything's gone, until my whole life is just half a memory. I'd be safe. I'd belong to nobody and I'd be so safe.

But that's not an option. Somewhere my mother never touched—good luck.

Gram turns from the counter and frowns at the sight of me. "Wait for me on the stairs," she says, a surprising gentleness to her voice. I must look worse than I realize. "I'll call your mother."

Please don't, I want to ask her, but it's no use. This has to happen. I don't have to watch, though. I leave her to reach for the landline and wander back into the entryway, collapse onto the stairs. The red runner is soft against the back of my thighs, worn nearly smooth. Just the feel of it comforts me, steadies the dizzy sway of the room. The knowledge that time has passed here, that Nielsens have come and gone. It isn't only me.

A long quiet from the kitchen, and then I hear a muffled swear, and the sound of footsteps. Gram, pacing. More minutes, more silence. How many times has she called by now?

Then: "Finally. You've been incredibly rude, Josephine."

Mom won't take kindly to that. Or she wouldn't if it were me saying it.

"That's all well and good," Gram says after a moment. "But I need to know how much you've said about—"

She breaks off. I can't hear Mom on the other end—

Gram's too far away—but to interrupt Gram, Mom must have come in strong.

How much Mom's said about what? About the girl? About the sister I seem to have?

"Nothing?" Gram asks. She sounds almost incredulous. "That's fine. That's in fact preferable." A beat of quiet, and then, more softly, Gram says, "That's well done, Jo."

Mom must hang up at that, because I hear Gram mutter something to herself, hear the phone land back in the dock before she steps into the entryway, sun streaking through the storm door to set her edges on fire.

"Jo's being Jo," she says.

I hold back a laugh. That's one way to put it.

"But there's nothing to worry about," Gram continues. "You're with family now."

Family. All this was waiting here for me, really really waiting, and Mom wouldn't let me have it. Wouldn't let me have it and her both. It must have been the daughter she wouldn't claim keeping her away. That girl here, me in Calhoun, and nothing more important than the distance between us. But why?

"Nothing to worry about," Gram repeats. She comes toward me and holds out her hand. When I take it, it's startlingly warm. She's real, I tell myself, and let her pull me to my feet. "Come on. Let's get you settled in. We'll work it out tomorrow."

116

ELEVEN

I follow her upstairs to a landing, off which sprout two hallways. Between them, a window seat overlooks the back acres of the farm. Gram leads me down the left-hand hallway, past a number of closed doors, until she reaches one standing slightly ajar. Inside, deep blue walls, white trim, and a white bedspread, delicate scrollwork above the bars of the headboard. It's been dusted but I can tell it was recently from the streaks left on the nightstand.

"It's nice," I say. And then, feeling silly, "Really nice. Thank you. Whose room was this?" It's not what I want to ask and we both know it, judging from the frown that flashes across Gram's face.

"Nobody's." She crosses to the bed and pulls back the spread. "For the most part. There's the dresser," she continues before I have time to ask what she means. She nods to the corner. Next to the chest of drawers, a crooked door is shut. "Bathroom's through there."

I wander over while Gram fusses with the linens behind me. Rest my hand on the latch and gently lift it, leaving the door open as I ease inside. A black-tile floor, and a claw-foot tub angled across the left-hand wall, black porcelain with brass taps. The lights are off and there are no windows, but I catch my reflection in the mirror over a pedestal sink to my right. The wall opposite me is taken up by built-in drawers and cupboards, stacks and stacks of them, the kind of storage you need when your family is too big to fit in a rundown Calhoun apartment.

"The water's all right in there," Gram calls. "We draw from two different wells. And I put a pair of pajamas in the dresser, and a few other things. They'll do until we can get you something of your own."

I come back into the bedroom, open the top dresser drawer and pull out a pile of cream silk. A pair of shorts and a matching button-up, a frill at the neck. Gram bustles past me into the bathroom and sets about pulling clean towels out of one of the drawers, not realizing what she's done. Because there, ironed onto the neck of the pajama top, is a small woven label, with a name handwritten on it in faded, bleeding ink.

Josephine Nielsen. These were Mom's.

"Sorry," I say, my throat tight. "I know it's early but I'd just like to rest now. And wash my hair."

Quiet, for a moment. "Of course," Gram says. "I'll see you in the morning."

She sidles by me with a touch to my back, then leaves me, and I listen as her footsteps echo along the hall, the stairs creaking as she heads down them. Outside, through the narrow window, the air is just starting to clear of smoke. I sit down on the bed, feel the springs separate underneath me.

This wasn't her room, I don't think. Not the one she grew up in. But these are her clothes, and this is her house, and God, I wish she were here. She should be here. Telling me stories, sharing this with me. Showing me all the spots where she carved her name, showing me all the secrets she and Fairhaven kept from my grandmother together. Instead it's just me. It's always just me, even when it was the two of us in our apartment, but I feel the emptiness next to me more than I ever have.

I pull the photo from the Bible out of my pocket, the one of Mom that makes my heart ache, and stick it in the drawer of the nightstand before I go into the bathroom and change out of my shorts and T-shirt. I leave my sneakers in the sink to keep the ash and earth staining them from getting everywhere.

There's no shower, so I run a bath. The water isn't rosy,

like what's downstairs. None of the texture, the grit. Once the tub is full, I ease in, my clothes strewn across the black floor, all ash and earth.

Heat licking across my skin, but it's like breathing again, and I remember the fire. The air clouding with gray, the earth gone dry, and no way out. Not for that girl. I owe her. I couldn't save her, so I should at least know what it felt like for her to die.

I take a deep breath and duck under the surface of the bath. Eyes squeezed shut, fingers curled into fists, the porcelain smooth against my back. The water stings the open sores across my forehead, sets my hair drifting. Stay under, I tell myself. Even as the air gets tight, as it bursts in my chest.

She couldn't breathe. She couldn't get out. She crawled and she crawled and she died, out there, she died, and I didn't save her, and I don't know who she is but she's mine, isn't she?

I burst up out of the water, gasping. Enough. Whatever should've happened, this is where I am. Nothing will change that now.

The water is thick with dirt. I can taste it, can feel it under my nails. I fumble for the shampoo, wash my hair as quickly as I can and hurry out of the tub. When I scrub myself dry, I'm so rough I tear my skin like tissue paper, leave blood behind.

Mom's pajamas slide on easily, just a little too big. I wonder how old she was when she wore them, if maybe she already knew, then, that I was on the way.

I avoid the mirror as I head back out into the bedroom. I don't need to see myself looking like Mom, like the girl I saw in the field. I just need to go to sleep.

But it takes me forever. Hours, until the moon is high, the sky blacker than black. I'm on my back, stretched out on top of the covers, sweating even with the window open. I can hear the breeze, though it's not reaching through to touch my skin. The fire engines are all long gone. Either the fire is out, or they've given up.

I can still hear the sirens, though. Faint, like an echo. Just the smallest cry, thin and wailing.

I sit up. It's not sirens at all. It's a person. I swear it's a person. For a heartbeat the fire sweeps across my sight, and there she is, my own body curled on her side, but I blink and she disappears. It's not that. It can't be that.

Still. I get out of bed, the floor cool against my bare feet. When I peer out into the hallway, the only light is coming from the landing, where the windows are letting in the moon. The opposite hallway, where Gram's room must be, is shut up, the door closed.

I tiptoe out to the landing. I can still hear the crying. And that's what it is, crying. Like an animal. Like a girl out there alone.

One set of windows overlooks the back of the farm, the acres I could see from the kitchen. I think that's where it's coming from. Glancing over my shoulder to be sure Gram isn't out here with me, I kneel gingerly on the window seat and peer outside.

The corn is nearly blue in the night, the breeze leaving meandering patterns across the top of the plants. The apricot grove I saw before is out on the horizon, maybe a mile away. That's it. Nothing out of the ordinary, just the wind on my skin and the lure of the moon.

I wait for a moment. Count the cries as they come, hitching and plaintive, drifting through the air like smoke from the fire. I can taste it still, lingering so thickly that sometimes a cloud of it will hold the moonlight inside, hovering in midair like breath in winter.

Too suddenly the cries go quiet. I jerk back from the window. My heart catching in my chest, breath coming quick. Whatever was making that noise, I don't think it's living anymore.

"Gram?" I say, into the emptiness around me. "Gram? Are you awake? Did you hear that?"

She must not hear me. She doesn't answer. And the dark stretches on, filling the gaps left in the silence until I'm sure I must have imagined them.

I go back to my room. Sit on the edge of my bed and wait for my nerves to knit themselves back together, but they don't.

It's a long shot. But I open the nightstand drawer and root through it, looking for a lighter. Matches, a candle. Anything. I need the calm of the apartment in Calhoun, the fan on low and the window open, the flame steady as I pour my whole self into it.

I get lucky with a banged-up lighter and a thin candle, the kind you hold at church during a vigil. My hands shake as I light it, and the orange glow wavers across the walls, casting strange twisting shadows.

There, I think, breathing easy at last. That looks more like home.

TWELVE

I swear morning comes earlier at Fairhaven. It tumbles through the window at the top of my room, crawls up the bed to open my eyes. My body aches, tired so deep down that I'm not sure it'll ever go away, and I dreamed about the crying I heard, about the moment it stopped dead. Next to me on the nightstand, the candle is piled up with fresh wax.

I didn't imagine it. Not any of it. Not the girl, and not the story of my mother, of what it means to be a Nielsen. Gram said family is honest with each other. But she hasn't really answered any of my questions. And I wonder if maybe I'm on my own. With this, just like with everything.

Take the easy explanation, that's what I should do. Of course Mom's been keeping secrets. Of course Mom stayed away from Phalene because of the daughter she left behind.

And Gram's part of this because Mom asked her to be. That's what makes sense, but I can't help feeling like it isn't right. I know Mom better than anyone, and I know that if daughters were what made her run from Phalene, she would never have kept either of us. Something happened here.

I get up already too hot as I slide open the dresser drawers, sorting through the piles of clothes in each. I'm not exactly looking forward to dressing in more of Mom's hand-me-downs, but anything's better than my dirty clothes.

In the top drawer, I find a little long-sleeved dress, lace tacked onto the hem, Mom's name written inside the high collar. I hold it up to get a good look, my chest going tight. It's familiar. Of course it is. I saw one just like it on the girl in the fire. A girl with Mom's face, dressed in Mom's clothes. I'd bet anything Mom's name was pressed to the nape of her neck when she died.

This is where she came from. It has to be. I can picture her here, sleeping in this bed. Just like me.

I put the dress back in the drawer. Gram said this room didn't belong to anybody, but Fairhaven told me the truth. Maybe the rest of it can tell me more.

I head to the top of the stairs. I mean to try the door to the other hallway, but before I can, I spot a police cruiser out the window at the front of the house. I watch as it rolls up the driveway, back toward the highway. They were here. Talking to Gram. Pressing her for answers just the way I want to. And I bet she didn't give them any, but I won't let her stonewall me. I have proof now, solid and real and something she can't get away from.

Fairhaven restless around me, creaking floors and peeling wallpaper. I go downstairs and pass through the entryway, hesitating by the front door. There's a pair of rain boots tucked in the corner, on top of a muddy towel and a ratty glove. I don't remember them being there yesterday, but then I don't remember much of yesterday at all that isn't the sight of my own face and the heat of the fire.

Gram's not in the kitchen when I get there. She *was*— the chair's pulled out, a mug of coffee still warm on the counter. I push open the screen door and step out onto the back porch. The wood is still cool, sun only just starting to reach under the roof. I stand there for a moment, breathing in, the air sweet with summer, spiked with a touch of smoke. It looks like it rained in the night, broke the heat and left the sky clear, left the plants glimmering and glossy. Maybe it put the rest of the fire out, tamped down the drift of the ash.

The ground slopes gently away from the porch, down into the spread of the fields, but even from up here the corn seems so tall, and so close. Across the crops I can see another house in the distance, one I didn't notice yesterday. It's off to the left, on a higher little hill, and though it's too far for me to see much, it seems almost like it was built to mirror Fairhaven. The same sort of porch, and the same white siding, although Fairhaven's is weathered with age.

That must be the Miller house. Tess said we're neighbors, and I can't see any other houses out here. I wonder what happened at the station after I left, with her and Eli. I can't imagine it went anything like it did for me in that conference room. Tess could've walked right out of there any time she wanted. But she didn't.

I squint up at the windows of the Miller house, small squares of sun. Maybe she can see me. I barely manage not to wave, just in case.

"Oh, good. You're up."

I turn, and Gram's there, leaning in the doorway, dressed in practically the same clothes as yesterday, a bucket hanging from one hand, a pair of work boots from the other.

"Get dressed," she says. "There's work to be done."

Not a word about the police who just left, or the fire. Not a word about the girl. And of course, not a word about my mother.

"Well?" Gram says, when I don't move. I came looking for her with a hundred questions waiting on the tip of my tongue, but I can't find my voice. Not when she's right there, and looking at me. "You waiting for directions back upstairs or what, Mini?"

It's the nickname that does it. I am not my mother. I

will not let a lie live inside me. I will carve it out, no matter what.

"What were the police here for?" I ask. "Did they have any news? About the girl?"

"Don't worry yourself with that," Gram says easily. "It's Thomas Anderson doing what he does best, which is being bothersome."

Fine. Fine, I'll try harder. Carefully, gently. I'm used to doing this, anyway.

"Look, you can tell me," I say, taking the words a parent should say and holding them on my tongue. Never mind that I'm in my mother's pajamas, my feet bare. I'm as old as I need to be. "I saw the girl. I know who she is. You don't have to cover for Mom anymore."

I don't expect her to give in right away, but I do expect more than what she gives me. Which is a blank stare and a tilt of her head.

"Cover?" she says. "Cover what?"

Oh, bullshit. Your house, Gram. Your land. Your face. Your girl.

"I mean, I get it," I say, even though I don't. "Mom was young and there were two of us, and she could only handle one. You can tell me the truth. I already know."

The only change is the furrow in Gram's forehead. "I have told you the truth," she says. "Are you feeling all right, Margot?"

128

"I'm fine," I say. It comes out too sharp. "I'm confused, though. Because you said family is honest. And aren't we family? Wasn't she?"

"She who?"

"The girl," and it's nearly a yell. I didn't think I would be here again. I didn't think it would be just like with Mom, with the world right in front of both of us and me trying, trying, trying to prove to her it exists. "I saw her. Tess saw. The police saw. You can't pretend she's not what she is."

"I am not trying to."

"You are," I insist. I have to say it. Let her try to get around this: "I saw the clothes in the dresser. Just like the dress that girl in the fire was wearing."

Gram looks baffled. "I imagine we could go to the thrift store in town and find you a half dozen more like it. What's this about, Margot?"

"It's about her," I say. "I'm not the only girl you've had here." Trapped, that's what I want to say. Hidden. But she wouldn't like that.

"That's right," Gram says. "Your mother grew up at Fairhaven."

"You know that's not what I mean. She came from here. That girl was wearing one of Mom's dresses."

"But how can you be sure?" Gram asks. She sounds like she really wants to know. "Did you see your mother's name in that dress?"

Even if i'd gotten a good look, that dress was too damaged for anyone to make out a little line of handwriting.

I hesitate. "Well, no, but—"

"Then it seems quite a fit to throw over nothing, doesn't it?"

"It's not a fit."

"No?" She frowns, purses her lips. "I thought you'd be
more mature than this. I really did."

I can feel it, that rushing panic I know from every fight
with Mom. Putting me on the defensive, when I came down
here with what I thought was proof. "Okay," I say, "then
why were there so many clothes in the dresser? You said you
brought me a few things, but that was—"

Gram waves me off. "They're just left behind from when
your mother lived up there."

I stop short. Victory sweeping over me until I'm smiling.
"You said that wasn't anyone's room. That's what you told
me yesterday."

There it is. A lie I've caught her in. It never works with
Mom, never gets her to back down, but Gram's different.
She has to be different.

"Did I?" she says. "Really?"

"Yeah." I shift from foot to foot warily. She's too easy, too
curious. I know what to do with defensive, with angry. Not
with this. "You didn't say it was Mom's, anyway."

"I'm sure I must have."

"You didn't. I know what I heard."

Gram tilts her head, eyebrows raised. "And I don't?"

I can't breathe right. Shallow and quick, a seizing in my lungs. How did I end up in this same fight? I've had it with Mom, over and over, and I left her, I left all that. This was supposed to be better.

"Margot?" Gram sets down her work boots and the bucket and comes toward me, her too-familiar face creased with concern. "Are you okay, honey? Come here. It's all right."

I just stare at her. Rooted to the spot, a hundred arguments playing all at once in my head. I've always told myself it's just Mom, just Mom who can't accept that things happened the way I know they did. But if it's the same with Gram, maybe the problem isn't either of them. Maybe it's me. I'm the one who's wrong over and over; I'm the one dreaming up hurts and picking fights. Maybe that notebook I kept in Calhoun was full of lies.

But it can't be. I saw what I saw.

"Let it out," Gram says. "Deep breaths." She takes hold of my shoulders, squeezes them gently and draws me into a hug. I stand there rigid in the fold of her arms, exhausted, afraid. For a second I want to apologize. If it were Mom, I would.

That, at least, can be different here.

"Good girl," Gram says, stepping back. "All right. Why don't you go get changed?"

She's smiling. The fight over, the conversation dropped. It's a relief, really, and I go without another word. Back to my room. Back to that fucking dresser. And that dress still matches what I saw on that girl. But it doesn't matter. It didn't prove a single thing.

I was stupid to think it would be enough to get answers from Gram. I shouldn't have played my cards so early. Shouldn't have let her make me wonder if I ever had any in the first place.

It's not giving up, I tell myself. I'll try again. But I'm not going at Gram without a hell of a lot more in my pocket.

My clothes from yesterday are still dirty, so even though it stings, feels like defeat, I pull open the dresser drawers and grab a pair of shorts, along with a T-shirt worn through with small holes.

I don't know for sure what Mom looked like at my age, but as I stand in front of the bathroom mirror wearing her clothes, in her house, I think it must have been exactly like this. Before her face narrowed. Before that scar marked her cheek. It's easier today than it was yesterday, to know I'm only ever what she already was. I can't have her here with me, but least I'll have this.

Back downstairs Gram is waiting. She doesn't say anything about the fight we had, if that's what she'd call it. I know I would. Even the smallest thing can come back bigger. Instead she just nods to my shoes, dangling from my hands by their laces, and waits while I put them on. As soon as I'm ready, she's leading me out the back of the house. We step onto the porch, and I watch her take the same moment I did. A breath, and a gaze, and the warmth of the sun.

"What's the work?" I ask, eager to fill the silence. The farm is nearly dead, from what I can tell. I don't know what there is to be done besides start it all over.

"Back acres need tending," she says, stepping off the porch and making for the side of the house, where the truck is parked. I take one last look at the Miller house before I follow.

I wait until we're in the truck, easing down one of the access roads, to ask her. The burned fields are off to the right, far enough that I can only taste the lingering smoke. The way the fire was burning, at least a third of her land must be gone, if it's even all the way out. But she doesn't seem worried. She hasn't since I met her.

"How do you make it work?" I ask. I'm facing her instead of the road, neither of us buckled in as the fields slip by, each one just like the last, like the ones by the house. Corn too golden for this time of year, somehow dead and growing at the same time. "The farm, I mean. It's just you, isn't it?"

We both know what I'm not saying. The girl like a grave dug between us, and for a moment Gram hesitates. I didn't mean to bait her. I didn't mean to start this again.

Then she shrugs, and the tension breaks. "It is."

I don't know exactly, but a farm this size—it would probably take a good seventy or eighty people to keep it running the way it should. Instead it's only Gram in a pickup, with crops that hardly seem like they'll yield anything at all.

"So how do you manage it all alone?"

Gram gives me a sidelong look as she turns the truck onto a road running toward the Miller house. "I should think you'd know the answer to that better than anyone," she says. And it catches in my throat, winds between my fingers like a hand to hold, because I know exactly what she means. Me, managing my own life, raising myself, alone in an apartment with Mom right there next to me.

"And the corn?" I want to ask in a way that won't hurt her, but I don't know where the mines are in her the way I do with Mom. I decide to try something broad. "It wasn't always like this, was it?"

Gram doesn't answer right away. It seems like an easy silence, but then I spot the white strain of her knuckles as she grips the steering wheel.

"Fairhaven's been running a long time," she says finally. "Things come and go. Money, family. It'll be good again."

Will it? She has no farmhands, no machines, no nothing. Whatever she's living on must be from generations back. Something she had that nobody else in Phalene did, and when Fairhaven dried up, she kept on. The town couldn't.

It's not long before we've gotten where we're going, and Gram brakes, dust catching us through the open windows. The corn presses in so close I can't see the sprawl of the fields, and here, this far back, it seems a little healthier, a little more alive. The grove I saw from the porch must be nearby, if I'm picturing the farm right.

But up ahead, that's what I'm staring at. The line between Nielsen land and Miller land. It's clear as anything, and would be without the low, ramshackle fence that runs down the middle of the ditch separating the two. On our side, the corn is cracked and golden. On the other, drifting, green.

I open my mouth, then close it again. What am I supposed to ask Gram? How'd you mess it up so badly when they didn't? What's wrong with us that isn't wrong with them? She wouldn't answer, no matter how right I'd be to ask.

There's a buffer on the Miller side of the fence, between the ditch and the crops. A stretch of maybe a hundred yards that's just long grass and weeds. I can see the Nielsen sickness bleeding into it, the creep of brown grass and parched earth, but it's gone, back to normal by the time the Miller corn starts.

I'm staring, but Gram's clearly used to it. She gets out, comes around the front of the truck, flipping off the Miller crops absently, like she's done it a thousand times and will do it a thousand more. Tess, the Millers, with land they bought off my grandmother, watching as she falls to pieces.

Gram raps her knuckles against the truck door as she passes, and I get out, follow her around to the flatbed. It's empty, lined with a blue plastic tarp that Gram seems to have fixed in place with a nail gun and a handful of frail-looking zip ties.

"We're doing what out here, exactly?" I ask.

She pulls the bucket out of the flatbed and slings it over her arm, waving me with her as she makes for the back field. "You made it just in time for the harvest," she says.

Harvest. What must it have looked like those years back, when Fairhaven belonged to the people in those pictures I saw hanging in the dining room? How much of the town would have been here, working, living off what the Nielsens paid them?

And now it's me and Gram.

There are no rows left in these fields. Nothing like what I can see of the Miller crops, where paths run between each furrow, as neatly kept as anything out here is. Gram's plantings have spilled from their beds, have crept under the earth to wind around each other, choking off the roots, breaking the stalks in half. I cringe as we pick our way through, try to keep the leaves from touching me. It's too much like the fire. The dry, papery brush, the slicing of the sky. I want to work at Gram, to get her to tell me what I already know, but I can barely keep myself halfway together.

"All right," Gram says, when we've only gone in a few steps. I swallow hard, grateful I can still see the truck from here. "Let's see what we've got."

She sets down the bucket and runs her hands up the stalk of the nearest plant. This one is just barely green, the velvet tassels starting to brown in the sun. The plant's bearing an ear, but it's small, nothing like what I expected. It could fit in the palm of Gram's hand. She doesn't seem bothered, though. She plucks it off the stalk, the husk making a terrible squeaking sound as it shifts.

"Open that up," she says, handing it to me.

I shrink from it, but Gram's watching me with her steady, dark eyes. Watching, and waiting, and if I'm not the girl she wants me to be, I don't think I'll be able to stay here very long.

Carefully, I start to peel the husk away. It's thin, each layer nearly translucent as I drop it to the ground, leaving the ear underneath. Soon it's bare, held loosely in my palm. Kernels blushing pink, same as the water from the kitchen sink, and crumpled, lined up like baby teeth. It's not how it should be. None of it is. Especially not the fact that the ear is two ears, two offshoots from the same plant, curled around each other in a helix.

I stare at it, at the rot spreading where the split cobs are pressed against each other. With my thumbnail, I bear down on one of the kernels. The film of it is clear—it's whatever is inside that's giving it that color.

It pops. Something pink and liquid spills out, pale and thin and cold under my nail.

I drop the corn, stumble a step back. The spiraled ear cradled in the dirt. What the hell is happening here?

"That's what I thought," Gram says. Just like at the station. So calm. Nothing ever surprises her. "This plot's no good."

I press my hands to my face. I feel like I've gone numb. "Are they all like that?" I manage.

"Not all." Gram touches my elbow, and the warmth of her, a real and living warmth, brings me back, urges me along with her deeper into the field. "Most. But not all."

"What happened? To make them that way, I mean."

She scoffs, and for a moment her steps take her out of sight. It lights a flare of fear in my chest. I rush after her.

"Look around," she says. The plants brushing my skin, reaching down the back of my shirt. Writhing up out of the ground. "Phalene got hit with a drought some forty years back. But Fairhaven got a blight worse than that."

"But the Millers—"

"Yes," she says, almost upset. "Well, you can spare yourself all manner of things with a bit of luck and a bit of money."

I don't really think Gram is one to talk about money.

Maybe she doesn't own half the town anymore, but she's not exactly hurting for it.

We find a few normal ears of corn. Those are the ones Gram drops into the bucket. It takes a long time to fill it. A long, long time, and we're nearly at the edge of the farm before we manage it.

I can see the apricot grove ahead, the beckoning of the shade so strong it's in my bones. I just want to sit, and rest, and feel something besides this pressing heat. But Gram starts back to the truck, and I follow her. Of course I do.

Years ago, a day's work would've filled the whole bed of the truck. And before that, even more. But all these acres, they've dwindled down to Gram and me, and what we can carry. She drops the bucket into the bed of the truck with a pitiful thud and we both try hard not to look at the empty space around it.

"Will you sell it?" I ask.

Gram shakes her head. "Anyone buying is looking for larger quantities than we can harvest anymore. This is just for me. For us."

"But you used to sell?" I try to fill in the pieces, try to sketch out what it was like when Mom was young. My hands braced on the side of the flatbed, corn silk stuck to a hangnail on my thumb. "When my mom was here?"

"Not even then." She sighs. "The last time we were pulling a profit would've been when my parents ran this place."

"What was that like?" I ask.

Gram waits a moment as the sun builds between us, staring over at the Miller house. Their corn grows too high for me to see the porch, to see the bright flowers I'm sure are gathered by every window. But we're close enough that I can imagine that picture of Mom I took from the Bible laid over everything, snow and blue sky as she smiled at the camera. At her own mother.

"Like that," Gram says, at last. "Just like that."

At the top of the house, as I'm watching, a window opens. "Hey," I hear, drifting over the field, before I realize there's a person, there's Tess, waving her arm so I'll see, leaning so far out the window it makes my heart skitter into my throat.

Gram's expression goes tight. They were polite to each other in the station. Even friendly, I think, by Gram's standards. But being civil can't go far toward easing the sting of living side by side.

"Margot!" Tess yells. I take a half step toward the house before I even realize it, my fists clenched with the urge to haul her away from the window before she falls out. "Come over!"

Gram is already opening the door of the truck, ready to get back to Fairhaven. But when I met Tess I didn't get the impression that she ever let people tell her no, and that doesn't seem to be any different even when she's barely more than a shadow against the sun.

"Get in the truck," Gram tells me quietly. "Before Theresa remembers her manners."

It's too late. "You too, Vera! My mom's got brunch." A pause, and then: "You can introduce Margot."

That seems to do it. Gram shuts her eyes for a moment, and when she opens them again it's to give me a sort of conspiratorial look of exhaustion. Two Nielsens, dealing with the Millers together. "All right," she calls back. "Just a minute."

Tess disappears from the window. I wait for Gram to get into the truck first. I don't want to seem too eager. But I'm anxious to see Tess. To talk to her about yesterday. To find out what happened after I left the station, and just what I have to be afraid of.

THIRTEEN

If the outside of the Miller house looks something like Fairhaven, the inside is entirely different. Fairhaven feels like a honeycomb, rooms blocked off and cloistered, but the Miller house is open practically from one side to the other. The living room, the kitchen, the french doors and the sweeping view beyond. All of it done up in varying shades of white, and I catch myself wondering if anybody's spilled anything anywhere in the last thirty years, if I might find tomato sauce and orange juice stains on the underside of every couch cushion.

Tess met us at the door and is just ahead of us now, wrapped in a blue summer dress and leading us across the plush white rug toward the kitchen. A woman is standing at the marble-topped island, wearing a stiff floral dress and staring down at a plate of fruit with a look of deep concentration. She must be Tess's mom, but they don't look much alike. Not compared to me and mine, at least.

"Hello, Sarah," Gram says as we get close, and Tess's mom looks up, startled, her fingers poised over the fruit plate with a strawberry pinched delicately between them. "Thank you for having us. This is my granddaughter, Margot."

Mrs. Miller hesitates, and I catch the moment of tension that takes hold of her body. Gram can't be an easy neighbor to have. Especially not now. Even so, it's only a heartbeat before she smiles and says, "I'm so happy you could join us," like she had any idea we were coming.

Tess skirts the island, snags the strawberry from her mother's hand and shoves it into her mouth. "You love company," she says around it. "My gift to you."

"Of course I love company," Mrs. Miller says. "And it's been so long since we've had the chance to see you, Vera."

That isn't hard to translate, no matter how thick Mrs. Miller wants to lay on the politeness. Gram and the Millers are not friends; they don't do this.

"But a better gift," Mrs. Miller continues, "might be washing your hands, Tess, before you touch the food I'm serving." She leans across and presses her palm to Tess's forehead. "How are you feeling? Better?"

"Fine," Tess says, batting her mom away and heading for

the sink. "Eli's coming down," she says over her shoulder as she rinses her hands. "He stayed the night."

Mrs. Miller's mouth goes tight. "You need to ask me about that sort of thing, Theresa."

"He's stayed here a thousand times."

"And we love him," Mrs. Miller says. "But until you live under your own roof, you'll ask me or your father before you invite someone in." She glances at me and Gram. "To stay the night," she adds, clearly for our benefit.

"Well, he's here," Tess says, shrugging. "So. Okay."

Mrs. Miller looks to Gram and smiles ruefully, as if to say, "Daughters," but Gram doesn't give anything back.

"I hope we're not imposing," she says instead. At Fairhaven she looks like she belongs, like she grew up out of the floor right there in the entryway, but here she has a tightness about her, an unexpected discomfort, and I wonder if she's feeling the same thing I am. Like I'm too much, too clumsy and too blunt to live in a house of white carpet and delicate words. Sure, I had to be careful in Calhoun, with Mom, but that was different. Nothing I learned there will serve me here.

"Don't be silly," Mrs. Miller says. She carries the fruit plate around the island, toward a long dining table in blond wood. "The more, the merrier. Richard should be off the phone any minute, and we've got Eli joining us too."

Tess grins easily from where she's leaning against the

counter, ignoring her mom's pointed tone. I just stare at the two of them, at the way whatever Mrs. Miller was trying to impress upon Tess slides right off. I didn't know it could work like that. I didn't know there are ways to keep everything from feeling like the end of the world. I look up at Gram, who's been quiet, and see her staring not at Mrs. Miller but through the french doors to the green sway of the Miller crops. We both want what's here. Just different parts.

"Margot," Tess says. She's opened the cabinet next to the fridge and is peering inside. "Come here and help me pick all the marshmallows out of my cereal."

"I made pancakes," Mrs. Miller says. "Don't ruin your appetite." But she doesn't stop me as I slot in next to Tess and watch her dump half a box of Lucky Charms into a bowl.

"How are you?" she says quietly, our backs to the adults, her hair a curtain, thick and dark. "After yesterday."

I shrug, drop a rainbow-shaped marshmallow onto my tongue. "Fine." She'll know I mean anything but. "What about you? Were you sick?"

"My stomach's been weird. It's nothing." She knocks my fingers away from one of the other rainbows and takes it for herself. "Look, I was at the station for a while after Vera took you home. I'm pretty sure the police are gonna come after you. Or her." She shrugs. "If there's a difference."

I knew that yesterday. At least, I was afraid that was

145

true. And I did nothing wrong. I know that. But there are things here Gram is hiding, and no way am I letting anybody else get to them before I do.

"Okay," I say, careful to sound as bland as possible. "So?"

"So," Tess says, drawing it out, "I want you to know it's gonna be fine. I said you have me, and that's still true. If you don't want them looking at you, they won't."

Behind us, Gram and Mrs. Miller are making painful small talk. I wait for a moment, to be sure they're not listening. It's not a secret, what happened yesterday, but I don't want Gram to hear me trying to dig deeper. If she does, she'll close up even more tightly. I understand that much, even if I don't understand why.

"Why would you do that for me?" I ask Tess. "You don't know a thing about me."

She shrugs, and for a second I wonder if it's something else between us. I never got good at recognizing attraction in other girls—it took me long enough to recognize it in myself, and even longer to say "lesbian" without blushing. But then Tess sorts through a handful of cereal, dumping most of it back into the box, and I wrinkle my nose, the tension evaporating. Sure, she rinsed her hands, but I don't think she used soap.

"Well," she says. "I know what it means to have your last name matter more than your first. To put it one way."

"Oh." I can understand that, even if Tess's probably gets her out of trouble and mine gets me into it. But still. There's an odd sort of shyness to her right now, like there's more she isn't saying. I nudge her arm. "And to put it another?"

She doesn't answer right away. When she does, it's just: "It's nice. To be part of it."

I think of her and her friends coming out of Hellman's yesterday. All of them gathered around her, watching to see what she'd do next. That's distance, isn't it? Even if it's not the kind I know.

"I'm glad you are," I say. I mean it. Back in Calhoun I never had anyone. Maybe Tess never really had anyone either. Or at least nobody who needed her the way I do.

The memory of this morning's fight with Gram flickers bright. I check over my shoulder. Gram isn't listening— she's busy looking offended as Mrs. Miller hands her a slice of honeydew on a pretty china plate. And maybe I should just let it go, but I can't. I want this life for my own, but to do that, to protect it, I need to know what the hell is going on.

"Listen," I say quietly, turning back to Tess. "I saw something. At Fairhaven. I really think the girl from the fire was living there."

I catch Tess's frown out of the corner of my eye. "What do you mean?" she asks. But I don't have time to answer. Mrs. Miller comes over, dusting her hands together and peering over our shoulders at the mess we've made of the cereal.

"All right, girls," she says. "Tess, would you go fetch Eli? I don't want the pancakes to get cold."

"Sure," Tess says. And then, to me, "Later. We'll talk more."

She slips up the stairs at the far end of the kitchen and comes back down with Eli just as Mrs. Miller is ushering us all to the table, where a tray of pastries is waiting. He stops when he sees me, and for a second I know exactly what he's thinking, because I'm thinking it too. That I died yesterday, and he saw my body.

"Eli doesn't get coffee," Tess announces, sidling by him to take a seat. She pulls me into the chair next to hers and drags the coffeepot closer. "Punishment for turning up the AC after I fell asleep."

"You keep it too cold." He sits down across from her, wearing the frown that I haven't seen him without yet. "I'm not trying to get frostbite."

"Whereas I absolutely am." Tess fills her mug, and mine without asking if I want some, before reaching across and pouring some for Eli, too. I watch, baffled, as she sets the pot back down and pulls a pastry from the bottom of Mrs. Miller's carefully stacked pile, sending a croissant rolling onto the table. She was joking, with Eli. I know she was. But still. To see a threat made and dropped so easily—it's nothing short of a miracle.

"Dad coming?" she says through a mouthful of pastry. Terrible manners, but then I don't imagine she's ever needed good ones.

Mrs. Miller is in the kitchen again, carefully stirring blueberries into a bowl of yogurt. "In a minute."

"I'll go tell him we have company."

"He's speaking with the chief," Mrs. Miller says, glancing sidelong at Gram. "Don't disturb him."

"The chief?" I say, and every pair of eyes flicks to me. Tess nudges my elbow, and I bet she means for me to back off, to not look so curious, but I can't help it. "You mean the police chief?"

"After yesterday," Mrs. Miller says, coming to the table and setting the yogurt down near the empty chair at the head.

"It didn't touch your land," Gram says from her seat at the foot of the table. It's the first real thing she's said since we got here, and I'm startled by how sharp it is, by how much else it seems to mean. "There's no need for Richard to get involved."

"Well, of course, but I didn't mean the fire, Vera," Mrs. Miller says seriously. She sits down next to Eli, adjusting her skirt and folding her hands. "I meant the girl they found."

My breath catches. How much does Mrs. Miller know, exactly? Did Tess tell her parents what the body looked like? From the reassuring squeeze she gives my hand, I doubt it.

"The girl?" Gram says, after a moment. "Yes, it's a shame. I heard she was a runaway. Wrong place, wrong time." I've never heard anything so bland, so carefully careless.

And Mrs. Miller jumps at it. "Poor girl," she says dreamily. Like she's eager to pretend it happened a million miles away. I recognize that, I think. Anything to keep the peace with Vera Nielsen. "I imagine it must be an inconvenience. Even Theresa was at the station for hours."

An inconvenience? Someone died. Someone died and nobody will acknowledge how much it matters.

"It was exhausting and terrible," Tess says over the rim of her coffee mug, "and I'll never recover." It earns her a stern look from Mrs. Miller.

"Hours?" I ask, before I can help it. "What did you talk with the police about?"

"Oh, it was all bullshit," Tess says.

"Theresa."

"What? It was. It was just all the same stuff they asked you, Margot."

It's a show she's putting on, I can tell. To prove she doesn't care, to prove it's no big deal. And I don't know why she would bother, or who it protects me from, only—

Gram. It protects me from Gram.

I go flush with it, anger and resentment and a gratitude so deep it embarrasses me. She's my family, and you don't need protecting from family. Except, a little voice reminds me, I know better than anyone that sometimes, you do.

"And then they had to ask me," Eli grumbles as he spoons a blueberry from the yogurt. "Like I had anything different to say. But why hear something once when you could hear it three times?" Tess snorts with laughter, and they share a wry smile. I wish I could thank him for playing along, for pretending. He carried that body out of the fire and everything since has clearly been more than he ever asked for.

"Is your mother with you?" Mrs. Miller asks me, and I know it's only small talk, but it strikes me between the ribs.

"No," Gram answers for me. She hasn't touched anything—not her water glass, not the coffeepot, not the food. "Margot's staying with me for the summer."

I am? I smile, wide, and it's nothing I could stop, even if I wanted to.

"Your daughter hasn't been home in a long time, has she?"

Mrs. Miller doesn't realize what she's asked. But I see Gram flinch the same way I do, and I feel Tess's eyes on me. Watchful, and quiet, two things I wouldn't have called her yesterday.

"Phalene's not for everyone," Gram says. "Especially a Nielsen."

"I'll never understand all that." Mrs. Miller looks at me and leans in a little, smiling. "More than fifteen years since we took the farm off Richard's parents. Tess was barely walking. And by Phalene standards I'm still just visiting."

"Did you know my mom?" I ask, and Gram makes a small sound. I might pay for this later, but I want anything anyone can give me of her.

"I didn't," Mrs. Miller says. "She was gone by the time we moved back. But my husband did."

"Really?" He would have grown up with her, known her before she could close herself off. Maybe back then, the smile in the photograph I tucked in my nightstand was something she wore all the time. He can tell me that.

And he can tell me, too, if it was really the fire that drove her away, or if it was something else. I can tell by now that there's no way I can talk to him with Gram here, though. But she'll stand between me and any answers that she hasn't already approved. I have to catch him alone—like he is now.

"Excuse me," I say to Mrs. Miller. "May I use your restroom?"

She gives me that gracious hostess look and sends me down a hallway that splits off a smaller family room next to the kitchen. It's narrow, cool and shadowed, lined with framed photographs of Tess posed on the porch, Tess by the Christmas tree, Tess younger and younger as I pass, until she's a toddler sitting on someone's knee. I think of the dining room wall at Fairhaven. Of the generations hung there, and of how none of those pictures seemed alive the way Tess's portraits do.

The bathroom is on the right, white tile and white towels with a white monogram. I hesitate in the doorway, my eyes meeting my reflection in the mirror above the porcelain sink.

I look like a mess, my hair straggly and slick with grease even though I washed it in the bath last night. Slowly I reach up and run my fingers along my cheek, the one where a scar would be if my mother and I were really matching.

Now it's me and Gram, and my somehow sister. I asked for this. I wanted a family. That body's a problem in my way, but all I have to do is solve it. Then I can make a life with Gram worth something. Then I can have what I want.

I leave the bathroom and turn back to the hallway. It ends in another pair of french doors, their glass panels mostly covered by a dark curtain. Through a gap I can see the glow of a computer screen and a burnished wooden desk, and there's a muffled voice coming from inside. It must be Mr. Miller talking to the police chief.

I lean back against the wall to wait, in a slot between two of the photographs. But something scuffs against the floor in the study, and it's only a moment before one of the doors is being pulled open. I straighten in a hurry, try to look lost and unsure. It's not really that far from the truth, anyway.

Mr. Miller isn't what I expected after meeting his wife. She's out of the pages of an old housekeeping magazine. But he's more like Gram. Faded denim and a button-down with the sleeves rolled up, the starch all but gone from the collar, if it was ever there in the first place. He's homegrown Phalene, just like her, I remind myself. That's why I'm here looking for him.

"Oh," he says, startled. "I didn't know we had . . ."

He trails off, and I know that expression by now. Wide, wary eyes, like I'm something between a shock and a haunting.

"Sorry," I say. "I was looking for the restroom." And then, even though I probably don't need to bother, "I'm Vera's granddaughter." I gesture to my face, the proof I was born with. "Margot."

"Margot," he says. "God." But he seems, then, to remember his manners, because he reaches out, and we shake hands, his palm calloused against mine, just like Gram's. "Welcome, Margot." He's still staring at me. It must be unnerving, if he knew my mother. To see me, just like her.

"Thanks for having us," I say. "Tess invited us over to brunch. I hope you don't mind."

"Not at all," he says automatically, and his smile is warm. "Have you been here long? In town?"

"No," I say, and if he was talking to the police chief just now, he knows this, but if he wants to pretend I'm just a new family friend, that works for me.

He steps past me, motioning for me to join him in heading back to the kitchen. I do, but slowly. I need more time to bring up Mom.

"How are you liking Fairhaven?" he says.

"It's all right. I wish I'd seen it before."

We pass out of the hallway and into a smaller family room, two couches and a fireplace. Mr. Miller comes up next to me, and for a moment we both stop, looking out the large bay window, across the porch and toward Fairhaven.

"My mom never told me much about it," I say. Mr. Miller is older than Mom—she had me early, after all—but their lives would've crossed, at least for a little, especially if he grew up here, and her right there at the house we both can't take our eyes off. "Did you know her?"

He gives me a once-over. "I assume you mean Jo?"

"Yeah," I say, and the oddness of the question is buried under the crush of hearing her name. Familiar, living. He knew her. He actually knew her.

"Then yeah," he says. "A bit, anyway. But she was a kid when I left Phalene for school. And by the time I came back to take over the farm, she was gone. Is she here with you?"

I want to laugh. "No," I say instead. "It's just me."

"Well," he says, "I'm sorry I can't tell you more about her. They always kept to themselves."

"Gram and my mom?"

He frowns. "No," he says, slowly, warily. "Did she not . . ."

"Not what?" I say, confused, and I watch his mouth drop open.

"Nothing." He clears his throat. "Let's get to brunch. I'm starving."

He doesn't wait for me, just heads down the hallway. And I follow, but I'm thinking about his expression, how it closed itself up in that way adults' faces do. How it said, *This is not for you. For your own good.*

Well. Fuck that.

Back in the kitchen Eli's half-asleep, his chin propped up on his hand, and Tess is building a stack of pastries, biting her lip as she concentrates. Gram looks like she'd rather be anywhere else, and for a moment I feel bad for her. But then it's there between us. Secrets kept and covered.

"Tess," I say, and she jumps, the pastry tower toppling over. "You ready to go?"

A smile lifting the corners of her mouth. Ready for anything. That's Tess, I think. Game, no matter what. "Remind me where?"

I knew I could count on her. "Around town."

"Right." She gets to her feet and steps around me, heading for the door, where a pair of absurdly white sneakers is waiting.

"Do I have to come?" Eli grumbles without opening his eyes. "Actually, don't answer that. I'm going back to sleep."

"Here?" Mr. Miller asks. He's circled to the kitchen

island and is busy toasting a bagel, ignoring all the food his wife laid out. "Have we officially adopted you yet, Eli? Your parents might have something to say about that."

Eli blinks, eyes bleary. "No, they'd be fine with it. I hear I'm expensive."

"Not as expensive as me," Tess crows from the door. She's got one shoe on and is halfway to falling over as she puts on the other. Mr. and Mrs. Miller laugh, so I guess that was a joke, but I don't talk about money like that. From the look on Gram's face, neither does she.

"What are you going into town for?" she says, pursing her lips. "You haven't seen enough of it?" Icy, and stiff, and nothing like the woman this morning who gave me a hug.

"I'm gonna show her the pool," Tess says. "Also the seedy underbelly. And the black market. The—"

"Yes," I cut in. "All that." I just want to get out of here, away from the press of my grandmother's gaze. Then I can find the gaps in the story, the ones I can get through.

Gram lets out a short breath and gets to her feet. She moves so differently than Mom does. Deliberate and sure. Mom is quick and Mom is sudden, and I wonder if people look at her and me and think we're as different from each other as she is from Gram.

"I'd rather you just come home with me," she says. She's being polite—we're in company—but I can hear the order she's wrapping her words around.

157

I put on my best smile. "I know," I say. "But it's my first time visiting. I want to see where my family's from."

I can do it too. Pointed and razor-sweet. I will figure this out, whether she likes it or not. I mean, she says she's being honest. If she is, she has nothing to worry about.

"Margot," she says, but Tess has the front door open.

"See you later," I say over my shoulder, just as Tess says, "I'll have her home by eleven."

Gram must be seething. She calls my name again, but I don't care anymore, because Tess is off ahead of me and she can help me figure this out. I don't have to be on my own.

The door shuts behind us. Bikes in Tess's garage, both of us laughing, giddy with knowing that Gram could be coming after us. It's barely a minute before the two of us are pedaling down her driveway. Fairhaven up ahead on the left, faded and yellowed against the bright sky. That's Gram's world, and my answers are there—I know they are—but I'll never get them from her. I have to find another way in.

Turn the corner onto the highway. Ash opening up on our left and the heat like cotton, like a clean sheet brushing my body, hotter and hotter, until there's nothing else. A haze, a fog, a shimmer on the road. Tess weaving back and forth, dress fluttering in the wind, hair long and loose. Sometimes life looks exactly the way you think it should.

And then we pass it and it doesn't anymore. The crime scene tape. The place where Eli laid her body. The scene is clear now, no cruisers and no techs, no camera flashes, but it was barely a day ago. Like it or not, it's easy to remember.

Tess slows down, her path taking her right to the edge of the road, and for a moment I think she means to stop, to put us back there. But I stay steady, and she catches up. Slides her bike alongside mine, and for a minute we just coast.

"Okay?" Tess calls to me over the rush of the breeze.

And I have no idea, but I say, "Sure."

FOURTEEN

Tess does take me past the pool, but I barely see more than the stretch of concrete and the flash of brightly patterned bathing suits before we're into the thicket of the houses and breaking out onto the town square. I wonder if she'd be back there on any other day, watching her friends put on sunscreen and shrieking as Eli throws her into the water. But now I'm here, and I'm asking for her help. Never mind that she offered.

She pulls over by the bike rack at the corner of the town green, and I follow. My mouth is dry from the ride, and I can still feel every place that yesterday's heat touched, but away from Gram, away from Fairhaven, I'm more of the person I was two days ago, before any of this happened. Just Margot Nielsen.

"So," Tess says, getting off her bike. "I'm showing you around town?"

She didn't ask on the ride here, with the wind and the road ahead of us, and I didn't explain. But I have to now.

"Yeah," I say. "Sorry about all that before."

"No, I should thank you," she says. I watch her slot her bike into the rack, wait for her to lock it, although with what, I don't know. Nothing to worry about for Tess, in Phalene. "You saved me from one of my dad's 'let's talk about farming' moods. Besides"—and the smile falls from her face, leaves the earnest girl I got a glimpse of yesterday and again this morning—"I saw what you saw. I'm not exactly fine about it, you know?"

That's one way to put it. I walk my borrowed bike up to the rack and settle it home. Yesterday it was her asking me what I knew. Now it's my turn.

"What I was trying to say before is that I found something," I say. "My grandmother told me I was staying in a guest room—that no one ever really lived there. But my dresser was full of clothes just like the girl was wearing."

Tess follows me toward the rack, leaning against it. "Did you ask her about them?"

"Yeah," I say, clearing my throat. "She had an explanation. She always has an explanation, except they don't make any sense. I think that girl must have been my sister. Maybe she was living at Fairhaven and I was with my mom."

Tess's eyes go wide. "Like . . ." And I can see her try not to say it. It comes out anyway. "Like some kind of *Parent Trap* shit?"

Jesus. "Sure," I say. "If that's how you want to think about it. But nobody's seen anyone else at Fairhaven. You haven't. The police obviously haven't."

"I'm guessing Vera hasn't had much to say about it." Tess sweeps her hair over one shoulder, a breeze catching the swing of it. "What about your mom? You could ask her. It's her shit too."

It is, but that doesn't matter. "I think," I say instead of answering, "that I need to figure out why she left."

"The fire," Tess says immediately, and then she winces. "Well, the first one."

"Right." That's not enough. Luckily, I think I know where to find more.

Anderson told Gram his father's old case notes were in storage, and that, Tess says when I explain, means the police station. Which is how we end up at the station's back door trying to pick the lock with a safety pin Tess found in the grass.

"I swear I'll get it," she's saying. "I saw this in a movie once."

I don't exactly have a better idea, but I take a step back

from her, press one hand to my stomach to settle the nausea there. I don't like this part of her, don't like how she can treat my life like it's an adventure she's on. No matter what attraction I can feel sparking sometimes, it'll never be strong enough to burn that away.

I step back, try to gather my thoughts. That's when I realize we're standing next to the parking lot, and it's empty of cruisers. Anderson and Connors and whoever else are all out in town. "Look," I say. "They're not here. Can't we just go through the front?" I have no doubt that Tess can talk her way past whatever receptionist is on duty.

Tess straightens, one hand going up to shield her eyes from the sun. *That's not as fun,* I can imagine her saying if I were looking at her with a little less frustration. Instead she says, "Sure. Hang back, though. Just in case."

I follow her around to the front and wait on the curb while Tess peers through the door to see who's on duty. The station looks just as imposing today as it did yesterday when I got out of Anderson's cruiser. The windows across the front of the lobby are dark, the blinds drawn, and through the door, over Tess's head, I can see the receptionist's desk, protected by a sheet of what must be bulletproof glass.

"Perfect," Tess says. "It's Judy. She's easy."

We head in, Tess shoving twice to get the door to open all the way when it sticks in the frame. A woman with bottle-even brown hair and perfectly painted red fingernails is sitting primly behind the counter, frowning as she fusses with the collar of her starched flowered blouse. She looks up as Tess approaches, leaving me just inside the door, under the blast of the air-conditioning. I ignore the goose bumps rising on my skin and focus as Tess settles into one hip and swings her hair over her shoulder.

"Hey, Judy," she says. "Hardly working?"

Judy's laugh is nervous. "Working hard," she says, but I catch an insistence in her voice, like she wants Tess to understand that she really is. She could be about Mrs. Miller's age, or maybe a little older. It's hard to tell from here.

"Listen, I know this is a pain," Tess says. It doesn't escape me that she's positioned herself between me and Judy, keeping our sight line from ever fully connecting. "But I left something in the bullpen yesterday when I was talking to Officer Connors. Can I go back and look for it?"

Judy's face twists, like she wants to frown but is too nervous. "I don't know, honey," she says. "I don't think I'm supposed to let you back there alone."

"No, it's okay." I can't see Tess's face, but it's not hard to imagine the winning smile she's giving Judy. "He said I could just duck in and out and it wouldn't be a bother." And then she knocks it over the top. "He said for you to call if you want to double-check."

"No," Judy says immediately. "No, of course. Go on back, and just give me a shout when you're done."

"Great." Tess looks over her shoulder at me and nods. I step up next to her as Judy presses a button under her desk and the door to the bullpen clicks open. Nobody had to let us through like that when Anderson brought me in from the fire. It must be just when nobody's on duty inside. And that bodes well for us.

"Oh," Judy says when she sees me. "Who's your friend?" But then her eyes go wide, and I know she recognizes me, just like everyone in this town does. "You must be—"

"She's here for the summer," Tess cuts in. "We'll only be a few minutes." She takes hold of my arm and pulls me through the doorway before Judy can say anything else. "Thank you!"

I give Judy my best approximation of a Tess smile as we pass. Judging from her stare, it wasn't very good.

"Okay," Tess says once we're in the bullpen and the door is shut behind us. "You wanted information, right?"

Nobody's in the conference room. Just a few scattered paper cups of coffee left over from a meeting and a whiteboard positioned at the front, my last name written across it in red marker. I look away.

"Yeah."

"We need the records, then, but I don't think they'll be up here," Tess says.

We check anyway, opening what turns out to be a supply closet and rifling through the desks in the bullpen.

Anderson's got a file folder with *Nielsen* misspelled and crossed out, and there's my name again, on that Post-it I saw on the file cabinet. But the folder's empty and the cabinet's locked.

"Now what?" I say to Tess. She nods to the corner of the bullpen, where a door leads to some stairs.

"The basement."

I follow her into the stairwell, down and down under flickering lights, one hand trailing against the wall. It's only two flights but it feels like more, feels like the summer has disappeared, leaving the air heavy with cold and shadow. Our footsteps echo as we reach the basement door, and for a moment I panic, afraid that Judy will hear us somehow. Afraid that Connors is waiting on the other side of the door to catch us.

I brace myself, but the stairwell door opens to no one. Just a hallway that runs barely a few yards before it corners sharply. The linoleum floor is water-stained and peeling, checkered in an unappealing teal and a gray that was probably white to begin with. Off the corridor is a handful of doors, all closed.

"One of these should be what we're looking for," Tess says.

She takes one side and I take the other, and soon enough we've found the door marked RECORDS and tried the handle. It's locked, because of course it is, but I stop Tess before she pulls out that goddamn safety pin again and lever my body against the handle. A door this old, this forgotten—it'll pop right out.

"You'll break it," Tess says.

I should care. But too many things have stood in my way, and this is something I can do, something I can take into my own hands. Tess talked us in, and she got me here, and I'm glad, but I have to do some of this myself. And so what if Connors and Anderson know it was me? I look guilty enough already. At least this time I'll have done something to earn their suspicion.

One push and another. I hear the door creak, and the rust on the handle is flaking off under my skin. I haul back on it, take a deep breath and throw all my weight right where the dead bolt would be. A snap. A jolt. The door tumbles open. I stagger, catch my chin on the frame.

"Okay," Tess says. "I was gonna go steal the keys from Connors's desk, but we can do this too."

I flush. Duck away from Tess and reach inside the room to flick on the lights. It's long and cramped, reaching away from the hallway, stacked to the ceiling with boxes and boxes of files and evidence. I can't imagine this is everything, but it's a start.

I take a step inside, and then deeper, the shelves rising like Gram's crops around me, edging in close. Shadows and dust, and a hundred lives in boxes. Sometimes it's like you can feel it, a history spiraling away from you in every direction, and Phalene has been like that every second. Right now, I'm almost relieved, because *this* I can touch. This is a room I can open and shut.

The boxes are labeled with what must be case numbers, and some of them have names and dates, too. It looks like they move backward, year by year, as I get closer to the far wall. Tess follows me, reading me the names she recognizes, which is all of them.

Mom had me just after she left Phalene. That means the fire has to have been before 2002. I'll start there, work back until I find what I need. I let my eyes unfocus, skim every date. The boxes begin to lose their shape, corners crumpling, duct tape peeling away. Ink running, paper curling.

Maybe it's not here. Maybe we broke in for nothing. Maybe everything about this was a mistake.

"Is there another records room?" I ask, hoping Tess will go looking and leave me to do this alone. I don't want her to see how nervous I am.

"Maybe." I hear her shoes scuff against the floor as she heads back toward the door. "I'll go check."

As soon as she's gone, I let my worry take hold of me. Let it send me to the very back of the room. I crouch in front of the lowest shelf, dust coating my fingers as I shove the front row of boxes to one side. There are more behind them, collapsed and mildewed. Something has leaked from the ceiling and dripped down to pool and dry here. But the dates are right. This could be it.

I check over my shoulder, make sure Tess is still gone. I can hear her meandering down the hallway, farther and farther. Good. I appreciate her help, I really do, and I know I'll need more of it. But I want this to be just me.

With a groan I heave the boxes onto the floor. I can barely make out the writing on the labels in the dim light, but there: on both, a name, the *N* large and clear even though the rest has blurred with time. *Nielsen*—it has to be.

I lift the lid off the nearest box.

Stacks of paper. Handwriting spread across the top sheet. Not Gram's. I'd recognize that now. These must be the old case notes. I spot another Anderson's name at the top of the page—that must be my Anderson's father.

Next I scan the few lines and Mom's name jumps out. But it's not the only one. The report mentions Vera, which I expected. And there's a mention of the Millers—they would be Tess's grandparents. There's a Katherine, too. That's new. Is that Mom? Maybe she changed her name to Josephine after she left Phalene. I wouldn't blame her for wanting a new start.

I squint down at the handwriting and, when it doesn't get clearer, sit back on my heels, hold the paper up to the light before tossing it aside. There must be a typed copy somewhere.

I find it in the next file folder. This one's bursting with binder clips that are barely holding sheaves of paper together. The first page is the same report, and I skim it quickly, aware that Tess will be back any second. It's not that I'll keep this from her. She should know too. But I want that first step into the secret history of my family to be one I take on my own.

Josephine and Vera, over and over. So—Mom was herself, then. Katherine was somebody else. I keep reading.

Josephine and Vera in custody, the papers tell me. Held for questioning. Vera reports having seen Katherine set the fire. Offers no further information when pressed. Josephine Nielsen corroborates Vera's account and reports having seen Katherine leave the house near midnight, around the time the fire is suspected to have started.

No body recovered. Katherine Nielsen presumed missing. All-points bulletin issued.

I sit back. Shock running through me.

Katherine *Nielsen*?

The paper falls from my hand. Lands on the floor next to my knee, but I don't move. Katherine. A name I have never heard anyone say. Family kept even further away than Gram.

Gram had another daughter. Mom's sister. My aunt.

And a part of me is saying, *You already knew. The girl in that field, the body you found. You knew sister wasn't right.*

Cousin, though. Katherine's daughter. Try that on. But that doesn't stop the questions. Doesn't stop the panic, stretching and strong, fizzing in my fingertips, building behind my heart.

I'm used to not knowing; I'm used to building my life around empty spaces, around locked doors and unanswered questions. And now this. An answer I never asked for. Blowing through every wall I've ever put up, tearing apart every memory I've ever kept close.

"Well," comes a voice from the doorway. I whip around. "If I wasn't sure you were a Nielsen before, I am now."

FIFTEEN

Officer Connors is standing in the doorway, watching me with raised eyebrows. My heart thunders, breath catching. I knew this could happen. I broke the door down because I didn't care. But he can't take me away now. Not when I've finally figured out the right questions to ask. What happened to Katherine? Maybe she left a daughter behind, not Mom.

"Shit," I say. "I . . ." There's no way to get out of this, though. Papers are still scattered around me, one box still open.

"You've been in town two days and been in trouble as many times," he says, coming farther in. "Should I expect Tess to jump out of the shadows?"

Tess. I forgot. She must be somewhere else in the basement. I hope she hears him, stays far away. There's no reason for both of us to get caught.

"I just needed to check something," I say, which sounds ridiculous. Connors obviously thinks so too. He huffs out a laugh and crouches next to me, picking up one of the stacks of paper and flipping through it. Over his shoulder, Tess peers around the doorframe. When she sees he isn't looking, she meets my eyes and tiptoes past toward the stairwell door, holding up crossed fingers and mouthing "Good luck."

She'll sneak out the back and step into the sun and everything will be the same for her as it was when we got here. And I'm here sitting in a whole new set of ruins. A cousin, maybe, and an aunt, and both of them gone before I ever had a chance to know them. If Katherine's anything like Mom, then nothing could bring her back here. Maybe that girl felt the same pull I did. Maybe she came looking, and Gram hasn't been keeping her hidden at all.

"So," Connors says. "This old chestnut."

"What?" He sounds so casual about this, this thing that's upending every part of me. More family than just the line from Gram to Mom to me. It could have been like those pictures at Fairhaven. Branches and roots both.

Connors ignores my surprise, and the flash of anger I can't put out. "We've been looking at this too," he says, and he starts piling everything back into the open box. Calmly, like it doesn't matter that I forced my way into someplace I shouldn't be. "Of course, most everybody from back then is already familiar to us. We don't need all this to keep it fresh."

I stand up with him and watch as he carefully slots both boxes back into place on the shelf.

"But a fire out at Fairhaven," he says, turning to me. "And you. And that girl. History repeats itself, you know? Only this time we've got a body."

This time. Me and that girl, history happening again, because we're just like Mom and Katherine.

Everybody fucking knew, didn't they?

It's a harder hit to take. Everybody. Every single person in this town, I bet. They knew, and they must have thought I did too, because why would Gram and my mom keep this from me? What kind of family would do that? Not a secret at all—just something so obvious nobody ever thought to say it out loud.

The missing picture on the wall in Fairhaven. *You look just like them,* from the pharmacy clerk. Them, them, and every time I thought it meant Gram and Mom. But it meant Mom and someone else. I'm shaking, goose bumps dotting my arms, and the room around me feels like that shimmer of heat on the road, like it'll disappear if I look closer. I've been careening through this town, breaking and oblivious, and I didn't even realize it.

"I have to go," I say. I have to talk to Gram. This is what she was protecting. Not my sister my mother left behind, but a whole other set of family. And there are still too many questions—how, how did nobody know that body when we pulled it from the fire?—but now that I know this part of the truth, there's no reason for her to hide anything else.

"You have to what?" Connors says. He looks almost amused. And I remember where I am—in a police station, in a room I broke into, surrounded by records I am very much not supposed to be reading.

I shove my hands in my pockets. "Sorry."

Connors settles back against the shelves and folds his arms across his chest. I remember that yesterday he was the nicer of the two. I think if Anderson had caught me here, I'd already be upstairs in the conference room being questioned.

"You're curious," Connors says. "I get it."

"I just found out my mom had a sister," I say. "So maybe you don't actually get it at all."

"Really?" Connors's eyebrows tick up. "Just found out? Seems like keeping secrets is a hard habit for your grandmother to break."

"She had her reasons," I say. Defending her, even though she's not here to reward me for it. My own habit, I guess.

"Whatever reasons those are, I'm not sure they're good enough. Everybody here knows about the twins."

Twins. Nothing new to him, but I see it in a flash. Mom and another, on the porch at Fairhaven with matching smiles. Of course. Of course it was twins. And Mom had me, and Katherine had her, that girl in the field. Another generation of Nielsen girls, and both of us strangers to Phalene. Both of us looking for family. Maybe Gram wasn't keeping her at Fairhaven, but she was still keeping her a secret.

"There's a lot that doesn't make sense about this," Connors continues, "if you don't know what happened here. Hell, there's a lot even if you do."

"Like what?"

Connors eyes me. I try not to let him see how nervous it makes me. Finally he sighs and straightens. "How do you think she died?" he says. "That girl?"

I can picture her there, in the field, curled on her side. And then later, on her back on the side of the highway. There was no blood. There were no bruises. She just wasn't alive anymore. "Smoke, I guess," I say. "Or something like that."

It was bad enough out there with safety just behind me. How would it be to be trapped, to know you'd never get out? To feel the life fade from you, and to think that even if you managed to keep breathing, the flames would swallow you whole?

"You're right," Connors said. "And I know you said you'd never seen her before." I open my mouth, and he holds up one hand. "I believe you. I mean, we haven't either. So I'm asking. Do you know why your grandmother's lying to us?"

Because she doesn't trust them with the truth. That much is obvious. But she's lying to me, too, and I don't want her reasons to be the same. I shrug, look away.

"The girl, then," Connors tries. "Let's start with her. I'll even do you a favor and ignore your resemblance, for the moment. Do you know why she might've been out there?"

"Wrong place, wrong time." That's what Gram said.

"Well, that's definitely true," Connors says, cracking a smile. He's easing back, trying to manipulate me into feeling comfortable. I spare a thought for Mom, a thank-you, because she may not have taught me much but she taught me how to understand this. "But the fire wasn't an accident, as it happens."

"How do you know that?"

His smile fades. "We do. It's hard to tell sometimes, but there are people who know what to look for. And they found it."

Okay. Okay, okay. The fire wasn't an accident. But that doesn't mean someone set out to kill that girl. There has to be some other explanation. Because if there isn't, I don't know how to handle that along with everything else.

"Why are you telling me this?" I say instead. Maybe it's not wise to turn this into a fight. But I'm too busy holding myself together to hold on to my patience too. "I've been with Tess from the second I got here. I've never even been to Fairhaven until yesterday."

"Take it easy," Connors says. "I'm not accusing you of anything. I know you didn't do this, okay? I know that."

I let out a breath. It's a relief to hear someone say it. Growing up with Mom, all the guilt she put on my shoulders—you bear it long enough, you start thinking it belongs there.

He nods to the boxes of files. "I'm telling you this because none of it's simple, Margot. Vera denies all knowledge of this girl. We have no idea where she came from. But I'm fairly certain that somebody set that fire on purpose, and it ended up killing her. And I think I'm beginning to see how this fits together, except for one piece." He looks me straight in the eye. "I need your help for that part. Can I show you what I'm talking about?"

I don't think I can say no. And more than that, I don't want to. If this is pointed at Gram, or at Mom, I need to know. Whether that's so I can protect them or so I can be the first to knock them down, I'm not sure. But I don't have to be right now. Not yet.

"Yeah," I tell him. "What is it?"

"The girl."

I snatch a quick breath. "She's still here?"

"Sure. Phalene County's not big. We do everything in the same place." He winces good-naturedly. "Puts a bit of a damper on lunch hour when you know the coroner's only one floor down."

I let his ease push away some of the tension hanging around my shoulders. Right now all I have to do is follow Connors. That is the only thing in the world, and I'm used to this part, to putting things away until I need to feel them. It's already happening. Katherine farther and farther away, the thought of her like pressure on a healing bruise.

I follow Connors out of the records room and to the right, along the hallway and around the corner to where a set of swinging doors leads to a large open space, about the size of the bullpen upstairs. We must be underneath it.

Inside, the halogens wash the world in yellow. A whiteboard stands streaked and dull in the corner, and a bland painting of a vase of flowers is hung crooked over a metal sink, like somebody put in the bare minimum effort at cheering the place up. But none of that matters. Because along the wall facing us are rows of metal berths, their rectangular doors shut tight. Stacks of metal coffins.

My breath catches. She's in there somewhere.

It's all right, I tell myself. I saw her once. I can see her again. And this time I know what she is.

Between me and the far wall is a long silver table with a channel around the edges. Despite my reassurances to myself, my throat goes tight at the sight of something there on the metal, dull and black against the shine. What is that? I don't think it's blood.

"Okay," I say, and I flush at the tremor in my voice. "I'm here. Let's get on with it."

Connors skirts the metal table and the little tray next to it holding a pair of magnifying glasses and a clean scalpel. I don't follow. There's a drain in the middle of the floor. I can't take my eyes off it. This windowless room, cold and empty—I could be here. It could be me. What's really different between me and her?

I don't want to look at her. It's sudden and strong, the certainty that I can't. Because if I do, and if there's really no difference, what will that mean? Who will I be then, if I'm a dead girl too?

"Come on," Connors says. His hand is resting on the handle to one of the berths, stacked in the wall like drawers in a dresser. A clipboard hangs from it, holding what must be the usual forms.

It takes everything, every ounce of will I have, but I force myself to cross the room and stand across from Connors, leaving space for the drawer to slide out between us. What am I nervous about? I've seen her. I've touched her. But I can't get rid of the prickle along my skin.

"Now, normally," Connors says, "I wouldn't be showing this to you. And normally you'd stay upstairs, instead of breaking into our records room. So I'd say we're a little past normal, aren't we, Margot?" I don't answer. He sighs. "Right. You ready?"

No. Never. But I swallow hard, set my shoulders. "Okay."

He grips the drawer handle and pulls. The tray inside comes rattling out.

For a second all I see is the white of the sheet. She's covered. I have that to hold on to, at least. But there are stains, that same black color from the table, leaking through the fabric. My stomach turns. They're right where her eyes should be.

"What . . . ," I start, but I don't get anything else out. Still, Connors must know what I mean.

"Her eyes? Yeah, I don't know," he says. "The coroner doesn't either."

He reaches for the edge of the sheet, but I beat him to it. I owe her that much, at least. My hand isn't steady, but Connors thankfully doesn't mention it as I lift the sheet and ease it back.

The smell of smoke hits the air. I blink hard to get the fire out of my eyes, focus on what I can see. Her hair, dark, smooth, gray threaded through. Just like mine, and I fight the urge to twirl the ends around my finger, the way Mom does sometimes with me. Take a deep breath. Gulp down the cold. I'm here. We're both here. And I'm alive.

I draw the sheet off her face. Drop it, and stagger back a step. My mouth suddenly dry and sour, throat working.

Her eyes are open. But they're wrong. Curdled. Black and seeping into her eyelashes, a liquid viscous and clinging. The stain on the sheet. The drips on the metal table. From this.

"What happened to her?" I manage, my voice raw. This isn't how bodies decompose, and even if it were, it's been barely a full twenty-four hours since we found her. Her eyes, running out of their sockets like thick black tears. How could that happen? The fire couldn't have done that. "She didn't look like that on the highway."

"No," Connors agrees. "She didn't." He takes the sheet from where I let it fall and lays it over her again, covering her eyes. As if that could keep me from seeing what's happened to her. My breath is coming too quick. Dizziness creeping in on the edges of my sight. But I can't look away. I can't. Because she'll be there when I do, and she'll be there forever, with something in her rotting.

"The coroner couldn't explain it," Connors says. "She couldn't explain a lot of things."

He slides the tray farther out. Her whole body between us, and his hand isn't steady as he flicks the sheet back from her legs. Pale feet, veins raised and delicate. And above, reaching down her left calf, thin white lines like a lattice of scars. They make a strange pattern, spirals made of spirals, all braided together, and they stand out sharp against the shiny redness of her burned skin.

That's where the fire touched her. The only place it did. When she came out of the field, the spark catching on her dress, on her skin.

That is not how a body behaves. Her eyes, these marks. Not a body like mine, or like anyone's. But I don't know what that means. Or what I'm supposed to do with it.

"You ever seen this happen to someone?" Connors asks. Like the answer should be yes, like I should be able to explain. Like I've ever stood over a corpse before and matched its face to mine.

"Of course not," I say. "Have you?" He shakes his head but doesn't move, and I can't stand it another second. "Can you . . . please, can you put her away?"

He waits a beat, agonizing and endless, before he slides the metal tray back into its berth and shuts the door. The latch clicks. I let out a breath.

"Maybe you haven't," he says. "But I think your grandmother might know something about it."

This, finally, gets me to shut my eyes.

"I don't know what you want me to say," I tell him. And then, because it's the only way I know how to ask for someone to take this out of my hands: "I don't know what you're waiting for."

"You read those files," Connors says. "Your grandmother said Katherine ran away, but she never went looking for her. Why not? What does she know that we don't?" He leans

183

against the wall, his hands in his pockets, the handle to the body's berth digging into his arm, the clipboard hanging there jostled to one side. "My bet is that Vera knows more than she's saying. And she won't tell me, but she might tell you."

I stare at the clipboard instead of at him, focus on the words I can read off its report instead of how he won't move, how he won't let me out of here, outside into the unbearable heat. *Notable conditions: inverted heart position, considered nonessential. Amphetamines: none detected. Barbiturates: none detected. Chemical compounds: detected, pending analysis.*

"Margot?"

I draw in a deep breath. Force my eyes back to him. Yes, something's wrong with Gram. Something's wrong with my whole family. But whatever they're hiding, it's mine to unravel.

"Ask her yourself," I say. "If you think she has something to do with this, then—"

"We did," Connors interrupts. He's frustrated now, and letting me know it. "We tried this morning. We've been trying to talk to her for years, since Katherine disappeared. We even had a warrant back then. Searched the whole place, which is how I know that a warrant's only gonna show me what Vera wants me to see. I need you. If I'm gonna get anywhere, it's gonna be with your help. And you need mine

184

too," he adds when I don't say anything. "Breaking and entering back there? Trespassing? That kind of thing could get a girl like you sent to juvie. But we can call it a wash. Like I said, I get it—you wanted to know. But so do I."

For a moment we just look at each other. I know he's right. But I won't help him. *Nobody but you and me,* that's what Mom always said. She's not here, but Gram is. And whatever secrets Gram is hiding, they're for me, not him.

"I can't," I say. "I wish I could help. It's not like I don't want the same answers you do."

"Not badly enough, I guess," Connors says.

I flush with guilt, feel it settle hot and stinging in my gut. But it's not enough to change my mind.

We leave then. Connors ahead of me, his expression grave and disappointed as he holds the door. It's fine. It's over. Nothing more to see. Just the memory of that girl's eyes, hovering behind my own. The gleam of the metal drawers, one of them hers. *Mothers and daughters,* she whispers in the back of my mind. Mothers and daughters and me.

SIXTEEN

Connors doesn't try to ask me any more questions. I can stay at the station, he says, if that's what I want, and he can try to call my mom. But I say no. I say get me back to Fairhaven.

He takes me to his cruiser, loads me into the front seat with reluctance written on his face. I feel strange, like I'm melting. When we pass the scorched earth, the proof of the fire, I want to look away, but I can't even blink. Every inch closer we get to Fairhaven, the closer Katherine gets to the surface. The harder she tests the lock of the door I put her behind. By the time we pull into Fairhaven's driveway, I'm ready to throw up.

"Ask her," Connors says, putting the cruiser in park. "You're the only one she'll tell."

"Yeah," I say, but I'm already halfway out of the car, and we both know I don't really mean it. I have questions for her, but whatever answers I get, I'm keeping for myself.

I wait until Connors is gone before going inside, to make sure he's really leaving. The door's unlocked, the front hall dark and cool. It's harder to hold on to myself now that I'm here. Here, where my mother and her sister grew up. Every room, every breath—they belonged to the girls, once. The twins.

There must be a reason Gram's keeping me in the dark, I tell myself. Please, let there be a reason.

"Hello?" I call. My voice is hoarse, heavy. Like it knows the pain of this, even though I'm doing all I can to keep it at bay. "Gram?"

"Up here," comes her voice from the second floor.

I go toward it. Step after step, my hand trailing along the banister. I'm awake, I know I am, but it doesn't feel like it. I could still be there in that room, in the station, with the girl's body out in front of me, her eyes liquid and black.

The landing is empty, no sign of Gram. "Marco," I call, and I hear Gram's chuckle before she says, "Polo."

She's in one of the rooms off the right-hand hallway, opposite the one leading to mine. I approach the open door, my heartbeat uneven, my breath coming quick. I hesitate before I go in. I have to be calm. Too much of me and I'm afraid Gram will shut down.

From here I can only see a slice of the room, but it's pretty much what I expected for Gram's bedroom. A flowered bedspread stretched neatly over a lumpy mattress, and a chest of drawers tucked against the wall.

"Can I come in?" I say, knocking gently. She'll appreciate that, I think.

"Of course."

When I step inside, Gram's sitting at a vanity against the opposite wall, a pack of Band-Aids on the counter as she carefully tapes up a blister on her palm. For a moment I don't say anything. Just watch her work, her expression calm in the mirror. She knows about the twins. About the girl. Right now. She knows she's keeping these secrets from me and she doesn't care. No guilt, no nothing.

"Did you have fun with Theresa?" she says, not looking up. Oh, she can pretend, but she's pissed I left the Miller house without her. I can hear it. "You're back quickly."

I go farther into the room, the floorboards creaking underneath me. "I learned something," I say.

Gram meets my eyes in the mirror. "Was it, perchance, something about manners?"

"No."

She turns to face me, one hand cradled in the other. "Well?"

It hurts to look at her, but I make myself keep steady. Her face, passed on to her daughters. How many women have been in this room? How many has she kept from me?

"Say what you mean, Margot," she tells me, when I wait a heartbeat too long. "This cryptic nonsense is for other people. Say it plainly."

The anger in me roars to life, hot and quick. I've been holding it in since the station. And I know some of it belongs to Mom, but she's not here now. Gram is.

"There were two," I say, stepping forward so Gram has to look up at me. "Mom and Katherine. Twins." There is so much more I could say. *Me and that girl, maybe my cousin, and you lied over and over again.* It would feel good, but it wouldn't get me what I want. I have to take it slow. Bit by bit. Answer by answer.

I can practically see her deciding how much to give me. Deciding whether she can lie. She must realize she can't. After a deep breath, it rolls out of her. "Yes," she says. "Your mother and her sister. Jo and Katherine."

It feels like the first sweep of a fan on a summer day, like cracking a window in our Calhoun apartment when Mom's out and she won't know. Not good, exactly, but welcome all the same.

Now for the next part.

"I know you told the police Katherine ran away," I say. "But I also know you never looked for her." I can feel my energy draining. This is too much. "You must know where she is, Gram. You have to."

"Nowhere," Gram says. So softly it's worse than if she'd screamed. "I'm sorry to tell you this. I really am. But she's dead, Margot. She has been for a long time."

I was bracing for disappointment. For Gram to call Katherine a mystery and leave it at that. But this? It feels like drowning. Like the end. "No," I say. "That's . . . You told the police . . ."

"I did," she admits. "It wasn't the truth. She died in that fire. Just before your mother left."

The apricot fire. Mom said Katherine started it, and Gram said she ran, and I can't fit any of it together. I can't. "Why would you lie to them?"

"They would never have understood." She smiles, reaches out to me. "Not like I know you will."

"I don't," I say. "And I don't believe you, either."

A flash of pure annoyance crosses Gram's face, startling me, and her hand drops. "Believe me or don't," she says sharply. "Neither one will bring Katherine back."

"Back from where? Where's her body?" Prove it. That's the Nielsen family motto, after all. You're hurting? Prove it. You deserve something better? Prove that too. "If she really died in that fire, why didn't they find her?"

"Those," Gram says, standing up, "are questions for your mother."

No. No, I am done with everybody passing me off to someone else as their problem. "Why? Katherine's your daughter."

"Yes," Gram snaps. "She was, in fact, my daughter, and
she's dead, and I don't particularly enjoy talking about it.
So perhaps we could be kind to one another and leave the
subject alone."

I wish being kind were what mattered. But there's
too much here that's not right. Too much I need to know.
"Please," I say. "Gram, you have to give me something."

Gram sighs, shuts her eyes for a long moment. "All right,"
she says, when she's looking at me again. "I can show you
their room, at least."

It's at the far end of the hall, behind a door with a silver
knob. Gram brought the key with her from her room, and
I stand back as she unlocks it, her touch lingering as she
eases the door open.

"Would you like me to go?" she asks. "If you want to be
alone—"

"No." And it sounds like I ripped the word right out of
me. "Please don't."

I need someone here to see it with me. I need someone
else so I know it's real.

Inside. My heartbeat loud in my ears. The only sound in
the world.

The first things I notice are the beds. Two of them, narrow and neatly made up. The headboards are matching—iron scrollwork, like the one in my room, but black instead of white—and the covers are the same. Yellow and white stripes, with a smattering of flowers across the top.

A large window sits between the beds, letting in the afternoon light. It faces away from the Miller house, looking out at the highway. In front of it, a large nightstand with two drawers is dusted clean. Two closets. Two vanities, the mirrors fresh and blazing with sun. Everything matching, everything just so.

"Which side was my mom's?" I ask.

Gram clears her throat. "Do you know," she says, "I don't remember."

I start to laugh. It's too loud, too much, but I can't keep it in. She doesn't remember. Or she does, and she's lying, and that's just as bad.

"Margot," Gram says. "You might have had a bit too much sun."

She sounds concerned. She sounds like she means it. And if she thinks I'm going to take anything she says at face value ever again, she's out of her mind.

I crouch in front of the nightstand. Two beds, a drawer for each. I reach out to the left one, pull it open to find a crumpled receipt and a pair of red plastic sunglasses.

I can't picture Mom wearing those. Can't picture her

ever being young enough, vivid enough. Maybe this was Katherine's side.

But then I open the other drawer. And there it is. A Bible, the same white cover, the same gold embossing. Just like Mom's.

I know what I'll see when I open to the first page. But I do it anyway. Shaking hands, a hitch in my throat. And there it is.

For my daughter on her twelfth birthday.

—With all my love, your mother. 11/8/95

No verse about a cup, about what the Lord wills. I don't know enough about what it meant in the first place to understand why it's not here. But the same handwriting. The same birthday. The same.

A sob breaks out of my chest. I shut the Bible, fling it away from me and sit heavily back on my heels. Josephine and Katherine. Sisters, and twins, and one of them my mother, and here is the room they lived in. Here is where they slept, where they grew. My mother's first and dearest secret. Gram's too.

"It's all right," Gram says from behind me. So softly, and it soothes me even as I try to shrug it off. She lied to me, I think, holding on to it hard, because if I've got anger wrapped around my bones, that's how I'll get through this.

"It's not all right." I lean on the bed next to me as I stagger to my feet. When I turn around, Gram is still in the doorway, her arms folded across her chest.

"I would have told you," she says, still so quietly that her voice drifts through the air like dust motes, golden and aimless. "But it should have been your mother. And she said that she hadn't. That she didn't want you to know." She steps toward me. "Besides. It doesn't really matter, does it?"

My mouth falls open. "What?"

Gram's eyes are steady on mine, and for a moment I see Mom in her so clearly. The will so strong I could throw myself against it for a hundred years and never do anything more than break my own bones.

Mom turned it in on herself. Used it to keep every door closed. Gram isn't quite like that, but I recognize it all the same, and I feel an ache so hard I'm afraid it'll never ease. Mom. I love her, I love her, because sometimes she's mine.

"Katherine died before you were born," Gram says now, one hand just barely reaching out to me. Every time she says so, it sounds more and more true. "It was all over before you even got here." A smile, warm and open. "It doesn't matter, Mini. It's all right."

"Of course it matters," I choke out. "What the hell, Gram?"

"There's no call for that," she says, but I'm done with this. She's not who I need right now.

Purpose urging me forward, through the collapse waiting for me in my body. Gram calls my name as I hurry past her, down the hallway and back out onto the landing. I pause for a moment, brace myself on the banister and try to take a deep breath. But my lungs feel heavy, feel like they did during the fire when the smoke was weaving thick. The feeling won't break until I get hold of Mom.

The landline is in the kitchen. I rush down the stairs, Gram's voice echoing after me. Whatever she's saying, it doesn't matter. Mom. I have to talk to Mom. To yell, and to cry, and to I don't know what, but I have to hear her voice. I have to make her hear mine.

The phone nearly slips out of my hands as I snatch it off the charging dock. Palms too clammy, fingers too quick, and I misdial twice, but soon the phone is ringing and the speaker is pressed to my ear. Ring after ring, endless. Gram arrives in the kitchen doorway as I wait, and she looks so sorry for me that I can't bear it. I push open the screen door and go out onto the back porch. She doesn't follow.

It's still ringing. The Miller house in the distance, afternoon spread like butter between. If I were Tess, none of this would be happening. If that were my life.

But it's not.

The line clicks, and my heart jumps in my chest, but Mom doesn't pick up. I don't know that I expected her to. Instead I get her voice mail, and the sound of her voice feels like a punch to the gut.

"Sorry," she says. "It's Jo. Leave a message."

Sorry. Of course she starts with sorry. To everybody but me.

The beep comes more quickly than I expect, and I'm not ready.

"Hi," I say, feeling immediately like an idiot. I take a breath in, wincing as it catches. I don't want her to think I've been crying. I haven't.

"It's me," I say, and the goddamn injustice of having to say that, of having to remind her of her daughter, suddenly lights me up. It's like that with me, sitting curled in my chest, until the smallest spark and the wick catches. I left, I know it was me who left, but where is she? Where's her concern? Why wouldn't she come after me? "Margot. Your daughter. The one you let just disappear two days ago. Remember me?"

As fast as it lit up, it goes out. I'm too tired. Too sad. Too buried under the things she kept from me.

"I'm calling," I say, "because I'm at Fairhaven and I found out, Mom. About Katherine. Why didn't you tell me about that? About her? Why wouldn't you want me to know my family?" I tip my head back, stare up at the porch light and feel a tear slide into my hairline. "I don't understand why you'd keep that from me. Do you really hate me that much? Do you really want to punish me that badly?"

I know what her answer would be: *Not everything is about you. Not even this.*

There's nothing left to say. I hang up. And I wait for a long time on the porch. For my heart to slow down. For everything to make sense. For this to hurt less. But that never happens.

SEVENTEEN

Gram is in the kitchen when I go back inside, steam billowing around her face as she leans over the water boiling on the stove. She's making dinner. Steamed potatoes and some kind of casserole. My stomach turns over at the thought of it.

I wind up outside the twins' room without meaning to. Half of me sure I never want to see it again, and the other so desperate for any clue to my mother and her life here that I could climb into her bed and never move.

I open the door gingerly. The air's gone dark, the sun too low to reach inside the room. That makes it easier to take my first step in. The floorboards groan, and I'm sure Gram hears it. I'm sure she knows where I am.

Carefully, I sit on Mom's bed. She always sleeps on her

left side, and in this room it would put her facing her sister. The Bible, Katherine's Bible, is on Katherine's bed. I reach across the gap and brush the cover with my fingers. Alive or dead? I can't be sure. And Gram's lied to the police over and over, lied as many times to me.

The thing is, I have to believe someone. I have to pick an answer and call it the truth, because sitting here, drowning in doubt—it's not doing me any good. That was real grief in Gram, when she asked me to let it go. Real mourning for a real death. Even Connors seems to believe that Katherine's dead.

He doesn't think it's the whole story, though, and I don't think it is either. And there's someone who can tell me more of it—Katherine. After all, Mom kept proof of her old life in her Bible. I wonder what Katherine hid in this one.

I ease it into my lap. When I open it, dust rises from the cover, and the spine nearly splits in half. It's been well loved, this one. Nothing like Mom's. I flip past the message from Gram and turn the pages one by one, their gilt edges slippery against my fingertips. There are scribbles in the margins of some pages just like there were in Mom's. Gram must have made them take Bible study, or taught them herself.

I'm into Exodus when I see the first one. Tucked between two lines of Scripture, so small I can barely read it in this light. I fumble on the nightstand for the lamp switch, and when it flickers on, a handful of moths dart into the air, hovering before they land again on the lampshade.

do you think we can ask the romans to crucify mom next

Next to it, in different pen, there's a tiny smiley face with Xs for eyes. I catch on a laugh, and an image slips into my head: Mom and Katherine, sitting on the porch, Gram pacing in front of them as she lectures them about Scripture. Katherine writing a note to her sister, and Mom reaching across when Gram's not looking to draw her response.

A family, together and together.

There must be more. More like that, little conversations and pieces of the past that I can take for my own. I flip through more pages, another, another. Please, I think. Just a sentence. Just a phrase.

I get more than that. Nearly a third of the way through the book, scrawled in blue ink across passages about burning cities. Katherine is talking. To someone, to God, to herself, and I push them out of the way. Katherine is talking to me.

i remembered it today which is weird because i feel like
if it was really that important it wouldn't have been so
hard to find but i was sitting there in bible study (hence
the bible) and mom was going on and on and on and i

was staring out the window at the apricot grove and i was
so so hungry like i don't know how they didn't hear my
stomach just going absolutely batshit but i was staring out
at the apricot grove and i remembered me and her out
there together

we must have been like four or five. or six? i'm not
good with ages and stuff like we could talk and walk so
how old is that

we were walking out to the grove and it would have
been after church because we were wearing those dresses
mom always used to put us in (and still does i mean
look in the mirror) and she was ahead of me because she
always goes first even though technically i'm older

she loves that grove and i get it i do because it's not
the house and that counts for something and mom never
goes there anymore which counts for a whole lot more but
i remember just feeling

i don't know

she climbed this tree that's the important part she
climbed the tree and i went up after her and i remember
asking her to come back down because we were walking
and talking but we weren't grown

but that didn't matter to her and i don't remember
a lot about the in between just grabbing hold of the
branches and trying to follow her and the look on her face
when she pushed me down

that's how i broke my arm

mom always said it was an accident on the farm which is technically true i guess but i'm looking at my sister and she's looking at me and i can see that expression on her face like "get out of here, get out of this place that's mine" and she's not making it now but that's because she's in her bed reading valley of the dolls and i'm in mine "reading my bible and writing my thoughts about jesus because i have so many thoughts about jesus yes i do"

mom must know that's how it happened she must know but i'm not supposed to and i don't think mini is either but i wonder if she remembers and i shouldn't ask her

i won't ask her

do NOT ask her

she'll get that same look because maybe we grew out of going to the apricot grove to hide from mom (i wish we hadn't) but we didn't grow out of mini wanting to rip my eyelashes out every now and then so just don't ask her

if she remembers let her keep it to herself

I look up from the page. Stare into the dark, across Katherine's bed, into my own eyes in her dusty mirror. Mini—Gram said it was something she used to call my mom. So that's her. That's Josephine. And she hurt her own sister.

She was young when it happened, if Katherine is

remembering right. And I'm sure it was an accident. After all, Katherine doesn't seem afraid of her. Instead she seems bright, and quick, and all these things I can almost see in my mother, if they weren't hidden in the places not meant for me.

The next entry, if I can call it that, is on the opposite page, running vertically down the margins. And all it says is:

good morning mini snored so loud that i have been awake since five thirty and i am going to put salt in her cereal to take my revenge and if i die i die

Sisters. Just normal sisters.

But I keep turning pages. I keep looking. Because there's a piece of Mom in Katherine's entries that I recognize. Was she always like that? Always defensive, always keeping people away from the things she thinks are hers? Katherine can tell me.

I have to turn all the way to the New Testament to find Katherine's handwriting again, this time in pencil and harder to read, dipping in and out around a passage about charity.

we took the x-rays today and mine were fine but they talked about mini's for a long time because i guess they

were weird (which oh great one more thing to add to the
"those nielsen girls sure are strange" script everybody
in town seems to follow) (it would probably help if mom
weren't still keeping us inside practically all the time and
dressing us like paper dolls from another planet)

dr howland sketched a copy of hers for her to keep
because he couldn't exactly give her the whole thing off the
light board but she couldn't even look at it

she threw it away so i grabbed it out of the trash and
stuck it in here because i think she'll want it one day
and i wish i could tell her it's fine that it doesn't make a
difference between us but she won't listen

she made me sleep in the guest room for the night
and it's not fair because this isn't my fault so why is she
punishing me

when i tried to talk to her she just kept saying "now
we're not the same now we're not the same" and i know
what she means i know why that hurts because she's mini
and i don't know how i'd recognize myself if i hadn't
learned to recognize her first but still

maybe it's not such a bad thing maybe it's fine you
know maybe this means that we can be whatever we want
and still love each other but i just don't know how to tell
her that

is it like this with brothers
we don't have a brother the closest thing we had was

204

richard but he went to college ages ago (probably when
mini broke my arm actually) and he never seemed like
this

    mom would tell me the bible has all the right advice
although she's been saying that less lately but when
we were like ten and eleven that was the answer to
everything

    "what does scripture say" like she didn't think she
could teach us how to be good people only this book could

    i don't think either of us is really a good person but
maybe there's time for that

    or there would be if mini would just TALK to me i
hate when she's like this i hate when she disappears i miss
her i miss her i'm pathetic

A pit opens in my stomach. I recognize too much of myself there, in that last line. Katherine, begging my mom to open herself even the smallest bit, and missing her, and hating it. She was always like this. I guess I shouldn't take it personally, then.

Tucked between this page and the next is another piece of paper. That must be the sketch Katherine mentioned, the one of the X-ray. I unfold it, find it still crisp and white, preserved. The drawing is carefully done. A rib cage. Bones shaded and spindly. And an arrow, pointing to the heart where it's tucked inside, on the left.

Wait. I've seen my own X-rays, at the doctor's the year I got pneumonia. They didn't look like this. The heart is on the left of the paper. That would put it on the right of her body, opposite where it's meant to be.

I blink, surprised. Mom's heart, mirrored. I had no idea. She never told me. And I guess she didn't have to, but still. It seems important. Like something I should've known.

And it's familiar somehow. I think back, scrape through every memory I can, and there—an opposite heart. Position inverted. I saw that at the morgue, written on the report for the girl's body. Her heart is switched, just like Mom's.

A shiver shakes through me. Of course everything knots together. I knew that. But this makes it impossible to ignore. Makes the possibilities I'd written off rear their heads. Maybe the inversion is genetic, is a marker that the girl really was Mom's. That I'm not.

Or maybe it's something else altogether. Maybe there will always be something about this family I'm not meant to understand.

I fold the sketch and slot it back where I found it. In a minute I'll go back to my room. Wash my hands, go down to dinner and try to forget everything that happened today. And when I go to sleep I'll cross my fingers and hope I don't dream about Mom's voice mail message, about her saying sorry over and over again as she pushes her sister out of an apricot tree.

EIGHTEEN

I wake up still in my clothes from yesterday, Katherine's Bible on the nightstand, the photo I found in Mom's propped up behind it. One of them dead, the other haunted.

I roll onto my back, stare at the ceiling. Gram said Katherine died before I was born. Before she could have a daughter who's my age now. So where does that leave the girl in the field? Not a cousin, and apparently not a sister. Nothing Gram will talk about. Nobody's again, nobody's but mine.

This is only my second morning waking at Fairhaven, but it feels like years since I got to Phalene. The fire, the girl, Katherine. I thought it would be easier without Mom, thought I'd find the answers I want. But all I've found are bits of the wreckage she left and more questions.

I will not spend another day here in the dark. I will

not let Gram lie to me again.

I change and head downstairs. She's already in the kitchen when I get there, standing at the stove, shucking corn and watching a pot of water as she brings it to boil. Fairhaven stretches out on either side of this room. Dark corners and locked doors, and I remember yesterday morning how I thought the house could show me something Gram didn't want me to see. I was wrong. This is the only part with any truth hiding inside. The only part that matters—the rickety table and Gram at the counter, a tiny smile just for me.

"You feeling better?" she asks. "You were quiet at dinner. last night."

I was. Wolfed everything down and went back upstairs as soon as I could, because I couldn't stand it, sitting there with her like everything was fine. I can't stand it now, either. She's keeping things from me, just like Mom. A lifetime of people deciding for me what I need to know. That stops now.

"What were they like?" Gram's proved she won't give me anything about the girl from the fire, so I start with the twins. Katherine told me some of it in those entries. But I need to hear it from Gram.

"The girls?" she says, looking up from the corn. I examine her for some relief, for something that suggests she's happy to be telling me the truth. There's nothing. Nothing

I can recognize, anyway. "They were inseparable. I suppose most twins are."

That's not what I'm here for. Not some rosy picture of two girls in matching dresses, laughing and holding hands. There's no way that's how it really was.

"But they must have fought," I say. I don't bring up the Bible, the broken arm. Maybe Gram's already read everything in there, but as long as I never find out for sure, I can keep it just for me.

"Of course they did." Gram picks up another ear of corn from the pile and begins to shuck it. I grimace, remembering the texture of it from the field, the way some of the ears split and spiraled around each other. "Some days they were Mini this and Mini that, and some days Katherine wouldn't stop stealing your mother's clothes."

Mini. Again. "Is that what Katherine called Mom?"

Gram drops the corn into the pot, and she doesn't even wince as some of the boiling water spatters onto her skin. "They shared it. They shared everything, most of the time."

But nobody shared a thing with me, did they? Not about this. So I try something else.

"How did the fire start, anyway?" I ask, sitting down at the table.

Gram raises an eyebrow. "Which one?"

"The apricot grove. You know, the 'accident,'" I add sarcastically.

"There is no need to take that tone." She pokes at the water with a wooden spoon, frowning. "Who knows why that sort of thing happens?"

"It's just a little weird," I say. "Two fires on the same farm."

"Well, the world is wide and full of happenstance," Gram says. I don't bother calling that the bullshit it so clearly is. I'm not getting anything here.

She pulls an ear out of the water by her fingertips and sets it on a plate, sprinkling salt over it. "Eat."

"For breakfast?" It comes out sharp, my frustration taking hold of me. She finds a way out of everything. Every single thing.

"We all make do with what we have." She lays it on the table in front of me and waits, like she's expecting to watch me until I finish. I ignore the plate and get up instead, going to the fridge. Gram gives a small exasperated sigh, and I hold back a smile. Maybe I can't get the truth out of her, but I know I can piss her off.

The fridge is alarmingly bare except for two sticks of butter, a plastic bag of wilting green beans and rows and rows of bottled water. None of this will do the trick. I want something I'm not supposed to have. I want to show Gram how much her rules mean to me. I shut the fridge and swing open the freezer.

"Margot," Gram says, "please leave that closed. It's not for you."

But I'm not listening. The freezer is stuffed full of apricots. Not an inch of space left for anything else. Some of them packed in plastic bags, some of them still fresh enough that when I reach out to touch them, they give under my fingertip. I want to ask about them, but the whole thing is weird enough that I don't even know what the question would be.

Gram takes hold of the freezer door and nudges me out of the way, shutting it firmly. "That's enough of that," she says.

It's the sputter of a car engine that keeps me from arguing. I recognize that sound. The whine, the choked growl. How many times have we scraped together enough money to get it fixed? How many times has it broken down again?

That's our car. That's Mom. A laugh spills out of me, giddy and terrified all at once. I called her, and she actually came. I can't believe it.

I run out to the front porch in time to see our gray station wagon, battered and covered in dirt, turn in to the driveway and screech to a stop. After a moment, it lurches forward again, but only a few yards before Mom must hit the brake.

I feel a reaching in my chest, and the acid of spite. Come on, I think. I'm right here. You have to come after me this time.

For a long moment it's just us, just her and me and the

space between. All I can hear is the sound of my breathing, of my heartbeat. And then the careful footsteps behind me, the swing and slam of the screen door as Gram comes out of the house.

"Who is that?" she asks me.

I don't look away from the car. Don't look away for a second, because if I do she could disappear. If I do she could turn and run, just like she always does.

"It's Mom," I say over my shoulder, and I can hear Gram's sharp little breath.

I can't see Mom through the windshield, not with her this far away, but I just know she's looking at me like I'm looking at her. I know she's hating that I got her here. I made her do it. Finally, finally, I got myself in her line of sight.

But there's one more thing, one more thing standing between me and winning this fight. She has to get out of the car.

Another moment, another beat of stillness.

"Maybe you should go inside," Gram says behind me. "I'll talk to her."

No way. I'm not surrendering now. If I go inside, she wins. If I move first, she wins. She has to want me enough to do this herself.

"Nobody but you and me," I say under my breath. "Come on, Mom."

It's stretching too long. The urge beating in my chest to just give up, to just go back to her, but I set my shoulders, bite my lip so hard I taste blood, and sit down on the porch, my movements exaggerated so she can see. I won't do it. This one's on my terms, not hers.

That must be what does it. I can't be sure, but it's barely a minute later—the click as the door opens, sound carrying down the dusty flat of the driveway. The stretch of her legs, and the shape of her against the sun, so familiar it hurts.

I have to grip the edge of the porch to keep myself from standing up. That is not enough. She has to come farther. I'm not asking for much here. I never am. Just one step, Mom. Just one step.

She takes it. That's all I need before I'm on my feet and heading for her. So quickly it's embarrassing, but I missed her. She's my mom, and I missed her.

The distance between us is long and maybe she felt it like I did, maybe she wants us close again too, but by the time I'm a few feet away from her, any proof of that is gone from her face. Just Mom as she always is, a statue an inch from falling apart.

The sight of it pinches my chest. Her familiar smell, like honey and salt. She looks like home, and I wonder what she sees when she looks at me. If I look like Fairhaven. If that makes her want me less.

"Hi," I say. And then: "You got a haircut."

"Dead ends," Mom says. Not a hitch in her voice. Not a flicker, not a fight. Just like Gram. "Needed a trim."

I don't think she means it to hurt me. So many times she does, and I know what that sounds like. And this time she doesn't, but she hurts me just the same. Because I remember it, I remember, good days and cold evenings, the fall snapping in quick, and Mom sitting me down in the bathroom, her scissors careful and cool against my neck as she snipped the split ends from my hair. Just like she taught me to do for her.

Her weight shifting from foot to foot, her eyes darting over my shoulder, to the house, to Gram back on the porch. She couldn't look more uncomfortable if she tried. I almost feel bad for her—the space in my chest is there, but the pity never fills it.

"I looked for you," she says at last. "In Calhoun."

Does she expect me to reward her for that? For doing the bare minimum?

"Okay," I say. "So?"

Mom folds her arms across her chest, meets my eyes for half a second before looking away again. "So you shouldn't have left."

"It was about time I did," I say. A mistake, I think as she straightens, draws herself up tall. I should have stayed soft. But I'm here now. I might as well commit. "Was I supposed to just wait for you to start caring?"

"That's it?" Mom's knuckles are white, her fists clenched. "That's what you have to say for yourself?"

I know what she wants. An apology for leaving, for not waiting, and all the groveling that goes with it—but like hell I'm gonna give that to her. She doesn't deserve that from me.

"I asked you about my family," I say. We both know I mean so much more than that last fight, in front of the pay phone in broad daylight. "But you never told me. So I found someone who would."

"Well, you seem to have figured it out." Mom looks up at Fairhaven, lets out a bitter laugh. "I thought when you called me maybe you were ready to apologize, but—"

"For what?" I say. I can feel it starting to throttle me, that anger I can't ever seem to shake in moments like this. It would be so much easier if I just let her win, but I'm the only person in the world fighting for me. If I don't do it, nobody will. "I'm not sorry at all. I got what I needed." Never mind that it doesn't feel at all how I wanted it to.

"You mean you got her," Mom says, and there, there, that's the weak spot I have to keep aiming at. "It's not worth it. I know you think you understand, but she can't ever give you enough to make up for what she takes."

"Oh, I understand that," I say. "I learned it from you."

"Fuck," Mom says quietly. She's desperate now, not

angry. That's so much better. "This is— I can't do this, Margot. Do you understand what it's costing me to be here?"

"No," I say, "because you never told me a thing. You never let me in, Mom." She won't bring it up on her own, will she? Not even after I asked her about it in my voice mail. Fine—I'll do it. Maybe this will get her to crack open. "Like Katherine," I say, and she flinches, full and sudden, like I hit her. "Why didn't you tell me about Katherine?"

"We can't waste time with this," Mom says, pleading, her gaze flicking to Fairhaven and back. "Okay? I tried to get us out of here and I can do it again, but we have to go, and we have to do it right now."

I stand my ground. "It's now or never, Mom. Why wouldn't you want me to know my family?"

"Because it's not any family at all. It's not real." My disappointment must be obvious, because Mom comes toward me, takes my face in her hands. Her thumb insistent on that spot under my left eye, where her scar marks her own skin. "I know," she says, soft and on the edge of crying. "I know it's not what you wanted. If I could change it, I would. But we have to go. You have to get in the car."

I bat her hands away. That's not loving me. Loving me is giving me what you owe me. "What happened to her? I am not going anywhere until you tell me the truth."

"Margot—"

"Do you think I don't mean it?" I step toward her and

she staggers back, and I hate feeling like this, like I'm about to break her, but it's the only way I ever get anything I'm after. And sure, maybe I can't make her want me. Maybe I can't make her love me the way mothers are supposed to love their children. But I can make her give me this. "Do you think I'm kidding? You had a sister and I had an aunt and you kept her from me," I say, my voice louder and louder. "You took her away, and I want to know why."

"Because I—" Mom's voice fails, and she covers her mouth with her hands, her eyes squeezed shut. "I'm what happened to her," I hear her say. Muffled, thick with tears.

I stand there. Mom at my feet. Sun in my eyes.

I'm what happened.

"What does that mean?"

But do I really want to know? I remember what Katherine wrote in her Bible. She was afraid, whether she wanted to admit it or not. Afraid of Mom.

The fires, the boxes of files. The trouble that people say comes with being a Nielsen girl. How does that make Katherine a secret worth keeping? And not from everybody. Just from me.

I don't have a chance to wonder. Mom straightens, swiping at the tear tracks left on her cheeks. "I don't owe you that," she says. And it's bullshit, it's such a mess, both of us standing there with our scales, trying to reckon with something that will never balance.

One day, I think, in a bolt of clarity I cannot stand, I will have to stop counting. For better or worse, I will have to let it go.

I don't want to. My whole life, it's been pushing against my mother that's kept me on my feet. If I let go there'll be nothing left.

"Yes," I insist, "you do." That's what I do. That's what I will always do.

"Katherine's dead," she says, with some difficulty, "and that's what you need to know."

"And the other girl?" I wasn't planning to bring her up, not when it's such an easy way for Mom to hurt me, but it slips out. I grit my teeth, keep on. "What do I need to know about her?"

Mom's brow furrows. "Who?"

Another lie. Another. Like I haven't heard enough. "Nothing, right?" I say, like she never responded. "You and Gram keep deciding what I need to know, and it's always nothing, and how the hell is that fair? Why wouldn't you ever tell me about her?"

"I have no earthly idea what you're talking about," Mom says. And the thing is, I know how she sounds when she's lying. I've heard it for years, felt swallowed by that rush of rage it calls to the surface. And she's not lying this time. But I'm sure that Gram is.

I don't understand. Her and Gram—I thought they were

keeping the same secrets. Where does it leave me if they aren't?

In the quiet, Mom reaches out and rests her hand on the roof of the car. "Now will you please get in? So we can go?"

I twist to look over my shoulder. Gram's there on the porch, leaning against the support post, watching us.

"Margot?" Mom says.

Those scales again, flickering in my mind's eye. Mom on one side, years and years stacking high. On the other, Gram.

And there, a shadow behind them both, Katherine and the body in the field, both of them waiting for me. Waiting for me to find out how they died.

"No," I say, turning back to Mom. "I can't leave right now."

Mom's face goes to stone. "Excuse me?"

I have to ask for it. "Can you wait?"

"Margot." She takes a deep breath. I can see her trying to keep herself in check. It won't work. "Margot, get in the car."

"No."

"Get in the fucking car, Margot."

"I'm not going right now," I say. I can't help smiling. Usually it's Mom going quiet and calm while I'm losing my grip. This feels better.

Mom shuts her eyes, and I hear her let out a disbelieving laugh, brittle and cold. "You have got to be kidding me," she says, before looking at me again. "This is what I get? I come back for you, I come to Phalene for you, and I get—"

"What you get is me," I say, every ounce of bitterness bleeding through. That calm I thought I had in my pocket disappears in an instant. "What a letdown. What a disappointment. I'm so sorry for you. Is there a support group you can go to? A hotline you can call for mothers with horrible daughters?"

Mom only looks at me for a moment and then purses her lips. "I'm not doing this," she says. "That's it. I'm done."

"You're done?" My voice rises. This whole thing has a hold on me so tight I could choke. "You started it."

She doesn't respond. Just goes to open the car door, and I feel myself start to disappear. She doesn't get to do this. To break me open and then act like she doesn't care, like I'm the only one feeling anything at all.

"Hey," I say. "Hey, you might be done, but I'm not."

She swings the door open. "If you want to stay with your grandmother, that's fine."

I lunge toward her, close the distance to grab the handle. "No, we're not finished."

"I said we are, Margot."

"I said we're not," and I slam the door shut. My arm hurts from the force of it, but it doesn't matter, because at least Mom is looking at me. And it feels good, because she looks afraid. Just like Katherine must have, that day in the grove.

"You don't get to call me ungrateful," I say, starting quiet. "Not when I've never asked you for a thing, not when I've taken care of myself for—"

"I didn't say that," Mom cuts in, with an exaggerated confusion. "Do not put words in my mouth."

"It's what you meant." She came back for me and I'm taking it for granted—I know how to translate her when we fight.

But she's shaking her head. "You can't tell me what I meant."

I struggle to take a deep breath. "But it sounded that way to me. Doesn't that matter? Doesn't it matter how you made me feel?" It's like I'm throwing myself at a brick wall. Mom barely blinks. "I don't just stop feeling bad because you didn't mean it."

I swallow the tears that are closing my throat. I can feel them pricking at my eyes, and I know they're about to fall, but please, please, Margot, get a grip. Mom doesn't care when I cry. It doesn't soften her. It only makes things worse.

"It's not my fault," Mom says, "if you can't hear what I'm saying without adding your own insecurities."

"I know," I say. "I know." We always end up this way. Me crumbling to pieces. "But doesn't it matter to you that you made me feel that way?"

"That's not the point."

"Answer me, Mom. Please." She just keeps looking at me like she's confused, and I can feel myself getting hysterical. My voice breaking, sobs starting to build up in my chest. "Doesn't it matter? Doesn't it matter to you?"

Nothing. Just quiet. Quiet, quiet, quiet, nothing coming out, and she's not even here. She's not even listening, and I can't feel for both of us. I just can't, and I scream, scream, "Answer me!" so loud it tears at my throat.

"Margot."

It breaks over me. The world gone like glass, cold and clear. I turn.

Gram. She's a few feet behind me, hands in her pockets. Relief, for a moment. That it's over. And then indignation, because even now Gram's not looking at me. No, she's looking at Mom, a frown etched so deep into her forehead that I wonder if it'll ever come out.

"If she wants to stay," Gram says evenly, "you can't make her leave, Jo."

Mom suddenly looks about two inches tall. She looks like the girl in the field, scared and lost. "She's my daughter," she says.

"And you're mine," Gram answers. "I couldn't make you stay. And you can't make her leave."

Mom looks back and forth between me and Gram. I can see everything now, every eddy of emotion across her features, like Gram is laying her bare.

"I'll be in town," she says at last. "Margot, I'll wait in town, okay? You asked me to wait and I'll wait."

I won't ever tell her what it does to me to hear that. How it makes my chest ache. How it makes me want to go with her after all.

"Okay, Josephine," Gram says. "It's time for you to go now."

We stand there in the driveway and watch Mom get into the car. We watch her reverse out onto the highway, watch her ease toward town, slowly, like she's hoping I'll call her back. I don't.

"Well," Gram says once the car has finally disappeared over the horizon. "That was quite enough excitement, I think."

NINETEEN

Gram doesn't say anything as we go back into the house. It feels like too long a walk, the ash plains hovering beyond Fairhaven, the Miller house bright across the fields.

I end up at the kitchen table again, shucking corn for Gram while my mind follows Mom into the town she left behind. Katherine, the fire, the questions nobody ever got answered—will people still hold it all against her? After all, I don't think the past ever really leaves, in Phalene. It breathes. It holds on.

It happens again.

Maybe I should've gone with her. She did come after me. And she's never done anything that big before.

No. Stop it. I always do this, anytime she gives me anything.

I tear the husk from the last ear of corn so hard it slices into my palm. I left her. It'll take more than one good thing to get me back.

Gram steps away from the stove and fetches a bottle of water from the fridge, holds it out to me. As I take it, she says, "It was wise of you not to go with Josephine."

"Was it?" I crack the cap of the bottle, take a long sip. Above me, the kitchen light is catching Gram's shoulders, her brow, throwing her face into shadow until she moves, leans on the counter with her hands folded in front of her.

"Yes. She's never been suited to motherhood." Gram shares a satisfied smile with me, like she expects me to join in. "Well, you know that better than anyone."

"I think we do just fine," I say. It's not true, but that's not the point. Gram doesn't get to judge Mom, not when she helped make her this way.

"Oh, you do?" Gram is watching me, a look on her face I know too well from Mom's, and I suppose from my own. Simmering resentment, almost an eagerness to be made angry.

Does she think I chose her? I know that's what it looks like. But I chose myself, chose getting answers. Not Gram.

"She's not perfect," I say. "But I love her. And I know she loves me."

Gram's better at this than Mom. The wound is there for only a second before she seals herself back up. "Does she?"

225

she asks. "Everything she hid from you—is that love?"

It feels like I'm waking up. Like everything since the morgue was a dream, a fever, and now I'm here, back in my body, alive with anger. "She didn't do it alone," I say, leaning across the table. "Katherine? The girl? And you're standing there like you haven't lied right to my face."

"Because your mother asked me to," Gram says. "I'd do anything for my family. Especially if it means protecting you."

I stare at her, my mouth open. How can all of that be true? And how can it still mean the fucking world to me to hear it, after everything I've seen here?

Gram straightens up then, brushing her hands on her jeans. "Actually," she says, "that reminds me. There's something I want to show you."

Another shot at answers, so here I am, waiting on the landing as she pulls down a rickety staircase to the attic. It's barely wide enough for one person. "Up there?" I ask, nervous.

"After you," Gram says. She's smiling.

"Okay," I say. Give her my best smile back and take a few tentative steps up. The stairs creak underneath me, the dark slithering down from the attic to clutch at my ankles. For a second I imagine Gram shutting the trapdoor. Leaving me up there.

"Is there a light?" I ask, hesitating.

"At the top," Gram says. So I keep going.

Up, up, step after step, until at last I reach the attic, and I edge forward, waiting for the floor to drop out from underneath me. Gram's footsteps follow me up the stairs. I let out a small breath of relief.

Finally, "Here," comes her voice from behind me, and I hear a click. Light ricocheting around me, spraying from the bare bulb above. The ceiling just beams and the roof beyond, the walls made of slats with insulation peeking through.

Just ahead of me a bookcase is practically empty save for a handful of picture books stacked on the bottom. Next to it, three plastic garbage bags that look like they're holding clothing, with the sleeve of a coat poking out the top of the nearest one.

Gram takes hold of my elbow, steers me to the other side of the attic. "Over here."

The light barely reaches this part, but it's enough to make out a collection of cardboard boxes stacked against the wall. Some of them damp with mold, some of them with newspaper spilling out the top. Gram lifts one of the boxes off the stack and sets it on the floor. I recoil as a mouse comes skittering out a hole in the bottom and disappears into the dark.

"What is all this stuff?" I ask as she sorts through the contents.

"Some of Jo's and Katherine's things," Gram says, her voice

muffled. I lean in eagerly, try to get a glimpse of what's inside.

Finally Gram straightens, pulling something out of the box. "Here it is," she says.

A dress, with a prim little collar and long sleeves that close around the wrists with a bow. It looks like the one the girl was wearing, like the ones I found in my dresser, dated and too formal for anything I've seen in Phalene.

Is this where that dress came from?

Yesterday I would've called this proof that the dead girl came from Fairhaven, that Gram was keeping her hidden. Now I know better. This isn't enough to force the truth out of Gram.

"Okay," I say slowly. "You wanted to show me a dress?"

"It was your mother's," she says. "Lots of this was. She barely took anything with her when she left." Gram turns around, tilts her head. "She almost didn't take you."

Shock punches through me. It doesn't matter that I've been thinking that my whole life. I've never heard it out loud before.

"She did, though," I say, once I've gotten my breath back.

"Well, after all that, I should hope so," Gram says. She steps toward me, the dress still in her hands. I go rigid as she holds it up to my shoulders, smooths it along the collar until her fingers are pressed against my neck. "Doesn't that look nice?"

Nice? Gram with a stack of clothes and a girl to dress

them up in, before she sent her out into the fields to die. It was something abstract yesterday, something I could pick up and put down. Now it's the two of them in the attic, Gram's hands soft on that other girl's cheeks, and maybe Gram didn't set that fire, maybe Gram didn't decide to end it, but the door just closed on any kind of innocence for me. I don't think there was ever any here to begin with.

"I don't know," I say nervously.

"Try it on, then."

"That's okay."

"No," Gram says, a hardness suddenly running through her voice. "I insist."

I look around, feel goose bumps rise on my skin even in the attic heat. "Okay, I'll just go to my room and—"

"Nonsense." Gram unzips the dress and holds it out to me. "I'm your grandmother. Nothing to hide from me."

No ground to give in her eyes, no frailty in her body. Mom is something breakable, but the woman she came from is not. I inch away from her, curl in on myself as I unzip my shorts and let them drop around my ankles. My shirt next. I drape it over one of the stacks of boxes.

"Stand up straight," Gram says. "You'll get a bend in your spine if you keep hunching like that."

I close my eyes for a moment. I could be buried now. I could be in a grave and this could be Gram dressing me for my funeral. But I'm breathing. I'm here.

"Fine," I say, and I reach for the dress, slip it on.

It's too small, like the dress that girl was wearing when we pulled her out of the fire. Gram makes a sound of disapproval and turns me by the shoulders. It won't zip, I know it won't, but she forces it anyway.

"Suck in," she says. "There's a good girl."

The zipper closes inch by inch, scraping my skin, until it finally hits the top of the collar. So tight I can barely move. For a moment the attic swims and stripes, here and somewhere else, me and someone else, everything happening over and over and over again, and I'm so dizzy I have to rest one hand against the wall to stay upright.

"Come on," Gram says, stepping back. "Let me see you."

I'm not sure what seeing she can do in the dim light from the single bulb, but I stand there and let her look. Let her think the sway of my body is more than dizziness. Let her think she's unsettled me—this is no worse than Mom's pajamas, than her bed and her room and her house.

"Are we done now?" I say, but Gram only purses her lips, considering me.

"I can't remember what your mother wore this for," she says. I go to undo the zipper, but Gram's grip tightens on my shoulders, and I can feel the seams straining. "It's a bit fancier than what she usually preferred. Your christening, maybe?"

I stop fussing with the dress. "I had one of those?"

"After a fashion." Gram shakes her head. "No, it wasn't that." And then she smiles, gently tucks my hair behind my ear. "Oh, yes," she says. "I remember now. It was when I took her to the clinic."

"The clinic?"

"Right." Gram's gaze is steady, her expression calm. "For the abortion."

I nearly choke. "Excuse me?"

"She changed her mind, obviously. They'd only given her the anesthesia when she came back out." Gram chucks my chin and steps away, starts stacking the boxes back up. "Aren't you lucky?"

My breath coming shallow and quick. I knew Mom never planned for me. She never mentioned a word about my father, like if she didn't tell me his name she could pretend he didn't exist. But it was more than just blocking out him, wasn't it? It was blocking out me, too. Because she never wanted me at all.

"Why did she change her mind?" I say, my voice hoarse and half here. Maybe she heard my heartbeat and couldn't do it, and maybe I have always belonged in her life. But Gram doesn't even turn to look at me.

"I'm not sure," she says, lifting the last cardboard box back onto the stack. "I never asked."

She leaves me. Goes back down the stairs, the light throwing her shadow across the floor, twisting it, shredding it, until it's just me in the damp heat, shaking in my little blue dress.

And now I know. This is how Gram punishes. This is where Mom learned it, only it's different here, sweeter and sharper at the same time, and I don't know how she survived it as long as she did, because I can't breathe, and I can't be here, and I can't do this for one second longer.

I claw at the dress, fumble over my shoulder for the zipper. One of the seams splits as I pull at the back, yank at the fabric until it tears along the zipper and falls away from me. My whole body hot, my skin itching, crawling, but the dress is off and falling to the floor. I step out of it, kick away the fabric tangling around my feet.

The air cold, sweat like salt in my mouth. For a second I stand there and catch my breath, my skin so pale it's edged in a glow. Not right. Something with me is not right. Gram and Fairhaven, and I've been letting it happen all around me, shutting my eyes and pretending, when of course that girl lived here, and of course Gram knew her, and loved her, and let her die.

I hurry back into my clothes, run downstairs and through the hallways, bang out the screen door and into the sunlight. I brace my hands on my knees, feel an acid sting in my stomach. But I won't. I refuse. Tears pricking my eyes, bile climbing my throat—none of it will ever sneak out. Fuck this family, and fuck this house. I don't have to stay here a second longer.

TWENTY

Mrs. Miller doesn't look surprised to see me when I turn up on her porch, breathing hard and on the edge of tears. It's around lunchtime, and over her shoulder I can see the table set for two, silverware gleaming, but she lets me in without a moment's hesitation and asks if I'm hungry.

"No, thank you," I say, my throat embarrassingly tight. "I'm sorry to just show up."

"Don't be silly. You're welcome anytime," she says, depositing me on one of the couches in the open living room and going into the kitchen. I hear the clink of ice cubes in a glass, and she's back in a second with water for me. I take the glass from her and try not to drop it when she smooths her thumb along my forehead. "I'll call Tess down."

I haven't seen Tess since the station. Haven't even

thought about her except to wonder if she got in trouble. But if Mrs. Miller's smile as she leaves is anything to go by, Tess is fine.

The quiet presses in as soon as I'm alone. My mom somewhere in Phalene, waiting for me. Gram at Fairhaven. And me here with the Millers, with a family whose roots reach almost as deep as mine. This is a family that can help me.

"Hey," Tess says, coming down the hallway from the staircase, her mom behind her. Tess only has one sock on and is in the middle of pulling on the other, her balance precarious, ponytail coming loose.

I get up from the couch, checking to make sure I haven't left any dirt on the white fabric. "Is Eli with you?" I ask. I have things I need to ask Tess, but I don't want to have this conversation with him around.

"Yes, is he?" Mrs. Miller adds.

"No, he's at his." Her tone is light and easy, but there's a strain to her smile I think I'm not supposed to notice. *Did* she get in trouble for being at the station? I was pretty sure she'd gotten away clean. "You said to ask next time he stayed. And I didn't ask, so he's not here."

"Look at that," Mrs. Miller says, and Tess sighs.

"I'm a very good daughter, you know."

"A very good daughter who's about to skip lunch, isn't she?"

"Yeah, maybe." Tess nods to the doors behind the dining room table, which open onto the back porch. "Want to go outside, Margot? Or more importantly, want to not be here?".

It doesn't sound like a joke, the way it's supposed to. I look guiltily at Mrs. Miller, but she doesn't seem to be bothered. "I'll leave plates for you both," she says, and before I can respond, Tess is pulling the back doors open and tugging me through.

It's just like Fairhaven. Or what Fairhaven must have been, once. The same kind of view, the same kitchen light behind me. But this place is still a working farm. Machinery waiting in the distance, a trio of silos far enough away that they look like toys. Gram must have cut Fairhaven in half when she sold this plot to the Millers.

"I won't ask you what happened," Tess says, and I jump. "But if you want to tell me, I want to know."

I'd forgotten she was there. Next to me, in a sweatshirt that's probably Eli's and a pair of basketball shorts that definitely are. Startlingly serious, her eyes red and weary.

"Are you okay?" I ask.

She waves me off and drops to sit on the edge of the porch, stretching her legs out into the grass, tracks left there by the mower still clear. "Fine. Come on. You look like you're about to keel over."

I join her, leaving space between us that she immediately fills, twisting to lean back against one of the porch posts and tucking her feet against my thigh, her knees drawn up to her chest. For a moment she just looks at me and I look right back.

I don't know what this is. The reaching in my chest. I thought I recognized it when I met her—the attraction I'm familiar with, the one I know from girls at school. But it's not that. Tess is . . . she's someone who knows. I don't want to be with her. I just want someone to see me, and she does.

"My mom came to get me today," I say. Turn away from her, stare into the afternoon. It's easier like this. "I left her in Calhoun to come here. And I didn't think. I didn't expect her to show up here. But she did."

"And?"

"We're not like you and your mom. I mean, I don't know your shit, and I know everybody has something, but—"

"I understand," Tess says. "Don't worry."

"She's everything," I say, and I knew it, I've known it for a long time, but saying it out loud, that's something else. "And we've fucked each other up for a long time, but I guess I thought that under it, somewhere, I was everything too."

Tess's hand brushes my arm. The barest touch, like she knows I'll shy away from any other comfort. When I look over at her, her chin is propped on her knees and her eyes are gentle. Just letting me tell her. Just wanting to know. That's a gift I could never have known how to ask for.

"And then today," I keep on, "today she comes back

for me and I think I'm right, I think I finally have the proof I wanted." Until the attic. The boxes. The dress. Yes, she kept me. But the trip to the clinic, the guilt she's put on me every day of my life—she's never forgiven me for existing in the first place. The original sin I will never, ever be clean of.

"You didn't go with her, though," Tess says.

"No." Because . . . I don't know how to put it. I try anyway. "The thing is, I'm starting to understand a lot more than I did. About her. About why she is the way she is."

Tess shifts next to me. "But?"

It spills out of me, ungrateful and nasty, and I hate that this is who I am, that this is what I can make out of knowing a person. "Does understanding her mean I have to forgive her?"

Quiet. I reach up, tuck my hair behind my ear and risk a look at Tess. She's staring out across the fields, a thoughtful expression on her face.

"I don't think so," she says at last. "I mean, maybe it helps. But maybe it makes it worse."

I tip my face up to the sky. Worse, to know that Mom hurt the way I did, that Mom had a mother like I did, and despite all that, to know that she didn't do better with me.

"Yeah," I say. "Maybe."

For a while we just sit there. I can feel Tess's body going tight next to me, can feel the tension coming off her. She's thinking about something. I want to ask what, but she just gave me the peace I needed, and I can do the same for her. If she wants to talk, she can. I won't make her. Not when there's so much else going on.

And sure, I ran here on nothing but instinct. Not Fairhaven, that's all I was thinking. Anywhere but there. But I've got questions curled in my throat, scratching each other deep as they wait their turn, and Tess can help me put the answers together.

"You get out of the station okay?" I start with.

She shrugs. "I should be asking you that."

The girl in the morgue, and Connors watching me as I took her in. His face, so unsurprised as I fell apart over Katherine. He knew. But I wonder if that story made its way out of Mom's generation. If it reached Tess.

"I found out about the fire in the apricot grove," I say. "And I found out about Katherine, too." A test, one I've given to Gram: how well can you lie when you're looking right at me?

Tess frowns, her mouth dropping slightly open. "Who?"

"Everybody knows." My voice too sharp, too near to breaking. "I get it. You don't have to pretend."

"No, seriously. What are you talking about?"

I let her sincerity ease through me, let it loosen the knot in my chest. Don't I know better than anyone how things can be kept over our heads? On the highest shelf, in a locked room. Jo, part of Phalene legend. Katherine, wrapped up and put away.

"My mom's twin sister," I say, and the surprise on Tess's face is real. "I found her name in one of the files, and when I asked my grandmother, she said Katherine died. But she lied to the police. It just . . ." I drop my head into my hands, press my palms against my eyes. "It doesn't fit together."

"What do you mean?"

I mean the girl in the morgue. I mean the way I need a word for her. Sister, or cousin, but neither one works. "Connors showed me the body from the fire."

Tess tilts her head, sun catching her eyelashes. "What does that have to do with Katherine?"

I think about the diary entry, about the X-ray sketch. How it matched the report at the morgue. "I don't know exactly. But I keep finding these lines, these things that must tie together. From then to now. Only . . ."

"Only what?"

"I thought that girl could've been Katherine's daughter," I say. It feels almost embarrassing somehow. "A cousin. But she looked exactly my age, and even if Katherine had her right before Mom had me, even if Gram somehow kept her hidden here all that time, or even if she just showed up, there was something else weird about her." I sigh, stare down at my hands. "Her body. She looked . . . I don't know. Wrong."

"Wrong how?" Tess leans forward. "She seemed fine on the highway. I mean, dead, but normal dead."

I snort, and catch a glimmer of triumph at the corner of Tess's mouth, despite the tightness that's lingering there. She wanted me to laugh. Too bad there isn't anything remotely funny about this.

I don't know how to explain it, really, but I do my best to describe it to Tess. The eyes, how they spilled down her cheeks. The odd scarring on her leg. "Connors asked me if I've ever seen anything like it before," I say, "and of course I haven't, but he just kept looking at me. And waiting. God, everybody here thinks I know something they don't."

"Well," Tess says slowly, "somebody has to know something."

"Sure, but—"

"I mean, Vera has to." There's a light in her eyes, one that sparks dread in my stomach. "You said she told you Katherine died, right? How does she know that for sure if they never found a body?"

It's the same question I have. But I don't sound like that when I ask it—entertained, excited.

"She just does," I say. It's the eager way Tess is looking at me that makes me say it. Makes me come to Gram's defense, whether she's earned it or not. "She saw the fire happen, after all. Maybe the body burned to ash, or—"

"Or maybe there was never any body at all," Tess cuts in. "Maybe Katherine really did run away. Maybe——"

"Stop," I say. A warning. This isn't a story. This isn't yours.

"No, maybe Josephine is the one who died," she says, picking up steam, "and your mom is actually Katherine."

I almost laugh, but the anger is too thick in my throat. Stop playing games, Tess. This is real for me.

"Okay," I say. "Okay. You've had some fun, but really, *stop*."

"I thought we were trying to figure this out."

"Yeah, figure it out," I snap. "Not make shit up."

"Oh, come on," she says, nudging my arm. "You don't have to get pissed over——"

"Over what?" I stand up, and she looks at me with wide, almost fearful eyes. "You picking my family apart?"

She holds up her hands. Like surrender, and it should calm me down. But it just leaves me even angrier.

"Why bring it up if you weren't serious about it? Is this fun for you?"

Because it isn't for me. It's my life. I don't have anything but this. Take it apart and I'm left with nothing.

"I'm just trying to help," Tess says. It's almost satisfying, how dismayed she sounds. "I don't understand, Margot. Why are you being like this?"

"Like what?" I say.

"Like . . ." She hesitates, drawing herself in close. Shoulders up, hands curled over her stomach. "I don't know. Like your grandmother."

It's not what I expected. And it hits me so hard I can't breathe. Like my grandmother. Like Mom. Is that how I am? Fighting with Tess the same way those women have fought with me?

"I . . . ," I start, but I can't find anything to say. She's right.

"Yeah," Tess says, getting up. "So. You want to apologize?"

I should. Should admit this day got inside me, made me overreact. Made me something else. But I think it just showed me who I've always been. I stay quiet. Shut my eyes to keep tears from welling up.

"Fine." Disappointment heavy in her voice. I hear Tess get up, hear the door open, and she sighs. "Go home, Margot."

I don't want to. But I don't have anywhere else.

TWENTY-ONE

I follow the road back to Fairhaven, dust coating my tongue. Finally, the reach of the back porch, where Gram is standing, leaning against the post, her arms crossed over her chest. I wonder how long she's been waiting for me.

"Welcome back," she says. A few feet away, her face impassive. For a moment we just watch each other. Will she scold me for leaving? Or will we pretend nothing happened?

"You hungry?" she asks then. "Or did Sarah feed you?"

I think of the lunch I missed at the Millers'. It'd be better by a mile than whatever Gram's got ready. But my stomach is empty, and Gram's offering me something. I'll take it.

"I could eat," I say.

She sits me down at the kitchen table, and I watch her at the stove as she cracks two eggs into a frying pan and scrambles them. We don't say anything. Maybe she's surprised I came back.

Gram scrapes the scrambled egg onto a plate. As it steams, she swings the freezer open and fishes an apricot out of a plastic bag stacked there. I frown, remember how she said it wasn't for me. But then the freezer is shut and her back is to me as she splits the apricot and palms the pit before dropping it into the trash in the cabinet under the sink.

Finally, she turns and sets the plate of food down in front of me. The eggs, with a fork speared in them, and the two apricot halves lying open next to them. It makes me feel almost sick. I'm not sure why.

The fruit is still frozen. I ignore it in favor of the eggs. Gram watches as I take a bite, and then another.

"Clean your plate," she says. "You look unsteady."

That's one word for it.

It should grate on me, the close observation, the almost distrustful way she watches to make sure I finish my food. But it's a relief. All I have to do right now is sit here and take one bite after another. No questions. No confusion. No bodies with faces like mine. Just someone who might have been a mother, once. And me.

When I'm done, Gram sets my plate in the sink and then comes back to crouch in front of me, so close that I can see the small ring of hazel at the center of her dark eyes, same as me and Mom.

"I wouldn't have told you about the clinic," she says in a voice that wouldn't sound gentle from anybody else, "if I didn't think you needed to know. Your mother might have come here, and she might have said she'll wait, but I don't want you thinking she means it. That will only get you hurt."

I don't answer. I can't. Gram is probably right. Mom came here not to save me, not to bring me home, but to score a point in the fight she is still having with her mother no matter what. If she really is still in town, it isn't for me, is it? Gram wanted me to figure that out. That's why she put me in that dress. To snuff out that last flare of hope. To show me how things really are.

"You know her," Gram goes on. Softer and softer with every word. "You know what sort of games she'll play. Don't let her fool you. You're too smart for that."

I shut my eyes and try to remember the look on Mom's face. It felt real, then. When she asked me to come with her. As real as the pride I felt in turning her down.

Gram reaches out and carefully lays her hand on my knee. I tremble, sway toward her before I can catch myself. "And I know," she says, "that things have been complicated. But you belong here, Mini. Remember that. It's better without her."

Not comfort. Not a threat, either. Just the truth. I feel it settle into me, wonder if when I look in the mirror it will be written across my forehead, in the marks my blisters have started to leave behind. This is the only place for a girl like me.

"I will," I say, and then, because I finally understand it all the way: "Nobody but you and me."

There is nobody else who will want me. There is nobody else who will give me half of what she will.

"Exactly," she says. When she kisses my forehead, her lips are dry. "That's exactly right."

She leaves me then. Disappears into the depths of the house, and I stay there in the kitchen, my heart beating too fast, my breakfast sitting horribly in my stomach, until I have to wrench open the cabinet under the sink and coil over the garbage as I dry heave. Nothing comes up, but I wait there a moment longer. Staring down at something small, tucked inside the eggshells from my breakfast. Shining and white.

A tooth.

For a moment I don't move. I just look, and look, feel a strange, detached curiosity well up and fade again. And then I shut my eyes. Sit back on my heels. I don't know what to do with any of this. I need someone to be here in it with me. I thought maybe that could be Tess, but I messed it all up.

And I know what I should do. Answers, I keep saying I want answers—I should be tearing this place apart. I can't, though. Not when it's all I have, not when I'm terrified of what I'll find.

I wish I could. I wish I were stronger; I wish I were better. I'm not.

I get to my feet. Climb up the stairs, back to my room, where Katherine's Bible is sitting on my nightstand. Maybe she can reach through the years and secrets keeping us apart. Maybe she can come back.

I flip to the last entry I read and then keep going, skip past sections where the pages have been torn out, past entries about Bible study, about fights Katherine had with Gram, about the weight of summer and how much Katherine wishes Gram would go for air-conditioning. Until *there*. I recognize it like it's my own face in the mirror: panic.

The other entries I read were fond. Maybe a little strained, and a little worried, but nothing like this. The handwriting is jagged. In a few places, the pen tore through the paper, and I have to press the page flat to read what it says.

> *i don't know what to do i don't fucking know what to do*
> *something's wrong with mini*

That's as far as I get before I have to stop. *Something's wrong with mini*—something's wrong with *Mom*.

> *i think i've known that for a while and god everybody in*
> *town certainly has a lot to say about it*
> *but honestly it's hard to tell because sometimes it's*

just that she's saying the things i want to say and doing
the things i want to do and sometimes it's that i don't
recognize her anymore

those don't sound like the same thing do they

but they are mostly

mini's always just been bigger and brighter and the
fun one i mean she would be if we had any friends and it's
freeing or something to see her fight with mom and run
out to the grove and scream and scream the way she does
and i like that she does that really i do that's not what i'm
talking about

what i mean is okay i woke up and she was gone and
fine fine she can go i'm not saying she has to stay by my
side every minute of the day

but i went downstairs to look for her because i wanted
one of those nights like we used to have when we were
younger when we'd sit out on the porch until the sun came
up just us and then never tell mom

that's what i wanted

and i get downstairs and i can't find her and it turns
out she's in the dining room and she had all these pictures
laid out across the table pictures of us

I turn the page eagerly as the writing cuts off. On the
back of that page there's the start of a word, now crossed
out, and the entry picks up again on the right-hand side,

where the ink hasn't bled through.

*she stopped when i came in and she started to put
everything back into these boxes she got from mom's study
that's where all the photo albums are*

*and she didn't say anything she didn't try to explain
anything but i saw it of course i saw it*

she was scratching out my face in every picture

*she even took the one from the wall the one of her and
me and mom when we're like fourteen the one we took to
put on the wall next to the rest of our family*

*she even took that one down and scratched me out
with an actual knife and i asked her what the hell she was
doing and she wouldn't answer me and so i*

*i made a mistake i guess i mean i know that now but
i reached out and i just touched her i swear that's all i did
and if she ever tries to say i did anything else i will show
her this because i swear i just touched her arm that's ALL*

*and she lost her mind i mean she actually lost her
mind i've never seen her like that before and i've seen
mini like everything i mean i was born with her and i've
lived every second after that at her side and i've*

*she screamed so loud i thought she would wake up
mom and she didn't hit me but she got so close and it's
ridiculous because she would never. she would never hurt
me like that. but there was a knife on the table and i*

was scared and i hate that i hate that i was scared of her
scared of my sister like i was scared of myself
   it's not fair
   fuck you mini for making me afraid

It looks like the entry ends there, but to be sure, I turn the page, and there's more. This time in carefully, deliberately neat writing, only in the margins of the Scripture so that it can be read easily.

today we are sixteen (lucky us) and as a gift mom gave us
a lecture about responsibility and taught us to drive stick
   then we sat down at the kitchen table which is where
we do everything now that mom's seen the scratches mini
left in the dining room one and no i never told her what
happened but i know mini thinks that i did
   and anyway she made us a cake which she never does
but sixteen is special or that's what everyone says
   and she told us the story she always tells us which for
posterity i will record here (hello older self yes it was just
as weird as you remember it)
   the story is that we were born in the apricot grove.
mom was pregnant but she wasn't showing much, and our
father—may he rest in Whatever the Fuck—was long
gone. she was out in the grove one day, collecting the fruit,
which was still growing (mostly) properly then, when her

250

water broke. she never made it back to the house, never mind to a hospital.

ta-da

two baby girls

we've always thought she must have been joking (i have anyway) or that maybe her water broke in the grove, but then she got in the truck and drove to the county hospital with her usual unbreakable practicality

today i think she wasn't joking at all and this is why

she lit four candles and she put them on the cake and she put the cake in the middle of the table and i was worried that my hair would catch fire so i let mini lean over to blow them out

(i am writing this very carefully. i want to know that this is what i remember. it is the kind of thing that very easily turns into something else. but this is what i saw.)

mom was behind mini holding her hair back because i had to get my neuroses from somewhere didn't i but mini still burned her finger

she saw one of the candles tipping over and she burned her finger trying to prop it back up and she didn't say anything because i bet she knew mom would fuss and fuss

but i saw later on her skin where the fire touched

like little lines or maybe scars running across her skin all coming from one spot and spiraling out to the edge of *the burn*

i only saw it for a moment
and then she put on a band-aid and she's left it on
since and maybe it wasn't anything
maybe it's just how burns are
but i don't think that's true

I sit back, frown down at the page. Does Mom have a burn on her finger like that? I can't remember. I should be able to remember.

What's fresh in my mind, though, is the girl in the morgue. The white spirals on her burned skin. Katherine's description sounds just like it. Another link in the chain, connecting everything. I just don't understand how.

I think of Mom leaning over the candle flame, the way Katherine wrote it. Of the scar that must be on her fingertip, locked away between memories. Mom wrapping my hand around my first lighter. Telling me "Keep a fire burning. A fire is what saves you."

Saves me from what?

From her?

I let out a shaky breath and keep reading. Whatever composure Katherine managed to find for that entry, she's lost it by the next, scrawled across the opposite page in the same ink.

mini's sick she hasn't come out of our room since after
cake yesterday and mom put all my stuff in the guest
room and said to pray about it and she said mini looked
like death warmed over which wasn't a very comforting
thing and now i'm panicked because she can't die mad at
me she can't

    we fight all the time of course we do we're sisters but
it's more than that more than being half of each other

      it's that sometimes i'm not sure which of us i am

        sometimes we are just mini and sometimes we are
something else entirely

      if we die it will be together if she dies i am going
with her

I shut the Bible. Katherine, holding tight to Mom. And
look at them now. One of them dead, the other one only half
living.

Gram said it was Mom's job to tell me how Katherine
died. And Mom didn't give me much, but it's enough. "I'm
what happened to her," she said in the driveway this morning. Mom, scratching out her sister's face. Mom, full of
anger and envy both. I'm scared I might know what she
meant.

I'm safer here, I tell myself. Safer without her. And
whatever Gram's willing to give me, that's all I deserve.

TWENTY-TWO

I stay in my room the rest of the afternoon. Skip dinner, and try to sleep, try to force this day into memory, but it nags at me all night. Mom, and the blue dress she wore to the clinic, and Tess, and I lie there, eyes open, until the sun rises again and the exhaustion is finally too much. It hits, takes me deep, wraps me in heavy, feverish dreams. Keeps me under until a knock on my bedroom door startles me awake.

I stagger to my feet, disoriented and dizzy. "Hang on," I mumble, and I hear Gram's voice say something back that I can't make out.

When I open the door, Gram's standing on the other side with a dress in her hands. Brightly patterned with blue flowers, fluttering sleeves and a skirt too full for my liking.

"What are you doing asleep so late?" she says, bustling past me. She's got a pair of sandals too, dangling from her wrist by their white straps. "We're due in town at five o'clock."

I check the clock. It's after four. I still feel like I could sleep another day, everything since arriving in Phalene a weight pressing me back into the mattress.

"Come on," Gram says. "Up."

"What?" It's too normal, all of this. I can still feel Gram's hand on my knee when she told me this is the only place I'll ever belong. And here she is. With a dress. Like a different dress isn't the reason I ran from her in the first place.

Gram turns to face me, holding the dress pressed against her chest like she's seeing how it looks on her. "The police fundraiser. The Millers have had it planned for ages."

That sounds like nothing she'd ever want to do. I know how she feels about Phalene. How Phalene feels about her. And I certainly don't want us to see the police any more than we have to. They're after Gram, and they want my help, and I'm scared that if they ask again I might give it. No, we're safer if we stay away.

"Why are we going?" I sit on the bed, throw the covers back and swing my legs up. "It's not like we're gonna be particularly welcome." Let's just stay here, I want to tell her. You and me and nothing else and that'll be the rest of our lives. I won't have to see Tess. I won't have to face the way I treated her.

"That's why we're going." Gram sets the sandals down, lays the dress on the bed and stands over me. "We'll show how little their gossip matters to us."

I'm sure there's something she's not saying. There's no way we're going into town just to be seen. Not with the body and the fire. And me.

"Sure," I say, because it's not worth a fight right now. Gram looks pleased and nods to the dress.

"Put that on," she says. "I got it just for you, in Crawford."

I frown. "When did you have time to do that?"

"After you left our breakfast with the Millers so abruptly," she says, her voice just sharp enough to let me know she's still put out. "I guessed the size. Come into my room when you've finished dressing. I'll do your hair."

She leaves me then. I get up, stare down at the dress. I can't tell if it's an apology for the blue dress in the attic, or if it's a reminder. A warning. You have lost your mother already; do not lose me.

No. I squeeze my eyes shut and undo the zipper. Not everything has to be picked apart. She bought this for me, even after I all but ran away from her at the Millers'—that's care. That's something to hold close.

The dress slips against my raw skin as I put it on, too carefully to hurt. I grab the pair of sandals Gram brought in with it and head back out to the landing. The door to

Gram's room is open, buttery light spilling out along with the faint sound of music.

The floor uneven under my feet, and I hear it creak as I near the door.

"Don't dawdle," Gram calls. "Come in."

Inside, the bed is neatly made, like the last time I saw it, and Gram is sitting at the vanity on the far wall, her long gray hair spread across her shoulders. She's wearing a dress like mine—I can see it in the large oval mirror—but hers is red. She's got a curling iron in one hand and is touching up the ends of her hair, making sure they follow the same exaggerated curve. She looks like she's from another age. Plucked out of time and put here in this room for me to find.

"Margot," she says, meeting my eyes in the mirror. "Don't you look like a picture."

"A picture of what?"

Gram gets up, crosses the room in stockinged feet and reaches out to tug on the bodice of my dress, smoothing a wrinkle. "A picture of your mother."

Everything in my life, a gift and a wound at the same time. When will anything just be what it is?

"Come on," she says. "Let's get some curls in that hair."

It's too hot in here, worse than in my room, even with the ceiling fan going. The blinds are drawn so low over the windows that I can't catch a glimpse of the sunlight or the fields outside. I follow Gram to the vanity. Its bench is plush and velvet, out of place in Gram's house, where everything is simply what it needs to be and nothing more. Nothing much on the vanity besides some old perfume, brown and dried along the sides of its glass bottle, and three tubes of lipstick. I reach for one of them.

Gram knocks my hand away. "Those colors won't suit you."

I sit still as she works the elastic out of my hair and undoes my braid. So carefully, each lock of hair laid gently over one of my shoulders. I shut my eyes. I'm afraid I might cry.

"Today's important," Gram says in my ear, her hands careful against my scalp. "I'm counting on you to keep things tidy."

I open my eyes, meet hers in the mirror. "Tidy?"

"As in," Gram says, "do not make a mess." She separates my hair into sections and strokes it with a stiff brush, smoothing it. I watch in the mirror as she sweeps it back from my temples, the gray streaks there stark. I don't know why—they never have before—but they set a blush going in my cheeks. Gram presses the back of her hand to my skin, cool against my rising heat.

"Just like a Nielsen," she says, something wistful to her voice. A dreaminess.

She picks up the curling iron then, and the whole world stretches out as she works it through my hair, piece by piece. Slow, pulling, the hum of the fan, the air beating against my skin. This is what being hers means. This is what I wanted.

I let it sink into me, wrap around my heart, until she finishes the last of my curls, sets down the iron. I lean back against her stomach. Matching dresses, matching hair.

"Look at you," Gram whispers. She bends down, kisses the back of my head, and she's holding my shoulders so tight that I can feel bruises setting deep under my skin.

I don't mind. It's about time love left a mark on me.

Once my curls have cooled, Gram herds me out to the truck. I still don't want to leave Fairhaven, but she won't be convinced, and besides, it feels good to walk next to her, looking like her girl. This is what I wanted when I came here.

Gram takes off her heels to drive. I hold them in my lap as she steers us down the highway, past the burned fields and into the center of town. Phalene looks just the same, but it feels entirely different seeing it through the window of Gram's truck. I know she's looking at everything and seeing something else. Seeing what it used to be when this was Nielsen country.

Is that how it looked to Mom when she got here? I know she won't be at the fundraiser—I can't imagine anything that would draw her there—but I feel a flutter of nerves anyway. What if I see her on the street? What if we pass wherever she's staying, a motel, or just our car parked by the side of the green? What am I supposed to do then?

But wherever she is, we park in the lot without seeing her. And I have other things to worry about. Tess, for one, the sting of our fight still fresh, and the police, for another. There's the station on the opposite side of the pavement, and for a second I wonder if Gram's really bringing me there, if she means to put me in the morgue alonside the girl she let burn, but it passes as Gram leads me in the other direction. Around to the front of the town hall, past the church with its broad marble steps and tall, arched double doors. Next to it, the town hall looks tiny and ordinary. Just a two-story brick building, its small, single door decorated with a pair of drooping balloons and propped open by a garbage can.

I'd think we couldn't possibly be in the right place if it weren't for the handful of people lingering outside, dressed up, like me and Gram. Farther down the sidewalk, a mother speaks sternly to her daughter, whose dress is about as wide as the girl is tall. Near the door, a collection of boys my age in blue sport coats and khakis are passing a cigarette around. Strangers, all of them, and I think it's the most people I've seen in this town. I wonder if they know who I am. If they care the way everyone else I've meet seems to.

I get my answer as Gram marches me by, her hand clamped around my elbow. The boys watch us approach, wide-eyed, and as we pass, the one nearest the door whispers to the others, smoke trailing from his open mouth.

Vera Nielsen, in the flesh.

I know how they feel.

Gram doesn't give them a second look. She ushers me inside and across a shabby beige lobby, following a sign tacked to the wall with an arrow pointing toward another door. I barely get a glimpse of the offices branching off the lobby before we're in the concrete stairwell, the only sound the echo of Gram's heels with every step.

"What am I supposed to do at this thing?" I ask, straightening the fall of my dress. " 'Don't make a mess' is kind of vague."

Gram ushers me down the second flight of stairs, into a small foyer with a flickering overhead light. A warped maroon door is just open, and inside I can hear the build of voices and music. "You and Theresa—would you call yourselves friends?" she asks, pulling me around to face her.

I don't know what my fight with Tess left us as. I don't even really know what we were before. I met her two days ago and maybe I should've been careful, kept myself away, but I was scared, and Tess was something to hold on to, so I didn't. And now it could be gone. Like closing a circuit with too much power running through it.

"Friends?" I say. "I guess." That's the best I can do.

Gram reaches out and adjusts the lie of one of my curls. "That's good. It's important that people see you here, see you with her. I have to have some difficult conversations, and Theresa's family can go a long way toward making them easier." She smiles, earnest and warm. "I'm talking to you as an adult here, Margot. I need your help. Can you do this for me?"

I can't deny the lure of it. The way she welcomes me into what she's doing, makes me part of it and of her. Like she knows I'd do anything for that. "Yes," I tell her, before I can catch myself. "I can do that."

Gram steps back, gives me a firm nod. "Right, then," she says. "Into the lion's den."

The room is packed. Round tables on a linoleum floor, with two well-stocked buffets on the far side and a bored-looking boy my age standing near a smaller table, where a phone is plugged into a pair of speakers playing cheery jazz. Across the walls are displays of children's artwork and motivational posters, like somebody decorated with whatever they could find on short notice.

All of Phalene is probably here, mothers quieting unruly children, fathers in clutches around the side of the room while a quartet of older couples dances slowly in the center. A table by the side is full of teenagers who would probably be in my class if I went to school here. Most of the police force seems to be here, too, congregated near the front, where one of them is setting up a box for donations.

The dress Gram put me in feels too tight, squeezing my ribs, the zipper rubbing the small of my back. I spot Eli off to the side, but Tess isn't with him. He seems to be looking for her too, searching the crowd with an anxious frown.

I have to talk to her. I have to apologize and make it right.

I catch Eli's eye and wave, and for a moment I can tell he's thinking about pretending he doesn't see me. But then he lifts a hand, gives me a wave back with a smile that looks like he's trying very hard to be polite.

"Can I—" I start, but Gram cuts me off.

"Back in the truck at six," she says. "Behave, Mini." And then she's practically prowling across the dance floor, making her way to a group of men bent together as they discuss something in hushed voices.

Mini. It should feel good. It almost does.

Eager to avoid talking to any of the police, I head for Eli, who is rearranging two stacks of cheese on his small paper plate with careful precision.

"Hey," he says without looking up. "Hang on. This is delicate work."

"Sure." I guess I should be glad he's even speaking to me without Tess here to make him.

"Okay," he says finally. I watch as he spears a square of cheese and holds it out to me, the colorful plastic frill on one end of the toothpick crinkling between his fingers. "Cheddar?"

I raise my eyebrows. "No thanks. You seen Tess?"

Eli shakes his head. He's keeping a good distance between us, like he wants everyone watching to know I'm making him uncomfortable. "No," he says. "But I'm sure she'll be here soon."

I check the room, but I just see the crowds of people, the police officers standing out in their dark uniforms. Anderson and Connors are probably here somewhere. I forgot, really, that Phalene would have more police than just them, but I recognize the third cop from the scene of the fire at one end of the table, assembling what looks like a pastrami sandwich.

No Tess. No Millers. I turn back to Eli. "Have you talked to her at all today?"

Eli removes the top layer of cheese from his plate and stuffs it into his mouth. "She texted me last night," he says. "But it didn't make a lot of sense."

Maybe she told him what's wrong. "Can I see?"

Eli's pause is too long. The answer is no.

"Never mind," I say. I bet it was about me. "I'll find her."

He looks over my shoulder, and his eyes widen. "I don't think you'll have to."

TWENTY-THREE

I turn around. There's Tess, coming through the door with her parents behind her. She's wearing a seersucker dress, a billow to the skirt and a cling to the bodice, with straps that have slipped just off her shoulders. Hair in a knot, and from a distance it seems like somebody was careful with it, but when she looks to one side, her expression oddly vacant, her eyes bloodshot, I can see a lime-green hair elastic barely managing to hold it up.

Flanking her, Mr. and Mrs. Miller look a sight better. They're each in fresh summer clothes. Striped shirt and slacks for him, and a pale blue dress for her that looks like a sister to Tess's. They're put together in a way she isn't, but when I look more closely, I see the same redness in their eyes. The same tightness in their shoulders.

What the hell? Tess was a little subdued yesterday, sure, but she looked nothing like this. Neither did Mrs. Miller.

Eli's watching them too, his mouth pulled tight. "That doesn't look good," he says.

They pass us, making for the front of the room. I spot Mrs. Miller's hand on the back of Tess's neck, firm and guiding as they head toward the gathered police officers. Her eyes land on Eli, and I'm startled by how cold she looks. No wave, no friendly smile to her daughter's best friend.

"Great," he mutters. "She probably got caught doing some ridiculous shit and blamed it on me. Like always."

It's possible, but I remember yesterday, the tension lingering in her shoulders. "I don't know," I say. "I think it's more than that."

"I guess we'll see."

An officer in uniform comes in, taking off his hat and scanning the room. It's Connors. I meet his eyes for a minute by accident and jerk around to face Eli, who wrinkles his nose at me.

"Don't be weird," he says. "Okay. I'm getting more cheese."

"Wait," I say, because if I'm alone, Connors will come over and try to wring information out of me, information I don't have. But it's too late. Eli's heading for the buffet and Connors is close enough that I can't reasonably pretend not to have noticed his friendly wave.

"Nice party," he says, slotting into the space Eli vacated. I glance down at his left hand, where his wedding ring glints. I wonder what his spouse is like, wonder which of the people milling around they could be. If Connors talks about the body, about Vera, when he goes home at night. How real is this to other people? Or is it only happening to me?

"Sure," I say. I wish I had something to drink, or something to do with my hands. As it is, I fuss with the ends of my curled hair and keep watching Tess. She's at her parents' table now, sitting between them, staring ahead. Not a twitch in her muscles, barely a blink. Whatever happened, it's beaten her down.

"Didn't see you around town yesterday," Connors says. "You okay at Fairhaven?"

I tear my eyes away from Tess and look at him. "Go ahead," I say. I can hear Gram, can feel her shaping the fall of my voice. "Just ask. You want to know if I've changed my mind. If I have anything to tell you about my grandmother."

Connors looks taken aback. "No," he says. "I want to know if you're okay. It was a lot, at the station. And you're a kid out there with Vera. That's not exactly the place I'd pick to process shit, you know?"

I don't answer at first; I can't. He called me a kid. I haven't thought of myself as one in I don't know how long. Seventeen, but I raised myself. Although I wonder sometimes if I didn't grow up at all. If all I did was survive.

"I'm fine," I say. And then, because the lure of it is too

strong, because Connors has seen exactly what I have: "I just keep thinking about the way the girl looked. Her eyes. The burn on her leg."

"So do I." A woman passes in front of us, carrying a bowl of ice cream she's served herself from the dessert table, topped with dark, oozing chocolate sauce. "Really puts you off some things," he says, laughing a little even though it isn't funny at all.

"They don't know what caused it?"

He hesitates. He's probably not supposed to discuss this with me, or with anyone. But I'm talking where I wasn't before, and I can see the gears turning in his head—maybe this is how he gets me pointed at Gram. The police haven't been back to Fairhaven since my first morning there, but after my break-in at the station, I know it's only a matter of time, and he'll want more ammunition for when they do.

"Yeah." He steps back, away from the rest of the party, and lowers his voice. I go with him. "The coroner's looking at some irregularities that could explain it. Some stuff in her blood that has no business being there. But I don't know, Margot."

What he wants to say next is implied: your grandmother does.

I ignore it. "Stuff in her blood?"

Connors waves a hand and then reaches out to snag a glass of water from a passing server—I recognize her as one of Tess's friends from the town green, dressed in a wrinkled catering uniform. He waits until she's gone to continue. "A chemical. We just got the results back on it—it's some farming thing, for planting sterile hybrids. Ridicine. You heard of it?"

I shake my head. Should it be familiar?

"It was banned in . . ." Connors scratches at his jaw thoughtfully. "God, I want to say forty years ago? Exposure killed a couple people out in Kansas. Made a whole big mess in the papers. So what it's doing here in that girl's blood-stream we have no idea."

A chemical. I saw the report, hanging from the drawer in the morgue. I let my eyes drift, turn my focus to that memory, but I can't make it take shape. And now Connors says it's been banned since long before she would've been born.

"But she was my age," I say. "That girl. Right?"

"Seems like it." Connors takes a sip from his glass, his expression grim. "That's what I'm saying."

We don't get any further. Across the room, Tess bursts to her feet. It jostles the Miller table with a clatter, sends a lemonade pitcher tumbling and a glass smashing against the floor, but she doesn't seem to notice.

"I told you!" she shouts. "I told you and told you."

"Theresa," Mr. Miller starts.

"It's not Eli. I have no fucking idea what's going on!" Her mother is looking up at her, mouth open, aghast. She doesn't move as Tess storms away from the table, eyeliner running as tears track down her cheeks.

Connors frowns, takes a step forward, but an officer is already crouching between Mr. and Mrs. Miller, and another two are gathering rolls of paper towels to clean up the mess. I take advantage of the distraction and hurry around the edge of the room, following Tess to where she's thrown open the back door and disappeared.

It leads to the floor of a stairwell, the flights above running up to the ground floor and beyond. I find Tess sitting on the bottom step, her forehead pressed to her knees. This close I can see a streak of blood down the side of her dress, and the long tear in her cuticle that must've caused it. I sidle inside and let the door swing mostly shut behind me.

"It's me," I say, and she looks up. Deep hollows under her eyes, sallow skin. She looks like she's barely slept. I won't ask if she's okay—I already know she's not. She was like this yesterday, too. Before I ruined everything.

"What's going on?" I ask instead.

For a moment she does nothing, and then she sighs, folds over and presses her forehead to her knees again.

"I can't believe this," she says, her voice muffled. "I can't actually believe this."

I sit down next to her, careful to leave room between us. "Believe what?"

With a huff, she straightens, her hair coming loose from its threadbare elastic. I watch as she sneaks one hand onto her stomach.

"This is," she starts, and then she breaks off. Laughs, incredulous and angry and near the edge of something. "I was feeling sick yesterday. I have been for a few days. Just like, on and off. It was nothing. It was absolutely fine. Except my mom freaked out about Eli staying over all the time because apparently that means we're sleeping together and she made me take a test and. Yeah."

Oh.

Oh.

"You're . . ." I trail off. I don't want to be the one to say it.

Tess does it for me. "Pregnant. With child. Owner of one oven containing one bun," she says, hysteria bubbling under every word.

"Um," I say. "I guess. Congratulations?"

"Go to hell," Tess says, but she laughs weakly, the air rushing out of her, and her body tips against mine. We fought, but we're here, and I can be this for her. I can be someone she counts on.

"So it's not Eli's," I say. I remember those boys outside in sports coats. Somehow I can't imagine Tess with any of them. With anyone. "Is it . . . Can I ask whose it is?"

"Go ahead and ask," Tess says into my shoulder. "And if you find out, let me know."

My eyes widen. I fumble for the right words to ask if she's okay, if she's safe. To make sure she knows that whatever she needs, that's what I'll do, but she keeps going before I can find them.

"I just don't get it. I don't know how this is happening."

"What do you mean?" I ask slowly. There's something else going on here. Something I'm missing.

"I mean, it's physically impossible." She twists her skirt in her fists, knuckles going white for a moment. I lean away from her, try to get a good look at her face. "I thought the test had to be wrong, right? But my mom made me take four, and they all said the same thing. I'm literally the fucking Virgin Mary over here."

I should say something. But I can't work past the shock. She's serious. She's really pregnant, and if I understand her right, she's saying there's no father. No nothing. Just . . . her.

The stairwell light catches her cheeks, pulling shadows across her eyes. Her fingernails have been bitten down, stripped clean of polish. She laughs, bitter and sharp. "How does this happen?"

"Okay." I do my best to sound calm. In control. One of us should be. "Let's take it in pieces. You said your mom made you take tests?"

Nodding, she shuts her eyes and lets out a breath. "This morning."

"And there's definitely no way there could be a father?" I say slowly. Her eyes flick open, and she shoots me a look that's half exhaustion, half despair.

"Please," she says. "It doesn't make any sense to me. So

don't ask me to make it make sense to you. It's too much. I mean, I've got my mom asking me about Eli and my dad won't even look at me, but God forbid we miss this fucking party, and—"

She breaks off as someone knocks on the other side of the stairwell door. I turn to look. Gram's face peers through the gap I left, arranged in the sympathetic expression I saw on her when I got to Fairhaven.

"Everybody all right in here?" she says. Bright and soothing and perfect. This is the grandmother I came here for, the grandmother who did my hair and dressed me up, but now it puts me on edge. This is a performance. I can see that now. And if she's like this, there's a reason.

Tess sniffs and wipes her nose on the back of her arm. "We're fine," she says. "Sorry to cause a scene."

"It's quite all right." Gram comes all the way in and presses the door shut, leaning her back against it. Keeping other people out, maybe. Or keeping us here. "They're just sorting the mess. It'll be back to normal in a minute." She smiles at Tess, warm and inviting. It feels more real for how small it is. "It seemed like quite an emotional thing. There was . . . well, let's just say there was some talk I recognized. About a situation I think you might be in."

"What?" I say. A situation? But Gram doesn't even look at me.

"My daughter got pregnant young too," she says. I stare

at her. How could she have guessed?

She crouches at Tess's feet, and I watch her lay her palm on Tess's knee. It's what she did with me, in the kitchen.

Exactly what she did with me. A sick, heady feeling sweeps over me, leaving chills in its wake. This isn't how it should be. "Gram," I say, but she waves me off, eyes fixed on Tess.

"I helped her through that," she says. "I can help you. You have options. Whatever you want to do," she says. "There are a million roads open to you."

It's the right thing to say. But it sounds all wrong. Because Gram isn't saying it to be good, or to be kind. Why would she choose now to look after Tess, when I don't think she ever has before?

"And the father," Gram continues, "whoever he is, he'll support you. We'll make sure of it."

No, I think, sudden and clear through the fog, through the confusion. No, Tess, don't, but Tess is already opening her mouth, and Tess is already saying, "That's the problem."

Gram's brow furrows. "What do you mean?"

"We should get back," I cut in. Tighten my arm around Tess's and tug, as subtly as I can. Don't say another word. Do not trust this. She is playing you the same way she played me. "Your parents probably want to talk to you."

She meets my eyes. I watch hers widen with understanding. "Yeah, you're right." Together, we get up and sidle around Gram, toward the door.

"No, wait a minute." Gram stands up, brushes invisible wrinkles out of her skirt. "Theresa, is there a father?"

Is there one. Not who is he. How does Gram know to ask that question? Here I am, still trying to get my head around how this could happen at all, and Gram goes straight to the heart of it. Like she already knows.

Tess turns. Her voice hitches, comes out in a whisper. "Why would you ask that?"

And Gram. She looks at me.

It's not much. The smallest thing, and she breaks away so quickly I think she couldn't have meant to do it. But it rips through me, echoes in the empty spaces where my own father has never lived. Not even a question I wanted to ask. Why would I, when I had Mom to figure out?

"I'm not sure what you mean," Gram says. "I'm just making sure you girls are all right. Let's get you back to the party."

I barely have time to move before she's nudging the door open and ushering us into the community room with a hand at our backs, firm and unyielding. Music too loud, air too cluttered with competing perfumes. I need fresh air. I need Gram to not be watching me so closely, like she's waiting to see what I'll do.

More than that, I need to get to Mom. And when Gram looks away from me for half a second, I'm bolting for the door.

TWENTY-FOUR

Outside. Evening coming on. I steal a bike from the rack in the green and ride through town. Breathing hard, every blink warping the world. Nothing's what I thought. No father, no father, and that never bothered me, and I wondered if he was out there, sure, and I thought sometimes about what he might've looked like, about what kind of face could have mixed with Mom's and disappeared completely.

No face at all. Just her, and then me. Is that—

I pedal harder, try to press everything down. The Nielsens in those photographs, in the dining room. They didn't look alike the way Mom looks like Gram, the way the three of us look like each other. And something is there, something is waiting for me to look it in the eye, but I can't do it alone. I need Mom.

I don't know exactly where she'll be, but I figure there can't be too many motels in a town this size. I've seen most of the west side with Tess, or in the truck with Gram. So I follow the highway east. Up ahead I can see a long, low building, white with blue trim and a small dusty parking lot. A sign flickers between VACANCY and NO VACANCY.

It's the only motel I've seen in all of Phalene, so she must be here. I pull in, careening over the unplanted flower bed.

Mom's car isn't in the lot to tell me which room is hers. Did she go for food, or maybe to find me? I leave the bike on the sidewalk and rush into the office. A boy a bit older than me is at the desk, his feet propped up on an old box fan while he nurses a beer.

"Shit," he says, tipping upright when he sees me. "I swear I'm legal."

The gray hair. It catches people sometimes, when they're not paying attention. "Sure," I say. "I'm looking for my mom." Don't bother with her name. It's probably obvious. "Which room is she in?"

"Your mom?" He frowns. "There was someone in the farthest room, but—"

"Thanks."

Down the walkway, past rooms behind weathered blue doors. Finally I reach the last one. The door stands slightly ajar, so I just barge right in.

I stop. I must have the wrong room. This place is empty.

No bags, no stuff. The sheets stripped from the bed and piled in the corner like somebody was about to change the linens.

But I'm in the right place, because it's there, in the middle of the mattress. The Bible. The one I left in our apartment in Calhoun. The matching one to Katherine's, back at Fairhaven.

Mom was here. And now she's not.

Panic rising in my throat, choking off the air. Her stuff must still be here. She can't have left. It's fine. It has to be fine.

I run to the dresser, yank open the drawers. Empty, empty, empty. Okay, Margot. Deep breaths now. She wouldn't do this. She wouldn't make you the first promise she's ever made and then break it just like that.

I check the bathroom. The shelves are bare, the towels dumped in the bathtub. They're damp. The shampoo is balanced on the side, the top still open. She was here.

"Mom?" I yell, and I know it's ridiculous, I know she won't answer, but I won't let that in. "Mom!"

Just an echo as my voice bounces off the tiles. I barrel back into the bedroom. The gleam of the Bible's gold embossing in the last of the light feels like a needle in my side. This was her room, but her stuff's all gone. Because she packed it up. Because she didn't wait. She left. And she took her whole life with her.

Her whole life, except me.

Every breath tearing something open in me, every second more painful than the last. She's gone. Mom's fucking gone. She packed up and she's not coming back.

She promised. She promised she'd stay. And I believed her. I can't believe I was so stupid. I really thought she'd still be here when I was ready to come back. I really thought it was different with us this time, that maybe we could finally understand each other.

For a moment I'm not sure what to do. Where to put the thrumming hive of anger living in my body. It's a gift, I tell myself. She finally gave me what I always wanted. My own life, away from hers. Celebrate.

I'm lit up with it, a rage sizzling in my body. I pick up the nightstand. Throw it against the wall. It's nothing, made of nothing, and it splinters into pieces. The Bible next. I hurl it at the mirror over the dresser. Shattered glass tumbles to the floor, scatters around my feet. So what if it cuts me? What's one more way to bleed?

How could she do this to me? We've spent all this time tearing each other apart, but we stayed, we stayed together, and now she bails? Now, when I need answers? Now, when I need help?

She can't have left. She can't, she can't. If anybody was gonna leave it was gonna be me, but it wasn't, really, because I'd never let go of her, not as long as I had a choice.

And I said I always wanted space from her, I told myself that every day in that apartment, wishing and hoping for a day without her voice in the back of my head, but I didn't fucking mean it, because she's my mom and I love her and I cry so hard my muscles tremble, cry so hard it sounds like a scream.

My mother, my mother, my mother who never wanted me.

"Come back," I hear myself whispering. Come back.

When I look up it's nearing sunset, and there's a cool breeze sweeping in through the open door. He must've heard me, that boy in the office, but he hasn't come to check. I don't blame him. I wouldn't either.

Slowly I pull myself to my feet. Wipe the snot and tears from my face with the edge of the motel comforter. I can break all I want, but eventually the only thing left to do is get back up. Get back up and find the answers I need on my own. I've been doing it for years. I can do it again.

I pick the glass from the carpet. Gather up the biggest pieces of wood from the broken nightstand and drop them in the trash can by the door. Hang the towels over the shower curtain rod so they'll dry better. Splash cold water on my cheeks to bring the redness down and tuck my curled hair behind my ears until I look closer to fine.

Back in the bedroom, I take one last look around before heading out. I should stop by the office to apologize. But something catches my eye. A square of white, sticking out from the Bible where it's splayed facedown. It's not the picture of Mom in front of Fairhaven—I took that with me when I left Calhoun—and it's not the money I left for her. It's something else.

I crouch, steady myself on the bed and pick it up. It's an envelope. *Margot,* written there in her handwriting. Shaky and lopsided, so different from Gram's.

I look around the room, the wreck I made of it, and swallow a hot rush of shame. She left me a note. Not that it makes any of this much better. But she did leave me something.

That something turns out to be a photo. Mom and Katherine, posed on the Fairhaven front porch, standing on either side of Gram. One of them in shorts and a T-shirt, hair long and loose. The other in a plain dress with wide straps. My breath catches in my throat—the face of girl in the dress is scratched out. So strong and so deep it rips all the way through.

On the opposite side of their mother, the other girl is looking at her sister, a fierceness to her face that I recognize from my own heart. That must be Mom. Mom from Katherine's diary, who scratched out her sister's face, who kept this photo because she cherished what she'd done.

Except. I look closer. I know my mother's face better than I know my own. And it's off. Just a little, but off. Everything on the wrong side. The freckle by the corner of her eye, the curve of her widow's peak.

My mouth goes dry. That's not my mom. That's Katherine. And the girl with her face scratched out is Josephine.

Everything hits me at once. Every word written in that Bible at Fairhaven—hers. Every bit of guilt and fear—hers. It was Katherine who scratched out those photographs. Katherine who broke my mother's arm, not the other way around.

My hands tremble as I open the envelope again and take out the rest. A bundle of paper, the texture thin and familiar. It has torn edges, is covered in careful letters inked in the spaces between the Scripture. This was ripped out of the Fairhaven Bible. The one I thought was Katherine's.

The pages unfold, and I lay them out on the carpet. Mom left the rest of the book there, in her old room. She took this. She took her sister's Bible like a memento. And she took these pages from her own. What's in here that she wanted to keep?

I take a deep breath. Start reading.

it finally happened
 i did it. i'm so sorry. i did it. i killed her. i'm so sorry
mini. i'm so sorry i'm so sorry i'm sorry i'm sorry mini
you have to forgive
 katherine
 katherine katherine katherine Katherine Katherine
KATHERINE KATHERINE KATHERINE

Mom killed her sister. Killed her sister and wrote it down. It's not a surprise, exactly. Not after what she said in the driveway. But that doesn't make it any easier to take.

I rest my fingertips on the place where Katherine's name turns ragged with grief. Everything I read back at Fairhaven—that was Mom, her fears and her worries, and if I were her, if I saw what she saw, maybe I'd end up where she did. I'm angry and I'm hurting, but it's always there in me. The reaching. The want to understand her.

Well, this is what I was after. Whether I like it or not, I think we've been standing on thin ice our whole lives, this thing she did waiting underneath us.

I set my shoulders, keep reading.

why didn't mom see why didn't she understand why did she make this mine to do

i have to tell i have to tell someone but mom doesn't want to hear and nobody does because nobody loves her the way i love her

i know it's loved now past tense and everything but it never will be, not really

i will love my sister and i will wish we'd died together i will always wish it could have been just us forever

And what she got was me. I couldn't have been much of a replacement for the sister she wanted to die with.

we turned eighteen. this is important. i know that even if i don't know why.

   things have been weird with us for a while but it was our birthday. it was the day we became the two of us. i wasn't gonna let it be anything but ours.

   we've been sleeping in different rooms. her in our old room and me in the guest room across the house, since the thing with the pictures (and everything after). i woke up and i got dressed in this hand-me-down from her, a dress she stopped liking and i started wanting. we've always been the same size. the same everything.

   i thought it would make her happy. i need to say that right now. i thought that it would make her happy to see me in something that was hers.

   i went into our room. ~~mini~~ katherine was still asleep. she's been sleeping so much since she got sick. mom says it's been a year, in and out of school, people talking about those Nielsen girls and their Nielsen mother, but i know better. since our sixteenth. that's when something happened to her. that's when she stopped being able to stand up, stopped keeping down food and started coughing up something that wasn't quite blood.

   so i woke her. i just wanted to see her. to talk to her. i would have climbed in bed next to her and stayed there all day. but she was so mad. she just wanted to sleep, or to not be near me, or both. i don't know. i'll never know.

i tried to get her to sit up. we could convince mom to let us watch TV, i think i told her. and she just started crying. she got out of bed and her legs were weak and her skin was so pale it was like she was disappearing right in front of me.

most of what she said i don't (want to) remember. but she told me that she hated how it was, that she hated our birthday because it only reminded her more how different we are now. we've had this fight before. it never sounded like this. she's never brought up the x-rays before. i thought she'd forgotten, honestly. that was my mistake.

"we're different all the way inside." i remember that exactly. we have known this for years. that we are like mirrors of each other, everything flipped. and i have never, ever cared.

but it ~~matters~~ mattered to her. because we were twins until we weren't, until she got sick and i didn't.

here, she said, and she picked up the prayer candle mom had lit for her and left on top of our dresser. and she said:

"i know what happens to me."

she must have meant the fire. i saw it the day of our sixteenth. i was right. i was.

then she said:

"come here"

and i went. i would go anywhere she wanted me

to. i watched her lift the candle. i saw that burn on her fingertip from our sixteenth birthday, saw the white lines spiraling across it and i promise you i'm not lying when i say i wanted them for my own. if that would make her happy. if that would get us back to how we were.

she pressed the flame to my cheek like someone putting out a cigarette. i can feel the burn there still. the skin is starting to scar, and i don't think it will ever fade.

i screamed. i'm sure i did. she let go. and i left. ran away, really.

she stayed upstairs the rest of the day. i didn't see her. mom didn't say a word about our birthday or about anything but she sat me down in the kitchen and patched up my cheek. she was gentle and she was steady and it still hurts.

i told her how the scratches got on the dining room table. i told her everything. i said, i remember saying, "something's not right with her." i said that. mom knew what i was talking about.

and what she told me was that someone would have to put an end to it. "sooner's better than later. she'll only get worse. it's the best gift you can give her." i'll hear that for the rest of my life. i'll always wonder what a different mother might have said.

it took me all night to decide what to do.

i think it should have taken longer.

i didn't know how i was going to do it when i woke
her up. i didn't know anything. i probably should have
planned. but i went into her room and this time when
i woke her she just seemed like herself. like me. and she
said "i'm sorry" the second she opened her eyes.

i told her to get up. i said i had a present for her.

that was the first lie i've ever told her.

she was in her pajamas still. i have the same pair—
mom got them for us both on our last birthday—but i've
never worn mine. they were too big for her (so too big for
us both) and she'd rolled up the cuffs of the pants and the
sleeves both. i could see the skin of her stomach through
the gaps between the buttons. i hated that.

she asked me where the present was and i said it was
outside and she trusted me. she followed me. we went
downstairs and we went out onto the back porch and i
could see the grove in the distance, a deeper dark than the
sky. it was almost dawn.

when we were kids we would stay on the porch and
talk all night. i thought that could be the present i gave
her. one little bit of our old lives for her to remember. but
it was too close to the house and to the light mom left on
under the stove hood. so i said we should go out to the
grove.

it used to be our place back when we were still young
enough that i'd give people the wrong name. so it seemed

like the right thing. all of it seemed like the right thing, is my point.

the grove is about a mile from the house. we walked it together, barefoot down the access road that cuts through the crops. halfway there she reached over and held my hand so tightly, the insides of our wrists pressed together. she did it. i never want to forget that. my sister and i walked side by side in the night once, and her pulse beat against mine.

but then we got there.

the place we started, the way mom tells it.

the grove has this smell to it that i don't know how to describe. it's like it's always just rained there. fresh earth, and something sweet. that night it was so strong it lingered in my hair for hours, until finally i took a bath in the black-tiled guest bathroom and changed into some of mom's clothes.

katherine looked happy. we stepped through the first clutch of the apricot trees and she let out this sigh. like she'd been holding her breath since i don't know when. since the last time we were there, maybe. and this i remember, this i cannot be wrong about: she said, "thank you."

that was the gift. bringing her there, that was my gift to her.

if she hadn't said it maybe i wouldn't have been able

to. but it felt like she was giving me permission. like this was the right way for it to be over for her.

so i let her go deeper into the grove by herself. i let her get ahead of me. and i picked up a rock from between the roots of an apricot tree. i meant to hit her on the back of the head so maybe she'd die without realizing what this was.

but i took too long, or she heard me, or something. i don't know exactly. all i remember is the line of her profile as she looked over her shoulder. mine. her and me. my mini.

i couldn't. not like that. i still had to.

i took her throat in my hands and she ended up on her back, me with my knees on either side of her. i was crying, and my hands kept slipping. but she was so weak that it barely mattered.

here is where i have to stop. it is too much. i can tell you i remembered the burn on her finger. and i can tell you i snapped off the dead corn from the fields and piled it over her body, right there in the grove. i can tell you i got a lighter from the kitchen and burned her down.

mom called the fire department. they came. they put it out. the police asked questions, and we told them it was all katherine, which wasn't really a lie. we told them she disappeared, which wasn't really a lie either.

i don't understand how, but when they looked for her body, there was nothing left to find.

that's the end of it. that has to be the end of it. but it's
been three weeks now, three weeks and seven hours since
i did what i did, and something is wrong with my body.
at first i thought it was her, getting what she wanted,
making us the same all the way inside again. but it's not.
it's not. i've already missed one period. already started
feeling sick every morning.

it'll be a girl.

i have no father and i have a mother i cannot bear to
look at and this is the only place i can ask for help. please.
i have sinned. that's what you say when you're confessing,
and i have. but my daughter hasn't.

It happened to Mom. Just like Tess, pregnant with no idea how. I wanted so badly to keep it apart, but it's all the same thing, isn't it? The past and the present, happening at the same time.

I stare at that last sentence, in my mother's handwriting. Me. That was me. Me she wanted to do right by. Me she kept, even though it scared her, even though she never asked for it. Even though I was only the echo of her sister. Not a father in the world, not for either of us. Just a choice to be made.

And it's in my hands now. Gram gave it all to Mom, said someone had to take care of it. Mom did her best, but there was so much she couldn't do. There was more than she could carry. So she passed the rest to me. Told me to keep a fire burning and locked herself away.

I close my eyes. See myself back at the table in Gram's kitchen. She built her family on sand and did nothing but watch as it fell apart. I won't do that. I won't be like that. There's a way this all happened, and it's there at Fairhaven, waiting for me to find it.

Okay, Margot, I tell myself. It's time to go home.

TWENTY-FIVE

I make it back to the house right as the sunset fades, the photograph of Mom and Katherine in the pocket of my dress. The driveway's empty, so I plant myself on the back porch and wait. Gram will be home soon. Every second stretching, endless, filled up with Jo and Katherine. With me, the girl with no father. The girl who grew in her mother's body all on her own. To not have chosen it? More than that, to not know how it happened? I'd have gone to the clinic too. I'm not sure I'd have changed my mind.

In the distance, the Miller house is well lit and shining, and my stomach tightens the longer I look at it. The same thing has happened to Tess. Whatever's causing this, it's not just our family. It's not Nielsen business gone Nielsen wrong.

A sputter, and the rattle of a truck coming in. Gram. But

she's not coming from the highway. Instead, her headlights hit me from the Miller driveway, running along the far side of Fairhaven. I frown, get to my feet. Maybe she brought Tess home from the fundraiser. Or maybe she went over to help her talk to her parents. Maybe she did a good thing, for once.

I wait, listen as the truck swings around the front of the house before settling in its usual spot along the side. The engine cuts, headlights die. I hear the door slam, and Gram mutters something to herself I can't quite make out.

"Hey," I call. Part of me hopes I scared her.

A pause. Then Gram sweeps around the corner of the porch, her heels dangling from her hand. The pattern on her dress seems deeper in the twilight. I blink against the shadows.

"What are you doing sitting out here?" she says.

I shrug. "Nothing. Waiting for you."

She walks past me and pulls the screen door open so hard that it smacks against the wall. Steps into the kitchen and tosses her shoes in the corner. I watch, confused, as she ignores the light switch and bends over the sink, washing her hands in the dark. But I don't dare touch the switch. If she's left it like that, it's because she meant to, and I need her loving me as much as possible when I ask her my questions.

"We won't even discuss the fact that you left the fundraiser to go God knows where" is what she starts with, voice raised over the water. She says it like I should be grateful. Putting me in her debt immediately. Even seeing it for what it is doesn't stop the rush of gratitude I have to fend off.

"Very generous of you," I say.

"Do not talk back to me, Margaret."

I ignore her. "Tess is pregnant. She's pregnant just like Mom was with me. And you know that."

She dries her hands on the dish towel hanging from the oven and turns to face me, her arms crossed over her chest. There's something caught in her hair, dotted dark along her temples, but with the lights off I can't make out what. "I don't accept your premise."

I do laugh this time. This is ridiculous. This isn't a debate. This is real, and it's happening to me, to the dead girl, and to Tess, and I will not let it go.

"What's happening, Gram?" I step forward. Hands clenched into fists, every moment of the last few days boiling up. "And what happened back then? To Mom? To Katherine?"

"That," Gram says, a warning in her voice, "is not your concern."

"How? How is it not mine?" I am so tired of this. Shut out and pushed in at the same time. "I found Mom's diary. I know what she did to Katherine. I know they had no father and I know there isn't one with Tess, and that doesn't just happen. That's not how it works."

Gram goes back to the sink and starts washing her hands again, picking carefully at something under her nails. That familiar feeling takes hold of me. *Look at me,* it says. *Look at me now.*

"Everything that's happening comes back to here," I say. "To you. Tess and Mom and that fucking girl, the one you said you didn't know anything about."

She doesn't even flinch. Just grabs the towel and wets it before dabbing at something on her skirt. "Best to leave all that alone," she says.

"Why?" I'm shaking, my whole body seized with anger. "She lived here, Gram. She must have."

"I said, leave it alone."

But I have lost the last of my patience. The question tears out of me, blunt and desperate, near to screaming. "Did you set the fire? Did you kill her?"

Gram sighs, deep and exhausted. Turns and sags against the counter, the water still running. "You don't understand what you're asking. Is it really killing when she wasn't . . ." She trails off, shrugs.

"Wasn't what?" Not a daughter. Not a sister. But she came from here, and I saw the report at the morgue. Her mirrored heart, just like Katherine. And something else, too. The chemical in her blood. "Gram, what's ridicine?"

Her face falls, goes clear enough that even in the dark I can see everything—the surprise, the fear.

"Where did you hear about that?" she says. If I thought panic would turn her fragile, the way it can with Mom, with me, I was wrong. "Answer me right now, Margot. Where?"

I lift my chin, set my shoulders. "Connors. He said it's some banned chemical. Were you using it here?" I throw my arm out, gesturing to the fields beyond the porch, to the crops bearing stillborn fruit. "Is that what made them this way?"

It's too big a question, and I don't even know quite what I mean. But I'm not wrong. I know that.

Gram looks at me for a long time. And it isn't pain in her eyes. It's something else, something older and deeper. I think I'm always two people to her and Mom. Myself, and the ghost of the girl before me.

"I have lived with my mistakes," she says softly, finally. "So has Jo. We've both done what we could. And it hasn't mattered at all." I watch, confused, as she pulls a bobby pin from her bra, gathers her curled hair into a knot and pins it at the back of her head. "Some things just get worse and worse, don't they, Mini?"

The nickname rips through me. "Stop," I say. "I'm not them."

"Oh, no?" She's mocking me, but there's no energy to it. "You're here, aren't you? You sent your mother away. You made yourself my girl."

I did. I tried so hard to be hers. To be anyone's, if Mom wouldn't have me.

"I sent her away because I know what she did," I say instead. It's not true at all—I didn't then. But I do now.

"And what's that?" Gram asks.

"She killed Katherine." It comes out easy. What a relief, to say it out loud, to let Mom be what she is. To stop pretending she could ever love me the way mothers are meant to love children. Mom's spent seventeen years hiding from what she did, and the whole time she had me right in front of her. Me with a face just like hers. Like Katherine's. How do you love the worst thing you ever did?

"Yes," Gram says with a strange sort of pride. "She did. That's where you come from. That's your Nielsen blood."

"No. No, I won't be like her. I won't be like you."

"You already are." She gestures to me, the wave of her hand encompassing me from head to toe. "You've done exactly what we have. You've put this family first, as you should."

She's right. I have decided that protecting this place is worth more than anything else. I have let Fairhaven wrap its arms around me, because nothing ever has before. But something isn't good just because it wants me, is it? Gram's not better than Mom. Her, kneeling in front of me, calling me her own—that's just the other side of the coin.

One day, I told myself, one day you'll have to let go. Maybe that's now.

"You're right. I have," I say. Gram raises her eyebrows.

"But I won't do it again." And I start walking. Out the back door. Off the porch and onto the grass. A glance around the corner at Gram's truck, a shovel and a shotgun in the flatbed. I could take it to grab Tess and bolt, but Gram probably has the keys, and I can't drive stick. It doesn't matter; I'm gone anyway.

I am leaving. I am getting Tess and we'll go to the police and we'll say this is how it is, and something will change. The driveway a stretch of dust ahead of me, the Miller house up ahead, and it feels so far but I'll walk as far as I have to, as long as Fairhaven's behind me.

"Margot!"

Don't. Don't turn around. I feel the urge to go back tugging at my feet, but I keep walking. You don't have to stay somewhere just because someone wants you to, I tell myself.

"Margot, you can't go." Gram is close behind me now. We must look ridiculous, marching through the evening in our party dresses, anger crackling like static between us.

"Why the hell not?" Another step. Just one after another, Margot.

"Please," Gram says.

That. That's what stops me in my tracks. I can hear the effort it takes her to say it. I can hear how much she doesn't want to.

"You don't have to look at me," she says after a moment. "Just listen."

I do, and I hear her skirt rustle as she comes closer.

"If it's spread to the Millers," Gram says when I don't move, "that means it's getting worse. I started this—you understand? So I had to stop it."

"It" what? I want to press her, but I know if I turn around, I'm giving up. Instead I take the smallest look over my shoulder. All I can see of her is the swing of her skirt, her hand slightly reaching toward me.

"What are you talking about?" I say finally. "Stop what? How?"

"I'm tying up loose ends," Gram says. Not really an answer, but there's a hoarseness to her voice I don't like. I frown.

"Loose ends like what?"

"Tess," Gram says. "Me." She takes a shuddering breath. "You."

The rush of air, the white of the stars and the black spread of pain as Gram swings the shovel and brings it down hard on the side of my head.

TWENTY-SIX

I come back to nothing. To the sky dark and blurry through a layer of dirt. It's everywhere, under my fingernails and in my mouth and I gasp, choking on my own hair. This is a grave. I'm in a grave.

Gram's going to bury me.

A rush of terror takes hold of me. She must think I'm dead, or she wouldn't have left me half-buried. And she's not here—she'd have seen me moving. I have to get myself out, have to run, and it has to be now, while she's gone. Before she comes back to finish the job.

The ground is still loose, and it tumbles away from me as I claw my way free, until I can breathe without swallowing a mouthful of grit. I push myself up, feel something give underneath me. It's too soft, too spongy to be the earth. It's

300

something else. My stomach lurches, but I force it down. Keep going, I think. You have to get out.

Finally I crawl from the dirt and tip over onto my hands and knees, feel a breeze brush my cheeks. My head is aching from the hit to my temple, the pain fresh. I'm alive. I'm still alive.

This is not how Gram wanted it. I can picture her with the shovel balanced in her hands, can picture the grim resolve on her face before she lifted it and swung it, hard. A loose end, she said. That's what I am.

I blink, wait for the world to clear in front of me, but it's blurry. I touch the side of my face, just under where the shovel cracked against my temple, and my fingers come away bloody. It's everywhere. Down my neck, in my hair, all coated in dirt. I'm dizzy too, nearly sick to my stomach with it. But I can't just stay here and wait to feel better.

Come on, Margot. Get up. You have to get up.

I take as deep a breath as I can and sit back on my heels. Long, slow breaths, my hands over my eyes until I get used to the throbbing behind them. I open them to heavy evening, to the winding green curve of trees. The apricot grove.

Gram never brought me here, but I feel like I know it from the way Mom wrote about it in her Bible. Here, where they were just the two of them. Here, where Katherine died. Here, where Mom burned her body.

I can see the remnants of the burned grove in the distance. The trees around me are young, bearing fruit, but as the grove reaches away from Fairhaven, they turn strange, broken and stained dark with ash. Trunks hollowed out, branches too short. The earth there is covered with grass, thick and bright, but that can't hide what happened here.

That's in the past, though. And I'm alive. It takes everything I have, but I climb to my feet, steadying myself on the nearest apricot tree, this one living and new. But then I look down at the grave Gram tried to bury me in. Reaching from beneath, pale and rotting, an arm, a hand.

A cry bursts out of me as I scramble back. That's what I felt under me. A body.

I shut my eyes. Hope it's not real if I don't look at it. But haven't I learned? I have to face this. I tried walking away and look where it got me.

I crouch, tuck my hair behind my ears. Ignore the gummy stick of my own blood, and begin to dig.

I hit skin first. A stomach, full of give and curdle. I recoil, feel a heave in my gut, vomit and acid and a sob building to a break, but I have to see this through. I have to. So I bend over her again, dirt up to my elbows, sweat on my forehead, and I brush the earth away from her face.

From my face. From ours. Because of course we're the same. Of course she's me, just like I'm her.

Her neck is bent, too far to be anything but broken, and

her eyes are half-shut. Under her lids I can see the pool of black, of liquid rot, clumping in her eyelashes, one tear of it sticking to her cheek. Just like the other girl. Naked, too, like the girl in the morgue, only this time I can't draw a sheet over her and leave her behind. I have to look. At her eyes, at her hands. At her mouth, loose, drooping down to one side of her face, a hole torn in the skin at the edge of her lips, gaping so I can see her teeth.

Everything else has felt so close. Overlarge in my sight, so I can't look away from it no matter how hard I try. This—I don't know. I'm here but I'm not, and it's not my hand reaching out, steady and still. Not my hand tapping lightly on the gleam of this girl's teeth.

Until it is. In a rush, dizzy and everywhere and all of my body prickling at once, like coming back from someplace numb. I can't hide from this. Not even in myself.

I cradle my hand to my chest and stare down at her. Like that moment on the highway, my first day here. Another girl, just like that. I had it making sense. That girl for Katherine, and me for Mom. So who is this?

It comes back to me then. My first night here, kneeling on the window seat. Looking out over the corn and hearing a cry. Hearing it stop. It was her. It had to be her. This girl, with her neck snapped, with her skin still fresh and gleaming. New, from nowhere. Another.

Dread like the slow build and whine of a siren. I have

to move this girl, even though I'm terrified of what could be underneath her. How many girls have there been? How many of me has Gram killed?

I crouch, empty stomach clenching as a wave of dizziness crashes over me. Get a grip on her wrists and tug, my legs barely staying underneath me. She's so heavy. Dirt pouring across her face and into her mouth. *I'm sorry,* I want to say, but she deserves more than that.

I get her just free of the grave, her torso sprawled on the grass, her legs still half-buried. And there. Underneath her. Another. My face. Gram's, and Mom's, and Katherine's.

This one's dressed, wearing a T-shirt and shorts. Nothing like the stained party dress I've still got on, but I recognize them. The same sort of clothes in the dresser in my room. I bite my lip and reach around to tug the shirt collar to the side. There, right where it was on every other T-shirt in my dresser. My mother's name.

This girl was inside Fairhaven. Gram kept her. Dressed her and fed her and then she ended up here. Just like I did.

I knew it. I knew it. But that doesn't make it any easier to bear. Heat races over my skin and I could throw up but I feel more like crying. I push the tears back and dig until I see her more clearly.

She's younger, this girl. Like me when I was thirteen, fourteen. My freckles before they faded, my hair before the gray really grew in. But her eyes belong to the girl in the fire, to the girl buried above her. Black and dripping, her flesh bloated and splitting, her clothes ragged, half-gone. And worst of all, pieces of her palm, sliced up separate like kernels on a cob of corn. Some have come loose, scattered in the earth around her. Pink at the root, white and tough at the top, black spread like blood from the hole left behind.

Like the harvest, the one Gram and I brought in. I try to breathe deeply, try to keep myself whole and here, but the trees are pressing in around me, the ground swaying under my feet. This is too much. I have carried so much and how am I supposed to understand this?

Easier to keep going than to think about it. And I'm so tired, so so tired, but I bend down, and I take hold of her arms. My sweat drips onto her brow. I smooth it back, but my touch strips her skin from the bone, pulls it clean away from her forehead.

I clutch my stomach, gather myself away from the grave and scream into the back of my hand. Every move I make, worse and worse. Every touch just hurting someone else. I should never have come here. I should never have climbed out of that grave.

But I did.

I lived, and they didn't. I'm still here, and they aren't, and whatever they are—sisters or something else—I have to bear witness. Have to see them, the way I wanted Tess to see me.

I turn around, make myself look. This is what happened to you. It was real then, and it's real now.

I keep digging. Bodies and bodies, younger and younger, stacked so close and all of it wrong, the smell too clean, too chemical as they decompose. One girl with bruises around her neck, skin pulling away from her bones, draping like fabric. Another unmarked like she died in her sleep, maggots dotted like rings on her fingers. And the deeper I get into the ground the less of them is left. Flesh pebbling to nothing, the roots of the apricot trees winding through their ribs. Until I find the last set of bones. Too small to be anything but an infant.

I sit back on my heels. My hands have finally started to shake. Gram put me here, where she put the rest of me. All those bodies, all of them living once, hidden in that house one after another. No wonder it was so easy for her to swing that shovel. She's done this over and over. Kept these girls and killed them.

Just the way she thought she killed me. And the girl in the corn, the girl whose body Eli carried that day, she was no different. Gram called the fire an accident, but I know what it was. A last resort. The only way for her to catch a girl who had started to run.

I wrench myself away from the grave and stagger down the path, farther into the grove. Toward the burn, the blackened reach of what's left of the trees. Tears hot in my eyes, but I don't know what they're for, because this isn't actually happening. It can't be.

I stop short when I see it. A small, flat white stone alone in the grass. A marker for a grave, I think, suddenly certain. And I don't need to dig it up to know who it must be.

Katherine. The only one of them—*us*, a voice whispers to me, *us us us*—anyone wanted to remember.

I kneel by her headstone and rest my palm against it, flinching for a moment as I remember the skin of the bodies behind me. Above us, the apricot trees reaching down. Some of them burned and some of them bearing fruit. I reach for the lowest of them, pluck the fruit from the branch.

Gram, with a hundred of them in her freezer. Why?

Carefully, I find the seam with my fingertips and pull the apricot apart. There, nestled in the center, in the gentle curve where the pit should be, is a perfect white tooth. Like the one I saw in the garbage at Fairhaven. There is no blood. No nothing. It never came from anywhere but here. Nielsen women, growing in everything.

I go cold with it. Waver and slip, and my eyes are open but there's nothing in front of me.

That story in Mom's Bible. About Gram giving birth in the apricot grove. And no father, not then and not ever, and not for me either. Did we all come from here? Is there another girl growing in the earth under my feet? I read Mom's diary, the passage she left me, and I came from her, I thought I did, but maybe I'm like the girls I dug up.

Or am I like Tess? Like Mom? Is my body waiting to bloom?

Tess. I get up, brush the dirt from my dress and peer through the apricot trees, try to spot the Miller house. Gram found out Tess was pregnant, said it had to be stopped now that it was spreading.

I nearly laugh. I'm just like her, aren't I? As long as it's only Nielsens, it's fine. But as soon as it touches someone else, it's gone too far.

There is so much I still don't understand. But before I get answers, I have to get Tess. The first name on Gram's list of loose ends, and I know what that means now.

TWENTY-SEVEN

The lights are on at the Miller house. It's closer than Fairhaven, but I can still only see the shape of it, the windows bright against the evening. I set off, at as close to a run as I can manage, bare feet aching against the earth.

I shouldn't have left her. I went to talk to Mom and she wasn't even there, and I left Tess alone, alone with her parents and with Gram. But I won't make that mistake again. I'll get her and we'll go to Connors. We'll sit in that station until the sun comes up, talk to the people we should've talked to from the start, and then, I hope, get the hell out of here.

I run up onto the porch and lean on the doorbell, knock and knock and call for Tess, for her parents. I don't care if they're in the middle of a fight. But the lights stay on, and the door stays shut, and I can't see in through the tastefully frosted windows on either side of the entryway.

Gram came from here. I watched her truck come up the road from this house, back at Fairhaven. If she's been here already, with that list of loose ends in her head . . .

I take a steadying breath and gingerly try the doorknob. It turns. The door eases open. It's strange to not hear Mrs. Miller immediately welcoming me in, polite to the point of frantic. It's strange to be here at all without Tess. Too quiet, too calm. Please, don't let it have happened. Don't let me be too late.

"Hello?" I call. "Sorry for barging in. The door was open, so I . . ."

Nobody scolds me. Nobody comes running. And it takes only a minute to see why. Because there's blood on the white floor, and blood on the white walls, and blood on the white flowers in their white vase, where they sit on a little white end table.

A numbness spreading from my chest, swallowing me whole.

I see Mrs. Miller first. Laid out in the entrance to the kitchen, on her stomach. A shotgun blast through her nice dress, one heel stranded behind her, the other only halfway on her left foot. Her left hand is reaching out, her phone faceup on the floor.

Gram. Coming back to Fairhaven, washing and washing

her hands. The dark patterns on her dress. A shotgun in the back of her pickup. It was already done. I left the fundraiser and went after Mom, and Gram did this. I let it happen.

"Tess?" I call. Please answer. Please.

The quiet keeps on. Cottony, thick, and I have to push myself through it. Past Mrs. Miller, past the stare of her open eyes. Through the smaller family room and down the hallway, following the footprints along the hardwood floor. Gram's footprints, in Mrs. Miller's blood.

I came this way that first day here, looking for Mr. Miller. It's the same now, only it isn't at all. Why would Gram do this? None of this had to happen. Not a single moment.

I should never have come here. To Phalene, to Fairhaven. I should have turned around the second Tess saw me. Or stayed out in that fire and died there, next to my own body.

The trail leads me past the bathroom, where a pile of white towels is crumpled in the sink, stained pink and red. Gram must've cleaned herself up some before coming back.

Farther then, to Mr. Miller's study, and I stop. Count the footprints as they lead inside and then back out. Something is in there.

I think I know what.

The door is ajar, showing me Mr. Miller's desk and his computer, the screen dark. Slowly, slowly, I open it a little more. File cabinets against the back wall, a thick geometric rug covering the floor. My stomach turns over as I step in.

This is worse. Worse than Mrs. Miller, worse than waking up in my own grave. Worse than all of it.

"Tess?" I say. Keep my eyes fixed straight ahead. Don't look to my left, where two slatted closet doors are thrown open. Don't, don't, don't.

Except I have to. I take a deep breath, and it writhes in my throat, like my insides are trying to force it back out. Tess saw you, I tell myself. She saw all of you. You owe it to her to see this.

I turn. Catch a sob between my teeth, feel it split me in two. Mr. Miller is slumped on his knees, crammed in against the corner of his closet. The bullet's torn through him so I can see chips of bone in the blood staining the floor. If I hadn't seen what I've seen today, I'd lose the will to stay standing.

It's not just him, though. Peeking out from behind him, the hem of Tess's seersucker dress. The pale stretch of her leg. He's wrapped around her, and those are her arms around his neck, her hands loose and limp against his shirt.

Dead. Both of them dead. One blast for two bodies.

At least, I think, they were together, and that's when I start to cry.

Tess. Tess, who needed my help, who gave me hers so freely just because she could. It should be her standing here, her standing in the apricot grove saying goodbye before leaving me behind.

How could Gram do this? How could she come here and turn this place to ruin? Lives, people, real things in a real world and Gram took them in her hands like they were game pieces on a board. Tossed them aside.

"I'm sorry," I tell them both. It's not enough. It will never be enough. I can never give them the time they deserved.

What I can do, what I have to do, is end this for them. For me, too. And I think of the lighter I found in my nightstand. Of every day in that Calhoun apartment, a candle held between me and Mom.

Keep a fire burning. A fire is what saves you—that's what she always said. She tried and tried to tell me.

This time I'm finally listening.

TWENTY-EIGHT

Fairhaven is sleeping when I get there. The front porch is dark, the upstairs curtains all closed.

I'm careful to stay quiet as I step up onto the porch and sneak through the open door, into the entryway. A radio somewhere upstairs, playing an old folk song. Like it's just a quiet evening in the middle of nowhere.

In the kitchen, the light is on. Gram must be in there, having her dinner. Is that what you do when you think your granddaughter and your neighbors are all dead?

I keep on. Upstairs, to get the lighter. The photograph of Mom and Katherine is still in my pocket, and I rest my fingers against it as I climb. She's here with me. They both are.

In my room I pause for a moment. Look down at the Bible, the one I thought was Katherine's. There is more of Mom in there. I'm sure of it. But it's not something she chose to share with me. I leave it where it is, pull the nightstand away from the wall so I can open the drawer, and grab the lighter.

Now what? Mom set the grove on fire, but she must have known it wasn't over. Must have known someone else would have to take care of it, have to find the roots and rip them out.

That's my job now, and Gram's how I do it. I'd be happy to never see her again, but she's got the information I need. And what can she do to me now? Every shot she's fired, every swing of the shovel, all when nobody was looking. Well. Look me in the eye, Gram, and see how far you get.

I go downstairs. Not trying to be quiet anymore. Through the entryway. Into the kitchen doorway. A light is on over the stove, and a dish of casserole is warming in the oven. There's a glass of half-drunk orange juice on the table. And a huddled figure. Gram.

I knew she would be here. Still. I freeze.

She straightens, a wash of yellow light sweeping over her face, and stares at me in the doorway. "Margot," she says. Low and gravelly. "I didn't think I'd see you again."

I could laugh. Instead I slowly lean against the door-frame, the smell of the casserole setting a growl in my stomach. "Life's full of surprises, I guess."

For a moment we just look at each other—the only Nielsens to weather the storm. The only ones strong enough.

"Your head," she says suddenly, nodding to me. "Does it hurt?"

"Of course it does," I say. I'm too tired to do anything but stand here, fresh blood leaking into my hair. "You hit me with a shovel."

Gram snorts. "Not hard enough."

She meant to kill me. Like she killed the Millers. How can this be the woman who did that? Both of us still in our party dresses, both of us bloodstained. And here she is. Drinking orange juice.

She takes another breath, like she's about to say something else, but then she just shrugs.

"No, come on," I say. "What?"

"Nothing."

"Tell me."

"I'm just surprised you came here," she says. "If I were you, if I'd survived, I'd have started running."

I've had a lot of strange conversations, I think, but this is up there. "I had things to take care of." I am tired of understanding only just enough to get by.

I fish the picture Mom left for me out of my pocket and cross to the kitchen table. I unfold it there, between us. Katherine in her shorts and T-shirt, Mom in her dress with her face scratched out. Gram's eyes go soft, and she traces the photo with a careful finger, lingering on Katherine.

"Look how young," she says, almost like I'm not here.

"What happened to them?" I say. Enough of being careful. Enough of trying to get it just right. "What did you do?"

Gram doesn't take her eyes off the photograph. But she starts talking. "I inherited Fairhaven when I was twenty-one."

That's hardly an answer. I force myself not to interrupt.

"We were doing well then. All that land east of Phalene was planted. Those storefronts in town were all rented." She sits back, pushes the photograph toward me, her eyes averted like she can't bear to look at it anymore. "But I was young, and my parents were gone. I made some poor decisions, the way anyone in my place would."

Anyone. Somehow I don't think *anyone* would end up where she's brought us.

"And?" I say, when she stays quiet for too long.

A blink, and a shake of her head before she looks up at me. "And. I can't remember exactly, so you'll forgive me if I get my dates wrong. I think it would have been 'eighty-one."

"When what?"

"It was a bad year for the harvest. The drought kept us from getting much, and what we did grow got hit with insects." She scrubs her hands across her face, and I can see her shoulders trembling. "It's been a long time since I picked through all this. I'm sorry."

I don't care. "That doesn't explain—"

"I know." She's sharp for a moment, before it drifts away. "We lost a lot that year. Had to lay off a bunch of people.

317

But it was one harvest. And we had plenty to fall back on."

I glance out the back door, toward the porch there and the fields beyond. "It was more than one harvest, wasn't it?"

Gram laughs, low and bitter. "Every year after that. Worse and worse. I sold half the farm to Richard's parents, hoped they might be able to keep it going. That way if I went under, there'd still be some work."

Richard. Mr. Miller. How can she say his name so simply, like she didn't wash his blood out from under her nails?

She gets up abruptly, takes her glass of orange juice to the sink and finishes it in one swallow before rinsing it. I watch the rounded shape of her shoulders, the white of her knuckles. "By 'eighty-one I'd stripped half of what I had left. Nothing out east would grow. So."

"So?" I press.

She sets the glass down and turns to face me. I can't see anything but the shape of her, the light over the stove catching her hair. "So then I heard about ridicine. You asked me before what it is. It's a chemical. It was meant to be used on hybrid crops. Sometimes you splice two kinds together and you get a sterile seedling. So you treat it with something like ridicine."

"It was banned," I say, and her head turns more fully toward me. "You used it anyway."

She takes a breath, and for a moment I think she'll deny it. But then she lets it out, so slow, and says, "Yes. I did."

"Why?" Connors said it could kill people. I don't understand what it could give Gram that would be worth the risk.

"It was meant for lab conditions," Gram says. "You'd treat a hybrid on the cell level. Tiny amounts."

That is not what happened here at all.

"But I needed my land to grow," she continues, her voice louder now, more alive. "I needed to get Fairhaven back to how it was. People were depending on me. This town was depending on me."

I picture the fields nearest the house. They're different from the others. The corn still living, but wrong. Off. Like the bodies in the apricot grove.

"It stimulated growth." Defensiveness in the hold of her body, in every word. "It turned sterile plants fertile. And yes, it was dangerous. I knew that. But it was just me. It didn't matter. I had to try."

No, you didn't.

"I treated the land with it. For at least two years, and nothing happened." She swipes at her cheek roughly, and I realize that she must be crying, the close shadows of the kitchen hiding it from me. "But you treat anyplace long enough with something and it'll start to build up." She pauses for a moment as she slips on a pair of pink oven mitts and pulls the casserole out of the oven, setting it on a rack to cool. Just like Gram, I think, to keep on as if everything is normal. "It built up in the land. It built up in me, too."

She laughs then, almost bitter. "Would you believe I

didn't care much for Scripture before all this?"

"Scripture?" Why are we talking about this now?

"Really," she says. "I went to church now and then, but . . . Anyway. I spent a good two years out there. Trying to work the land on my own. Trying to get it to give me something back. And then it did. It gave me Jo."

This. This is what I need. This is how I understand myself, and Tess, and all those girls in the grove. "Gave you Jo how?"

Gram makes an exasperated sound. "Do I need to explain the mechanics of birth to you, Margot?"

"You're the one talking about Scripture," I say, but Gram's already going on.

"The ridicine did what it was supposed to. Gene duplication. Only, in me." Gram's hand drifts across her stomach. "I had your mother right there in the apricot grove. I didn't realize she was coming until it was too late. There was quite a lot of blood."

"But that's only one," I say. "And they were twins."

"Yes." She sounds exhausted. "Katherine came differently. I went back out to the grove the next day and there she was. Half buried. Just a little thing. Just like her sister."

It cracks open in my chest, something I've known since I saw those girls in the grove. Katherine and Jo. Mirror twins. One born from Gram and one born from the earth. Pieces fitting together, everything I've seen and tried to ignore all part of the same puzzle.

Blood on Nielsen land. Give it enough, and it might give something back.

"Is that why?" I ask. "Why they were different?" Why Katherine got sick and Mom didn't. Why the fire ruined one and saved the other.

"I'll never know for sure," Gram says, and I tamp down a flare of frustration. "But chemicals break down. They decay. And that certainly happened to Katherine. Not Jo, though. I always supposed it processed differently in her. Passed itself on." She nods to me. "After all, here you are. Come from your mother just like she came from me."

But not the girls in the grove. The ridicine kept inside or sent down the line—it doesn't make a difference. Damage done no matter what, and we've all ended up back here, haven't we?

I shake my head, ignore the flash of pain and get up, cross the room to lean against the counter next to her.

Gram looks at me. In the yellow light her skin is sickly and thin. Tear tracks fresh on her cheeks, wrinkles at the corners of her eyes. I feel like I'm seeing her for the first time.

"I'm sorry," she says. I haven't heard her sound old until now. It makes my heart clench, an ache I recognize from years with Mom. "I really am." She reaches out, touches the edge of the cut she left me.

I step back. I don't want that from her. I want answers. "They didn't show up with Katherine and Mom, did they?"

321

"No. No, it was just the twins," she says softly. "Until Katherine died. Until your mother put her back in the grove. Like planting a seed, I suppose."

The truth of what happened like a black hole, both of us walking the rim of it. Katherine didn't just die. Mom killed her, and she did it because Gram said someone had to.

"But Mom burned the grove down," I say. A reminder to myself that Mom tried. She did.

Gram nods. "She thought it would be over that way. We both did. But the grove grew back, and it's never really over, is it? You're proof of that. They all are." Gram settles back against the counter, and her shadow reaches out, blends into the dark. "It was easy enough when they were young. I could take them in, give them a few months of a good life before I put them down."

I flinch. Putting them down—that's exactly what it was.

"But they got older and older," she goes on. "I'd find them in the grove and they'd be, well. Your age, I imagine." Her voice goes tight, frustration wound through. "There was an order. There was a process. I had it under control."

She never did. Not for a second. Doesn't she understand? The apricots, teeth inside like pits. The corn, growing like blood and body. It's everywhere. A whole living system, all of it linked together. She took those girls, made their cradle a grave, and it just kept tumbling over itself. Worse and worse. But she won't admit it.

"I did," she says. "I had it. And then one runs away right when you get here and—" She breaks off. I watch her swallow hard, watch her composure come back. "I was going to have another chance, with you. I wasn't going to lose you like I lost Jo, after Katherine. I never thought I'd see her here again." She laughs, the sound empty and harsh. "But what a lucky thing."

"Lucky?" I wouldn't call it that. I've never felt lucky in my life.

"That mess with the body, out on the highway. Your mother came here just in time. I was going to point the police to her and they'd leave us alone." She wipes her palms on her skirt, adjusts the lie of it. "Then Theresa decided to make a scene."

"It wouldn't have worked anyway." I smile, happy to have this over her. "Mom's gone. She left."

Gram snorts. "I suppose that's no surprise. I'm surprised she came at all. She barely lasted two months here, after Katherine. I don't think she could bear being here. Especially not once she knew about you."

"And is that what's next for me, then?" I say. "Another Nielsen girl?"

I don't miss the way Gram's eyes drop briefly to my stomach. "Not," she says, "if we put a stop to all this. Which is what I was trying to do. I didn't realize it was spreading past my land. If I'd known sooner . . . Well. I didn't."

"And you had to kill the Millers for that?" She looks a bit startled. I keep on. "I saw. I went to the house. Gram, how could you do—"

"I didn't need all of them," she says. "Just Tess. But it didn't work out like that."

Mr. Miller, wrapped around his daughter. The phone by Mrs. Miller's hand. I will never forgive her for that. Whatever else I make myself understand, that will never be part of it.

The Millers—one name on that list of loose ends checked off. Then me.

There's another, though. We both know it. Her.

I watch as she reaches into the nearby cutlery drawer and takes out a fork before spearing a bite of casserole straight out of the dish. There's a weariness to her, so heavy she can barely stand upright.

Like planting a seed, she said about putting Katherine back.

But if that were true—if Katherine was really the start of everything—wouldn't it be over by now? Mom knew enough. She'd seen the fire mark her sister's skin. She'd seen what it could do. And she burned Katherine's body.

I came along anyway.

There's something else to this. I shut my eyes. Put myself back in the grove, at the nest of Nielsen girls. All of us with the same face. With mine.

But it isn't mine, is it? And it isn't Mom's. I've always

thought I looked like her, but the truth is that really, we both look like Gram. We both have her face.

Vera Nielsen, over and over again. Every one of us, just her. Mom, Katherine, me, those girls. Stranger than daughters. Stranger than sisters.

And of course it's that way. Her genes, her DNA, warped by the chemical but still just hers—nothing else added in. Gram, and the rest of us. Branches off the root; patterns in the ink. Copies of the original.

I'm looking at Gram and I'm looking at myself, at my own face in fifty years. Watching myself as I turn to the sink and wash my hands again, as I try to get clean of Tess's blood.

"I'm . . . ," I start. "We're . . ." I can't finish, but Gram nods anyway.

Mom, living with her own copy for seventeen years. Does she know? Does she know we're both just Gram all over again?

And that's where the worst of it is hiding, where I have to fight a sob down my throat, because maybe I'm not a daughter at all. If we're the same person, what does that make us to each other? All I've been for my whole life is a daughter, and what's left if I'm not that?

I look down at my hands, half expecting to see them gone translucent and decayed like the girls in the grove. But no. I'm still in my body. I'm still myself. And I won't let this take me apart. I know who I am. Margot, I'm Margot, and that's the truth that matters. I have hurt and I have loved in ways that Gram never will. I am someone all my own.

And she's something else. She's Gram, the beating heart in a living system. Gram, pushing the Nielsen blight further with every breath she takes. Gram, Gram, sitting in this house and doing nothing.

She's how it stops. How nothing like Tess ever happens again. How I make it right. I think she knows that too. Mom certainly did. A lighter in my pocket. Her rule, ringing in my head.

I came here for Gram. For a family that might love me. And I could have it. I could stay here, I could wrap myself up in my last name and watch the mess we've made swallow the whole town. Watch what happened to Tess happen to a hundred other people, and one day, one day, have a daughter of my own, and pass it on to her. Isn't that what I want? To be somewhere only I can belong?

But it's not love, to give your wounds to someone else. I won't be part of it. Not anymore.

"I'm going," I say. And Gram, she just watches me. Steady, and still, and if I didn't know better I'd say she looks relieved.

"All right," she says.

I take the lighter from my pocket. Flick and catch, flick and catch.

I leave the photograph to burn.

TWENTY-NINE

When the fire department finally arrives, they're too late. I'm at the top of the driveway, shivering and barefoot, and I know without looking that the fire has climbed from the front porch, where I set it, to the second floor. Every door still open. Every window still unlocked. Gram still inside. She won't ever come out again.

At the station they sit me down in the conference room with a blanket around my shoulders. Officer Anderson can barely look at me. He's across the table from me, the blinds pulled down. The station has an interrogation room, but nobody wanted to put me in there. Nobody wanted to make this into something they had to handle. Fairhaven burned down with Gram inside. The fields leveled and black. The Miller farm flickering with police lights in the early morning.

I tell Anderson about finding Gram at Fairhaven, after the fundraiser. About the strike of the shovel against my skull. He takes pictures of the side of my head, of my hands, of the dirt under my nails from clawing my way out of the ground. And I spin it like this—that after I came to, I went back to the house and found Gram, full of remorse for what she'd done to the Millers. That she set Fairhaven on fire and wouldn't come out. Penance, I say. I can't tell if Anderson believes me, but it's not like he has other stories to choose from.

"Why did she do it?" he says when I'm done. "Did she say anything about that?"

"She said she was angry with them," I say. "For doing so well when she was failing."

Not quite a lie, but not even close to the whole truth. I sound like I'm a hundred miles away, my voice quiet and thick. This is shock, I know. But knowing that doesn't break me out of this bubble, this careful, deliberate calm. I'm glad for it.

"Three people dead, because of that," Anderson spits, coming around the table to sit down again.

"Four," I say. This matters. Maybe not to anyone else, but it does to me. "You weren't counting her." I want to lie down. I want to shut my eyes and wake up in a hundred years. "So what happens now?"

"To you?"

No, not to me. The police will call my mom. She won't come back for me. I know that already. "To the land," I say. "To the town."

Anderson raises his eyebrows, like he didn't think I'd care. "Nothing, to the town," he says. "Vera was dangerous. We're better off without her."

I wait for the flare of anger, for words defending Gram to fill my mouth. But they don't come. I might be better off too. Or I will be.

"And the land?"

"You mean your future inheritance?" Anderson watches me for a moment. This is nothing like our first conversation, here in the same room. Gram's gone and he's exhausted, and I think he'd rather be anywhere else, but there are things that need doing. Questions that need asking, just for the sake of saying he did.

"I guess," I say. My inheritance came to me in a different form. It never occurred to me to wonder about land, or money, or anything I could touch.

"Well, there are wills for this sort of thing," he says. "Provided Vera's didn't burn to a crisp. But I'd imagine you or your mom can expect—"

"We don't want it." What I want is for it to disappear. To never be anything again but ash. To sit there for years and years until it gets back, somehow, to what it was. "And the Millers? What will you do about them?" I ask. "It was my

329

grandmother. You know that."

"Yes," Anderson says. He shuts his eyes, tips his head back. "But she's dead."

Thanks to me. Because I did what had to be done. What my mother taught me to do.

Maybe I should be the one to call her. Maybe I should be the one to tell her I did what she never could.

"Do you need me to give you her number?" I say. "You probably have to call her, right?"

Anderson shuts the folder and looks up at me with a frown. "Who? Your mother?"

"Yeah."

"We don't have to call her." He gets up, nods to one of the rooms off the bullpen. "She's already here."

I feel half myself as I watch him open the conference room door. As he leads me into the bullpen, my legs unsteady, my hands clutching the blanket. She's here. She's here. She left but she's here.

The room Anderson leads me to is somebody's office, but they've put Mom there. She's behind the desk, slumped over, and by the number of seltzer cans on the desk in front of her, she's been there a while.

How long has it been since they took me from Fairhaven? It could be years, or heartbeats.

"Miss Nielsen?" Anderson says, and my mom jerks upright. Circles deep under her eyes, grease thick in her hair.

She lurches to her feet the second she sees me. I stare at her close-bitten nails, at the raw skin of her cuticles. A wreck of a person. That's what she is.

And we're the same. That's me, standing on the other side of the desk. And I'm her. And we're both of us really Vera underneath it all, and I don't know how to hold that together. I don't know how to look at Josephine Nielsen and not see my mother.

I bet Anderson expects one of us to say something. But we just look at each other, the promise she made and broke echoing between us.

"I'll give you two a minute," Anderson says at last. "Let me know if you have any questions."

Just a few, I think, and he shuts the door.

"So," I start with. "Hi."

Three days ago I'd have done anything before making the first move. It would've been so important to me to make her go first. To make her be the one to reach out. It doesn't matter anymore.

"Hi," Mom says. She sounds hollowed out, her voice rough. When I found her room empty at the motel, I thought she'd be happy to have left me. That's not what this looks like.

Maybe it's a chance to change things between us. After all, she's not really my mother, not when we're both pulled from Gram like Adam's rib.

But then, this is who we are. Mom and me, the imprint of that left in both of us. There's no changing that. There's only moving forward.

"You know you didn't have to come back," I say suddenly. "I can handle myself."

Her expression crumples into something too soft. I have to look away.

"I know," she says. "I know you can."

"So you can leave." I shrug. "Tell Anderson I'm fine as I am. I'm almost eighteen anyway."

A breath of quiet, and at first I wonder if Mom's considering it. But when I look at her again, it's something else. She's biting her lip. She's nervous.

"No," she says. "No, I'm here."

Her hand shakes as she tucks her hair behind her ear, and my chest tightens. Everything about me, Mom and Gram is the same, down to our blood, but this, the way Mom tries and tries to hold herself apart. It's only hers. Because Gram could do it—Gram did it every day—but it's hard for Mom, and I can see the work she has to put in.

"Here *now*," I say. "Where did you go? When you left the motel?"

"Um." Another pause. Maybe she doesn't want to tell me. "Rapid City, I think."

"You think?"

"It's been . . . ," she starts before trailing off, looking

away. And I hate that I know exactly what she means. "Actually," she says, so loud it startles me, "I brought you something." She ducks down behind the desk and comes up with a plastic bag.

I just stare at it. Of all the things we've said to each other, all the scenarios we've run, I never expected this.

"It's a shirt," Mom says, when she realizes I'm not going to open it. She pulls out a giant navy blue T-shirt with *Rapid City* written on the front in that stylized font they use on postcards.

"You brought me a shirt from Rapid City," I say. That's all I have in me. Because she was supposed to stay here. She was supposed to wait. I would rather have had that.

"I know," she says, deflating. "I panicked. I got a call from your grandmother and I just . . . I'm not proud of it."

She sounds so tired. Usually we'd have hit a wall by now, but we're both too drained to do anything more than talk. Just talk to each other, like people do. Maybe this is what we needed all along.

"I know it doesn't make up for anything." She drops the shirt back into the bag, sits down heavily in the desk chair. "I made you a promise, and I broke it. I just wanted to fix it somehow."

"That would be a first."

She recoils, and I wait for the warm rush of pride, another point scored, but it never comes. She wanted to fix it.

She tried. With Gram, with Fairhaven. She tried to tell me.

"I followed your rules," I say. Tremble and quiver, my chin crumpling. I will not cry. I will not cry. "Keep a fire burning, right?"

Her breath catches. "Margot?"

"I know everything. I did it, Mom."

I watch her wilt with relief. Wait for her to reach for me, to share this, because it's only us. We're the only ones who will ever know what this means, or what this feels like. But she collapses in on herself like she always does. And I get it. I do. She's spent my whole life watching me grow, watching me turn into her, into Gram, into the sister she killed. Even if she didn't know exactly how deep the sameness runs, even if she doesn't now, it's there in our faces. An echo in our voices. I don't think I'd reach for me either.

She takes a deep breath, lets it out slow. "And the Bible? The record I left? Did you find that?"

"Yeah." I don't tell her about the other entries I read. I don't think she meant for me to see them. But I'm so glad that I did. That I found my mother when she was young, when she was joking about Gram and when she loved her sister more than anything.

"Good." She drops her gaze, fidgets with the pencils in a cup on the desk. "I know it's hard to understand, but—"

"It's okay." I mean it. "It was the only thing to do."

"Yeah," she says, the worst kind of laughter in her voice.

"It was. Nobody ever should have given me something to look after. Not Katherine." She looks at me now, resolve holding her body tight. "Not you, either. And I wish I could tell you I'm sorry I didn't do better, Margot. I wish I could say that. But I did the best I could."

I try to hold it back. But I can't. "It wasn't good enough."

"I know that," Mom says plainly. It doesn't seem to hurt her the way I thought it might.

"And you can't say that you're sorry?"

She looks at me for a long moment. "No," she says. "If you'd grown up like me, Margot—"

"But I did." If she can't understand this, this most fundamental thing. If she can't be sorry for it, then I don't even know what we're doing. "I grew up with you, Mom. You took everything Gram put on you and passed it on."

Like the girls in the grove. Everything happening over and over, and I have to break it. I asked Tess if understanding a person meant I had to forgive them. And I do understand my mom. I know how she saw what happened to her sister, how she killed Katherine with her own hands. I know how she kept me, even though I bet she's spent my whole life wondering if she would have to kill me too. I know what fires she walked through now.

"You're right," she says. "I did. But you're stronger than me, Margot. You are. You bore what I never could."

And the thing is, I know she means it like praise. Like

335

pride. But it isn't to me. Because yes, I bore this. I fixed it, but there's a voice in my head, one I've never really heard before, and it says, *I shouldn't have had to.*

I shouldn't have had to be strong. Not like that. I should have been able to break. Maybe one day all that strength can just be a gift my mother gave me, and not the tool I used to survive her. But I don't think it's today.

"Well," I say at last. "Thank you for coming back."

She fidgets with the plastic bag, watching me. "And are you? Coming back?"

I want to say yes. I want everything to be fine, but whatever we do today to bridge the gap—it won't hold. Not when I can still feel my whole life with her in every heartbeat.

"Not now," I say instead. "Not yet." It's what I can say instead of "I love you." It's what I can do to look after myself.

Her face crumples for a moment. I watch as she blinks away tears, feel my own well up.

"Not yet?" she says. She swallows hard, her knuckles white. I wait for the fight. And it's there. I can see it in the tremble of her body, in the shut of her eyes. But she says, "Okay." And she says, "Not yet."

It's the kindest thing she's ever done.

THIRTY

The Miller funeral falls on the hottest day of the summer so far. Eli and I go together, sit side by side in the first pew, a few feet from where the three coffins are set up across the front of the church.

"Don't ever tell me," he said this morning when I showed up on the church steps in a black dress his mother lent me. "I'll ask. But don't ever tell me what you saw in their house."

It's been a week, but it seems like yesterday. Mrs. Miller, still reaching for her phone. Mr. Miller in the closet, his body between his daughter and a shotgun. Gram told me she wasn't there for all three of them, only for Tess. He could've stepped aside, but he didn't.

"I won't," I said. It's not a hard promise to make. I never want to think about it again.

There was no funeral for Gram. Mom left Phalene that night, went back to Calhoun and our old apartment. When I think of them now, I think of them together, standing on the porch at Fairhaven in the light of an unending afternoon. I'm too far away to see their faces, but I know they're watching me.

I've been staying at Eli's house, in his room while he sleeps on the couch. Every day Connors comes to pick me up, and he takes me to the station, and he tells me something new. Empty bank accounts one day. Piling debt the next. It is so easy to make this something Gram did.

And it's true, and it's what happened. Gram killed the Millers. Gram treated the earth. Gram, Gram, Gram. But the fire caught the ridicine, turned the bones to something smaller than ash, and when I told the police to look in the grove, they didn't find a thing. Just like Katherine. Mom knew what she was doing when she told me what would save me.

It doesn't sit right, that nobody will ever know all of it. Even the parts that were mine.

Next to me Eli clears his throat and edges closer to make room in our pew for Connors and his wife. The church is packed, all of Phalene turned out to say goodbye to its brightest family. This would've been the Nielsens once. Way back, before any of this. Now the police won't release what they found of Gram's body, and why should they? So I can mourn her? I'll do that just fine on my own.

Tess's coffin is between her parents'. White and shining, and next to it, what must be her school picture, blown up and encircled by a floral wreath. It doesn't look a thing like her. But Eli's staring at it like he can't breathe, and so I reach over, squeeze his wrist once.

The reverend takes the pulpit and the service starts. I shut my eyes, let it look like I'm praying. But really I'm not here anymore. I'm there, in that afternoon that lives at the back of my mind.

Three more weeks until my eighteenth. Three more weeks at Eli's house, of helping him sort through Tess's belongings and find pieces of her to keep. They chose each other, he and Tess. Built a world between them and decided it was worth something. Whatever's next for me, I want it to be like that.

The reverend keeps talking. This will be over soon. I will walk out the door and I will go where I want and I don't know where that is, but I have time, now, to figure it out. Time to build my own life. Time to decide how much of Mom I want in it.

A summer afternoon, sunlight and sway, the crops growing green. Fairhaven bright with fresh paint, and two—no, three women on the porch, wearing the same face. A fire on the horizon. I could live here forever, in the memory of something I never had.

I open my eyes, a breath unfolding like wings in my chest.

Leave it there, I tell myself. Let the fire come. I'm on my way to being brand-new.

ACKNOWLEDGMENTS

I wrote this book so many times that I can't quite remember what's inside it, but what I do remember is the unfailing support I was so lucky to receive from the people around me. First, of course, to my patient and brilliant editor, Krista Marino, who read this book over and over again and let me take it in all the directions it wasn't supposed to go before we found the right one. I don't know where the book would be without you—presumably entirely in the second person and without an ounce of clarity inside.

Thank you to my agents, Daisy Parente, Kim Witherspoon, and Jessica Mileo, and to the teams at Lutyens and Rubinstein and InkWell, who are so wonderfully supportive and who know the answers to my questions before I even realize what I'm asking.

Thank you so much to Beverly Horowitz, Barbara Marcus, Monica Jean, Lydia Gregovic, and everybody at Delacorte Press for providing such a wonderful home for this book. To Emma Benshoff, thank you for being an incredible publicist and for being someone I can email about Taylor Swift albums. Thank you to the whole marketing and Underlined team—Elizabeth Ward, Kate Keating, Jenn Inzetta, Kelly McGauley, Jules Kelly, Josh Redlich, Kristin Schultz, and everyone else—for being the most incredible crew. You are so generous with your time, so kind, and so deeply fun. I'm beyond lucky to be working with you.

Thank you to Regina Flath, genius designer, Alison Reimold, the artist of my dreams, and Trish Parcell, who knocked the interior out of the park. I am forever in your debt. Thank you so much to all the talented bloggers and Instagrammers who have supported both *Wilder Girls* and this book. I'm in awe of the content you create and of the work and dedication you put into your posts.

Thank you to Sara Faring for listening to a hundred versions of this idea. To Diana Hurlbert, Rebecca Barrow, and Maggie Soares-Horne for reading early drafts and pretending they made any sense. To Emma Theriault for many hours of sprinting and shared misery. To Christine Lynn Herman for enduring an astonishing volume of direct messages about corn, and for your support, which I could not have done without. To a great many more friends, too, to whom I owe so much. I love you all.

To my mom, who always shows up, no matter what. Thank you for meeting me here.

ABOUT THE AUTHOR

Rory Power grew up in Boston, received her undergraduate degree at Middlebury College, and went on to earn an MA in prose fiction from the University of East Anglia. She lives in Rhode Island. She is the *New York Times* best-selling author of *Wilder Girls* and *Burn Our Bodies Down*. To learn more about Rory, go to itsrorypower.com and follow @itsrorypower on Twitter and Instagram.